THE
SERPENT'S
BRIDE

BOOKS BY KATHRYN ANN KINGSLEY

THE MASKS OF UNDER SERIES

King of Flames

King of Shadows

Queen of Dreams

King of Blood

King of None

Queen of All

THE IRON CRYSTAL SERIES

To Charm a Dark Prince

To Bind a Dark Heart

To Break a Dark Cage

To Love a Dark Lord

For a full list, visit www.kathrynkingsley.com

THE SERPENT'S BRIDE

KATHRYN ANN KINGSLEY

SECOND SKY

Published by Second Sky in 2025

An imprint of Storyfire Ltd.
Carmelite House
50 Victoria Embankment
London EC4Y 0DZ

www.secondskybooks.com

The authorised representative in the EEA is Hachette Ireland
8 Castlecourt Centre
Dublin 15 D15 XTP3
Ireland
(email: info@hbgi.ie)

ISBN: 978-1-83618-736-3
eBook ISBN: 978-1-83618-735-6

PROLOGUE

Her wedding bouquet was the color of blood.

The crimson roses were wrapped in delicate champagne lace and detailed with black pearls perched upon the thinnest of wires. They almost seemed to be floating.

It wasn't what she would have chosen.

A string quartet was already playing as dark wood doors swung open in front of her, light glinting off their brass inlay as they moved.

Rows of faces turned toward her, some with expressions of curiosity and others with vague disinterest. They didn't know her. None of those in attendance were her family.

The hall was flanked by soaring granite columns supporting an arch overhead. Angular chandeliers hung down, filling the space with a deep amber glow. The walls were decorated with flowers that perfectly matched her bouquet.

What attention to detail.

With the tempo of the music, she walked on, and the faces of the guests followed her.

At the end of the long aisle, standing beside the priest, was the groom. Her husband. As she approached, she felt his red eyes boring into her.

Vampires always seemed to stare right *through* people.

She moved to stand across from him. And in spite of everything, she couldn't help but appreciate how handsome he was.

Raziel Nostrom might be a monster, but you couldn't deny that he was beautiful.

Sharp cheekbones, long black hair held back with a silk ribbon. Tall, broad-shouldered. And those blazing eyes.

His tuxedo was perfectly tailored and likely worth more than most humans would make in a year. His suit was such a deep red that it was nearly black—of course—and accented by a black silk undershirt that starkly offset the white bowtie at his throat and matching handkerchief.

And tucked into his buttonhole was a rose that matched her bouquet. A flower the color of blood.

"You look dazzling, Monica." His words were quiet, intended only for her.

Monica.

For a moment, her smile almost faltered. Was she really doing this? Marrying a man who didn't even know her real name? She felt adrenaline coursing through her veins, heard her heartbeat rushing in her ears. But she pinned her smile in place and looked up into Raziel's eyes.

She had to be perfect. If he doubted her now, years of planning and patience would be wasted.

Turning away, she passed the bouquet to her maid of honor. Raziel's sister. From the front row of seats, the rest of his family watched on. Mother. Brother. Cousins. The whole blood-drinking lot of them.

The priest stepped up to begin the ceremony.

This was her wedding.

Her name was Nadi.

And she had come here to murder them all.

ONE

ONE WEEK EARLIER

"Again."

Raziel danced the gold coin over the backs of his knuckles. It was one of his favorites. Moving the coin to his thumb, he flicked it into the air, sending it whirling up into the light of the Father, the larger of the two moons, before catching it in his palm to repeat the action.

A familiar sound. Then a whimper of pain.

Turning on his heel, he looked at the man sitting in the chair across the room from him before letting out a long, heavy sigh. Tilting his head to the side slightly, he clicked his tongue. "Marley, Marley, Marley... you really are terrible at this, aren't you?"

The man in question let out a growl of rage and defiance as he clung to some pathetic shred of dignity. "What I'm upset about is... He sent the Serpent to deal with me? I didn't even warrant Mael coming in person to do the deed? Doesn't Mael understand I never meant—" He choked off in pain.

"Never meant what? Insult? Offense?" Walking across the plush carpet, Raziel went over to the large house plant Marley kept in a vase by the window in his office. It offended him for several reasons. One, it was needlessly ostentatious. Two, it stank of the Wild. And third, Marley was clearly forgetting to water the damnable thing and it was beginning to brown at the edges.

That Marley would bring a piece of the Wild into his *place of business* only confirmed that Raziel's brother Mael had been right about his suspicions. Not that it mattered anymore.

"Come now. I've heard it all. What kind of excuse are you going to invent this time, Marley?" Raziel moved to half sit on the edge of Marley's desk, putting him only inches away from his victim. "Mael spared your life once. He sent me to make sure he wouldn't be fooled a second time."

Marley wasn't restrained; Raziel had no need for anything so mundane as protection from humans. And, clutched in one hand, Marley held a pocketknife, slicked red with blood that had come from the several fresh holes in his right thigh.

Marley didn't respond, just whimpered.

"Now. Stop changing the subject. Tell me who you were working with, and I'll let this be quick." Raziel smiled warmly, casually tucking his hands into his pockets.

Marley grimaced. "*Fuck you*, Serpent. Fuck you, and your whole vampire family. Yeah. I sold you out. I've been selling you out for years. And I'd do it again in a heartbeat."

Laughing, Raziel shook his head. "Humans. You get so petulant when cornered. *Again.*"

Marley picked up the knife and stabbed himself in the thigh without a moment of delay. He had no choice, after all. Raziel had told him to do it.

"Who were you working with?" Raziel's power applied to physical actions—but sadly not *words*. It was quite obnoxious. He *could* command someone to speak, but what would fall out of their mouths would just be nonsense. He might as well tell them to bark like a dog.

Which was usually quite amusing, but he was not in the mood at the moment. He was in a bit of a rush.

Marley was shaking now. He was going into shock, despite his absolutely *miserable* aim with the knife.

But he stayed quiet.

Very well.

Have it your way.

Taking Marley's face in his hands, Raziel tipped it up to look at him—firmly, but not forcefully. He smiled again. "Marley, you and I both know you're going to die tonight. Give me the name of the fae *scum* you sold Mael's shipment to, and I will let you die quickly and peacefully. Don't, and you know how painful I can make this for you. It's your choice. Your part in all of this is over. Loyalty will get you nowhere."

Marley shut his eyes, tears streaming down his cheeks and onto Raziel's hands. "Th—the Iltanis..."

Straightening up, Raziel patted his victim on the shoulder. Heading for the door, he took his pocket square out of his pants' pocket and cleaned his palms. "Thank you, Marley. Be a dear and slit your throat. Deeply. Don't want you to spend all night gurgling on the carpet. Now, if you'll excuse me, I have a wedding to plan."

The quiet *thump* from behind him was the last time Marley ever crossed Raziel's thoughts. Folding the pocket square and tucking it back into the pocket of his pants, he headed down to street level where his car was waiting for him.

A wedding to plan.

What a *joke.*

To a woman he'd never met—one served up to him like a sacrificial lamb. She'd been traded away by her father like so much meat at a market. He wondered how much this *Monica Valan* knew about the deal. He almost felt bad for her.

Almost.

* * *

Nadi walked into the expensive hotel room, quickly glancing over the space. A luxurious king-sized bed with decadent, golden silk sheets. Large glass windows tastefully tinted to avoid any onlookers seeing anything... untoward.

An expensive and discreet hotel.

It catered to a very specific kind of clientele. Which meant that it wasn't her first time in the building, though her first time on such a high floor. In the basement there was a jazz nightclub that was the talk of the metropolis, all brass and rose granite and flapper dancers in shining sequined dresses.

The man who had booked the room walked in behind her. *What was his name again? Danton? No, Denton. Mark Denton.*

Denton locked the door, throwing the series of large and newfangled deadbolts. They wouldn't be disturbed until morning.

Very discreet.

Turning, she smiled at him, knowing it wasn't her expression but her low-cut top that was catching his gaze. Her dress plunged down between her breasts, and he hadn't stopped staring at her cleavage all night.

That was fine. That was why she had chosen this body and this dress in the first place.

Walking up to him, she slipped her hands up his chest, smoothing them over his shirt, before unbuttoning his coat. "Can't imagine how stressful it must be, working for the Nostroms... such a powerful family. So many *connections*. What's it like to be so close to them?"

"You know how it is. A job is a job. Mael is a slavedriver. His sister is worse." Mark grunted. "Usually, Mael has me running all over the city, delivering messages for the mayor. Like he couldn't just pick up a damn *phone*. But right now, get this, he has me handing out invitations for his psychopathic brother's wedding."

What. A cold chill ran down her spine. She forced warmth into her voice. "A wedding? That's romantic, though."

"Sure, normally." Mark snorted. "Except this poor dame isn't a vampire, sweetheart. Do you *know* what happens when a human gets married to a vampire?" He sighed. "Best you don't."

"I read a moontale like that once. Maybe they'll fall in love and he'll turn her." She tried to play the idiot routine. It seemed to work, as he just shook his head. "Sit, let me give you a shoulder rub." She motioned to an upholstered bench over by one wall. It was a deep green velvet, lined in brass, and matched the same hyper-modern detailing as everything else in the room. "I'm *fantastic* with my hands."

Mark chuckled. "I can't wait to find out..." He moved to sit on the bench, shrugging out of his coat and tossing it aside. "Give me a little show first, though, yeah? Show me what I'm renting this room for."

Disgusting.

Her smile didn't flinch as she stood in front of him, just out of his reach, and slowly slipped out of her own coat, letting it pool on the floor. She turned her back to him and, taking her sweet time, bent over, unlacing her shoes.

"Fuck. *Yes.*"

Her jaw ticked. She was very glad he couldn't see. As she straightened up, she slid her hands up her legs, making sure he could imagine his hands in their place, riding her dress up her thighs. Kicking off her shoes, she let her dress fall back down before turning to face him.

"Aww..." He stuck out his lower lip in a comical pout.

"Have to leave something for the main event. Besides. Seems like I have you excited enough." She chuckled at the obvious state he was in.

With a shrug, he leaned back a bit to undo his belt and unzip his fly, releasing some of the pressure on what must be an uncomfortable situation. "I've always appreciated a beautiful woman who knows how to use it to her advantage."

"Mm." Walking around behind him, she stroked her hand up his arm and to his shoulder, kneading it.

"Anyway, you know what the funny part is, about the whole wedding fiasco? He hasn't even ever *seen* the broad. She's from one of the outer cities. Some rancher's daughter. Never even visited the metropolis." He let out a low groan, tilting his head forward. "Harder."

She obliged, grasping both his shoulders in her hands and giving them a good squeeze. That drew another low groan out of him. She went on like that for a moment, waiting until his muscles eased and relaxed. Waiting for him to slip his eyes shut.

Reaching up, she pulled out the two long pins that kept her long locks curled up in a bun.

And drove them deep between his ribs and directly into his lungs.

Mark went rigid, arching his back, doing more damage to himself. He jerked, trying to spin and grab her, ripping bigger wounds in himself. It was already too late; he just didn't know it yet. His lungs were filling with blood. He let out a strangled noise, went to shout, scream—and could only suck in liquid instead of air.

"Sorry." She smiled. "You know how it is. A job is a job. Especially when the Nostroms are involved."

Mark lurched for her, but his knees gave out. He coughed, red staining his lips. It was amazing how quickly a person could drown in their own blood. If a victim panicked—which most of the time they did—it could be over in a matter of moments.

"Try not to bleed on the furniture. None of this is the maid's fault." Sighing, she grabbed Mark by the wrist and tried to pull him over to the corner. He was already going weak, but he still tried to ball up his other hand into a fist and punch at her. It was easy enough to move out of the way of the pathetic swing.

By the time she dragged him into the corner, he was twitching in the last throes of death.

Brushing off her hands, she looked down at his crumpled form. Blood was seeping through his shirt. It'd likely be a decent-sized puddle on the black marble floor by the time she woke up in the morning. But, importantly, it wouldn't get on the carpet.

Reaching down, she pulled her hairpins out of his back. They were custom-made, and she was hardly going to let Mark keep them. She let her glamor drop—well, part of it, anyway—as she headed to the door to ensure the deadbolts were thrown. There wasn't any need to keep wearing the face of the prettiest woman she'd ever seen, now that her target was taken care of.

Being a shapeshifter was useful when one was an assassin.

Though the shapeshifting had definitely come first in her life before the killing-for-hire had.

Heading to the bathroom, she tossed the two bloody weapons into the sink and switched on the hot water. She'd have to boil them when she got home, but scrubbing them in soap and hot water would do for now.

Oh, shit. The bathroom was *nice*. Mark hadn't been cheap. The tub was enormous. Definitely meant for more than one—and very likely more than two.

Extremely discreet.

Shame to let such a wonderful tub go to waste. Sitting on the edge of the marble platform that surrounded the large oval basin, she reached over and flipped open the brass taps, letting the water rush out. Smiling, she decided there was only one thing that could make it better.

Booze.

Humming to herself, she headed back to the main room.

There was a silver bucket by the wall filled with ice, and an uncorked bottle of white wine shoved into it.

First, she figured it didn't hurt to go through his coat. She had *plenty* of money. Being an assassin paid extremely well, and she really didn't know what to do with what she had, so she didn't *need* to raid his wallet for cash. But after growing up fae in the darkest corners of the city, it was hard to turn down free money. And there might be something useful in his pockets.

His wallet had a few paper bills amounting to a not small but not incredible sum of money, a few business cards that seemed uninteresting but she'd keep just in case, and a paper ID card she'd leave with the corpse. She had no need for it. In fact, better if it weren't on her person.

It was the other pocket that had something more interesting.

A crimson envelope with a broken black wax seal that had a stylized decorative N stamped into it. She knew that symbol. She knew that symbol *very* well.

Flipping open the envelope, she pulled out the card and read the delicate crimson text scrawled across the expensive off-white linen card inside.

Of course it was blood red. Of *course* it was. Egotistical shit.

You are hereby cordially invited to the wedding of Raziel Nostrom and Monica Valan on Everdeen the 4th, 3435, at the Wellingham Estate Courts.

It didn't even include instructions on how to RSVP. He just *assumed* whoever was invited was coming. Naturally. *Egotistical shit.*

Tossing the card onto the bed, she took the whole bottle and one of the delicate crystal glasses, then headed back to the bathroom. Flipping off the electric lights—they tended to hurt her eyes, though she preferred them to the smell of the oil lamps they were replacing—she let out a sigh as the darkness flooded the room.

She was used to the darkness. She had grown up in the

Wild, after all. Placing the bottle and glass on the edge of the tub, she stripped out of her clothes and tossed them aside.

The Wild stretched for miles underneath the island of Runne, sprawling in endless caverns, rivers, oceans, lakes, and fields. Larger than the humans and the vampires who all lived topside could probably imagine.

Filled with creatures and wonders the likes of which they could *never* dream of.

And it was where most fae clans lived. Those that hadn't overtaken the plains between the walled cities where the humans and vampires had driven them out, at any rate. It was dangerous in the plains, and while there was always a chance for war and raids anywhere in the Wild, the plains were notoriously worse.

But being underground, where it was *supposed* to be safer, meant that most fae never saw the light of the sun. So they adapted to live without it.

It was another advantage she had over those that lived above. Even the vampires, who were also creatures of darkness, had poorer night vision than her kind.

Her clan had lived underground.

Had being the operative word there.

Oh, by the two moons, this place had that soap that made the water all bubbly!

She'd been in this hotel before, but never in *this* nice of a room. "Mark, you really know how to treat a lady you planned on fucking once." Laughing quietly to herself, she unscrewed the top of the glass bottle and poured the contents into the bath, loving the feeling of the steam rising off the surface of the water.

Slipping into the water, she let out a satisfied groan and sank into the liquid up to her neck. She could really stretch out in the enormous tub. Once it was full, she turned off the taps and poured herself a glass of wine.

She sipped it, leaning her head back against the lip where

the porcelain met the marble and let out a sigh. Her good mood didn't last long as a name came into her mind as it had so many times over the past eighty years of her life.

Eighty years that she had spent learning to kill. Learning to hunt. Learning to survive. Because of *that name*. That *one name*. And the face that went along with it. She had spent eighty years honing her skills. Knowing that someday she would have a chance to take her revenge. On *him*.

Raziel Nostrom.

Her stomach twisted in hatred at the thought of him. She had to bite back the memories. The night that ruined her life—that took everything she cared about.

She remembered those red eyes—his silhouette. The look in her human mother's eyes as he told her to slit her own throat.

And his laugh as she'd done it. That monster's *laugh*.

Downing another mouthful of the wine, she swallowed too much and coughed.

Raziel had destroyed her life.

And she had been on a quest to destroy his ever since.

Nobody wakes up one day and goes *"You know? I think I'm going to murder people for money."* Everybody had a reason. She didn't talk much with other assassins. It was a pretty lonely trade. But the few she'd bumped into—usually because they were going after the same mark, which was always extremely awkward but usually wound up with a game of rock-paper-scissors followed by beers at a bar—all had similar sob stories to her. Some were better, some were worse. But they all had a name to point to. The names were always different—but there was always *someone*.

Point being, Raziel Nostrom was a difficult hit for several reasons.

He was a vampire. While his two siblings were older and *arguably* stronger, that wasn't saying much. Raziel was powerful, ancient, and notorious for being able to hypnotize his victims into effortlessly killing themselves. And he didn't just have his victims kill themselves quickly—that wouldn't be brutal enough to prove a point. Not to mention, usually Raziel didn't simply just target the victim. He wanted to ensure that the message was sent loud and clear.

Crossing him usually meant losing more than just the right to continue living. It usually meant losing everything else, first. Family. Friends. Loved ones.

Even after over eighty years, the sound of her father's screams, begging for mercy, still woke her from her nightmares.

She had vowed, a long time ago, to make sure that Raziel suffered just like his victims. She wanted him to watch everything he loved be taken away from him, bit by bit, before she ended his life.

And she was going to kill his bloodsucking, criminal family first. Just like he had hers.

For the longest time, it had seemed like that was impossible. That there was no way that she could get close enough to the Serpent to exact her revenge.

That was, until she'd met the dead fuck in the other room.

The wedding was in a week.

That gave her not a lot of time to go to work, but she had all the information she needed. But for tonight? Tonight, she could relax, enjoy the luxurious hotel room, and rest. It might be the last night of good sleep she'd get in a while.

So, for the first time in a long time, and probably for the last time, she let down her glamor.

All of it.

She felt the knot of tension between her shoulder blades, which was seemingly always there, slowly release. She didn't fit in the tub anymore, enormous as it was. But that was fine.

Her long tail draped over the edge and along the marble platform and over the side. She'd get cold eventually, but it was worth it for now. Sinking as far down into the water as she could, she shut her eyes and basked in it. It felt like bliss.

Animal. Beast. Savage. Abomination. Liar. Cheat. Murderer.

Okay, that last one was accurate. But it wasn't her fault. She hadn't wanted to be this way.

There was a mirror on the side of the tub. Lifting it, she looked at her reflection in the silvered glass. There was just enough moonlight drifting in through the big, tinted windows to see by.

Some parts of her might have almost passed for human, as fae went. Many of her kin were monstrous, twisted things—with too many arms or eyes, or who had their bones on the outside or all their organs the wrong way around. She looked fairly human...

Her hair was the color of pure onyx, flowing down around her in long waves and currently floating in the water, reflecting back shades of green and blue in the faint light. Her ears were only a little pointed and easily hidden within her hair. Her skin was pale, and only in the direct sunlight did it seem tinted just slightly sea-green around her temples or at her wrists. Even her eyes, which were the color of black opal and flecked with every color in nature, could be disguised with tinted glasses. She could almost be mistaken for a human at a glance, if nobody looked down.

Since it was her eight-foot-long gods-damn fucking *fish tail* that generally gave it away.

It was the same color as her hair. Pure black and shining in the moonlight, tinted like spilled oil. It was like the tail of the colorful "laced fish" that her mother had brought her to see one day. Their fins had flowed through the water like the most delicate fabric, and many of them had more than one. As a child, they'd looked like elegant dancers to her.

Lifting the end of her tail, she studied it for a moment before dropping it back down. Sighing, she rested her head back and thought over her next steps. Memories of a home she no longer had weren't going to do her any good.

Shutting her eyes, she took a deep breath and put the glamor back over herself that only altered her appearance enough to remove the tail. It was one she had been used to wielding ever since she was a child, as being an aquatic fae with a land-based clan was... inconvenient. Pulling her human legs into the hot water, she felt the tension return to that spot between her shoulder blades like an old friend.

She hadn't hunted Denton with the intention of it leading to anything. She had only been pursuing him because he had an association with the Nostroms and a decent price on his head. It had been a way to both secure a few months of funds, and be a thorn in their sides, if even just a little.

But now? Now that the stupid wedding invitation had landed in her lap?

A plot was forming in the back of her head. It was insane. It was absolutely *ludicrous*. And if she succeeded, she would probably wind up dead. This was a one-way trip. She didn't have time to plan or to take care of any kind of contingencies. But this might be the best chance she'd ever have.

This "Monica Valan," the human who was being married off to Raziel, was coming from one of the outer human cities. The trains would have to move through contested areas, which was dangerous. Nadi doubted Monica's family would risk making the trip with her.

That meant Monica would come alone for the wedding.

And that meant a switch could be made.

Nadi chewed her lower lip.

A bribe and a switch.

Raziel had a... reputation, when it came to partners. A reputation that would precede the Serpent even in the distant settlements where Monica lived. And Nadi could use that to her advantage.

Her thoughts flashed back to the first time she had set eyes on the vampire. On the grin that had been burned into her soul. That too-smooth, fanged smile when he'd seen her. And the one word he'd spoken that had cut through her very soul.

"*Run.*"

Her jaw ticked in rage.

Nadi was going to make Raziel Nostrom suffer.

Or she was going to die trying.

TWO

"I *told* you."

Raziel shrugged. "Do you want a trophy?" He stared out the glass of his brother's high-rise office, looking down at the street below. The cars in this area of town were like the buildings themselves—huge, new, clean, expensive. Far away from the soot and grime of the people who made them.

Far away from the homes of the laborers who cheered when the girders of each skyscraper were riveted together. But they weren't Raziel's concern. Nor were they the concern of his brother.

Mael leaned back in the leather-padded chair of the office he occupied in the metropolis' statehouse. The piece of furniture creaked with the strain of his weight. Raziel was taller and broader than most but looked like a rail next to his elder brother.

He would never admit aloud how much he *hated* that fact.

Flicking a coin into the air, Raziel caught it as it danced back down toward his palm. "Fae will never be happy with the scraps we let them scavenge. They will always try to claw up from their holes like the fetid beasts they are." Grimacing, he fought the urge to extend his fangs. "We should have exterminated the Iltanis when we had the chance. Every last one of them."

"They can be useful, brother. You know that."

He rolled his eyes. "There are other beasts down there who will bring us the narcotics we need. We don't need that *thing* who fancies himself a man. He grows too bold. It's only a matter of time before he does something remarkably stupid."

"No." Mael stood from the chair behind his desk. Raziel glanced over at him. A stranger on the street would never think them related. Raziel with his long dark hair and red eyes, and Mael with his blond strands and golden orbs. "Luciento Iltani is a dog. One we've trained to obey. He snaps at his leash from time to time, and we correct him with the rod."

"And I am the rod."

"Yes." Mael smirked. "You are. And you like it."

With a heavy sigh, Raziel headed for the door. "Someday, this rod might snap, brother. Then what will you do?"

He didn't wait for an answer.

* * *

Sneaking onto a train filled with armed guards was easy... when you could *become* an armed guard.

Well.

Sort of easy.

The first step was to find a man posted on the edge of the security checkpoint where the train was going to be stopped to be searched. Someone of lower rank on the edge of the outpost, who had his back turned. Taking the man's shape was easy enough.

Even if suddenly having a dick and balls was *really distracting*. How men walked around with those things dangling around all day, Nadi would never know.

One quick hit upside the back of the head with her pistol

and she dumped his unconscious body behind the checkpoint building. By the time anyone found him or he woke up, she'd be long gone and wearing another face.

Taking his place, she waited until his superior officer walked by. "Sir? Sir, a moment in private?"

"Keep it brief, the next train is almost here." The older man rolled his eyes. He jerked his head toward the small station building and she followed him inside.

A few minutes later and he was unconscious underneath his desk. And she walked out wearing *his* face. And trying not to scratch *his* crotch.

She seriously hated having to glamor as men.

Putting on her best scowl, she waited for the train to arrive and barked the appropriate orders for "his" troops to search the train.

Gods forbid any *fae* get inside the city, or any smuggled goods—well, any that the bastard Nostroms hadn't bribed them to ignore, at any rate.

Climbing aboard, she was pleased when the train staff stepped aside to let "him" on board with no questions.

The train was packed.

From the informant at the telegraph office she'd paid off, Nadi learned that Monica would be up near the front with only a couple of guards. How much Raziel had paid for a private cabin for *eight*, Nadi had no idea. But it must have been absurd.

It would make her easy enough to find.

Especially with how heavily guarded the train car with the one said passenger would be.

Getting the contact information of the informant had required burning a lot of leads. The one that hurt the most was cutting off her contact with Betty, the woman she got her assassination contracts from.

The older woman had sighed when Nadi had briefly explained what she was after, but she hadn't tried to stop her.

Mostly because she didn't care *that* much if Nadi wanted to throw her life away. And part of the older woman understood that revenge was what drove them all to do what they did, at the end of the day.

"A shame to lose one of my best," Betty had said through her cigarette. Nadi hated the smell of them, but she put up with it without complaint.

Betty was as close as Nadi had to a friend, sad as that was.

And it was pretty moons-damned sad.

But now was time to focus on the present, on the train, and on finding Monica. The only thing that might have given her away was the small bag she had slung over her shoulder. But as "captain," no one would question her as she peered in each window going along the front of the train.

This was the right train. Monica was in here *somewhere.* Nadi didn't know what the young woman looked like, but there couldn't be two trains with a young woman with guards posted outside and—

There.

Two hired goons standing outside of a door, doing their best to look both serious and incredibly bored at the same time. They weren't any of the Nostroms' usual hires. Probably from wherever this Monica Valan came from.

With a sigh, Nadi reached into her pocket, produced out a wad of cash, and peeling off a few thick bills, stuffed a handful each into the hands of both men. "Get lost for the next half an hour."

The two guards glanced at each other. At the apparent captain of the guard. At the large sums of money they'd just been paid... and then they both obediently shrugged and walked off. Funny thing about hired goons. They could always be rehired by other people.

Let them think the captain of the guard was about to do something lascivious and horrid with the single, unescorted woman on the train. The truth was somehow both worse and better than that.

As Nadi glanced through the door of the room, sure enough, there she was. She *had* to be Monica Valan. A single woman, sitting in the train car by herself, was peering out the window of the train, up at the tall buildings like she'd never seen skyscrapers before.

Opening up the door without warning, Nadi stepped in and shut it behind herself with a click. "Papers." Her voice matched that of the captain of the guard perfectly.

"Here you go, sir." The woman handed her up a folded stack of papers with a bright and beaming smile. Yep. Monica Valan. The young woman was very pretty with a round, friendly face and giant puppy-dog eyes. *Painfully* innocent. She was looking up at Nadi with such wide-open curiosity it almost made her heart bleed.

Raziel would absolutely destroy her. Snap her into tiny pieces, drain her of blood, and leave her an empty, soulless husk. The Serpent delighted in breaking his partners—men or women, anybody stupid enough to sleep with him.

Pulling the curtain down on the door, Nadi sat next to Monica and, in the same movement, pulled a silenced pistol from her pocket and dug it into Monica's side.

Then she smiled at Monica with Monica's own face. "Hello."

Monica squeaked, her hands flying over her mouth.

"No screaming. No running. I'm not here for you. You're going to walk away from this unharmed and with a *lot* of money in your pocket if you do what I say."

"Wh-wh-what do you want?" Monica stammered. "Please—please, I—"

"Do you know who and what Raziel is? Do you *really* know what you're walking into? What happens when a *human* is married off to a *vampire*?" She arched an eyebrow.

The way the other woman chewed her lower lip told Nadi that she did know who Raziel was. And what was going to happen to her.

Monica's shoulders slumped. "I don't have a choice. Papa…"

"Sold you off like cattle?"

Monica nodded.

"Here's what I'm offering you." Nadi shifted, dropping her canvas bag from her shoulder onto the ground at her feet. "In this bag I have cash, credits, a new identity, and priority passage rights from here back to anywhere else you want to go. Monica —you're going to feel 'sick,' and I, as captain of the guard, am going to take you off the train to recuperate. The guards will assume I'm having my way with you or something disgusting."

Monica snorted.

Nadi shrugged. "From there, you leave. Go anywhere you want. You'll be free. And I'll get back on board the train to take your place."

"You—you want to switch places? But… but why?" Monica blinked, astonished.

"I have a bone to pick with your fiancé." Nadi gritted her teeth.

"And if I won't…?" Monica asked the obvious follow-up question.

"Then I kill you, stuff you out the window, and I go on in your stead, anyway."

Would she? She honestly didn't know. Probably. Monica didn't deserve to die. But that was the nature of revenge, some-times. The Serpent and his family needed to be stopped—how many lives could she save by stopping them?

Monica looked down at the bag at Nadi's feet. "How… how much exactly?"

Greed really was fantastic, sometimes. "One million." Nadi smiled, still wearing Monica's own face. "Call it a wedding gift."

"I don't want to marry that vampire *fuck*." Monica's cussing sounded surprisingly natural on her. Farm girls—always full of surprises. "One million dollars to go live my life, and not get tortured and murdered by that unholy monster?" She shook her head. "I don't know how I can say no."

Nadi let out a small breath of relief. "Great. Then I'm going to lower the gun. I'm going to take the shape of the guard again and follow you off the train. Do *not* do anything stupid. Please."

Monica didn't do anything stupid.

In fact, after they had gotten off the train, she *hugged* Nadi.

Fucking *hugged* her.

And thanked her for saving her life.

Nadi killed people. She didn't *save* them. She was doing this out of a selfish need for revenge—to make Raziel pay. Not out of charity. It kind of put a damper on the whole exchange.

But the real Monica headed away, toward the center of the metropolis, bag of clothing and supplies slung over her shoulder, a smile on her face.

And Nadi, now wearing Monica's face and using her voice, got back on the train, and shrugged at the rented goons that had resumed their positions either side of the door. "He wanted to play a round of cards," she said to one of them with an innocent giggle. "Nice man. Very lonely. And here I thought he was going to do something *dastardly*."

The two guards glanced at each other, not sure what to do with that statement. "Are you ready to go, miss?"

Walking into the cabin of the train, she took a seat exactly where she had found Monica.

"Ready as I'll ever be."

* * *

Raziel watched his black automobile pull into his driveway from his vantage point on his balcony. His driver had returned with his new piece of *temporary* property. He was leaning on the railing in curiosity, walking his gold coin back and forth over the knuckles of his right hand.

His bride-to-be was about to arrive.

His blood sacrifice.

When mortals were wed to vampires, one of two things happened. Either they were remade in the holy tradition... or they were devoured and joined in blood and blood only.

And Raziel had no intention of keeping a wife underfoot for longer than he had to.

Monica Valan's father had been foolish and crossed the Nostroms. And it had cost him dearly. Not only his daughter, but all of his wealth and his businesses—the legal ones and the less legal ones too. Even the outer cities were not out of the Nostrom family's reach.

After the wedding, whether or not Monica lived, all that belonged to the Valans would become Raziel's. And therefore, by extension, his family's.

And he was *quite* certain Monica wouldn't live long.

Mortals. They were so fragile. So easily killed. He had lost track of how many human toys he had *accidentally* murdered over the centuries. But that was just part of being a vampire.

Cracking his back, he let out a breath. The circular head-lights of the car flicked off as its petrol engine rumbled to a stop. Many areas of the metropolis were still easier to access by horse and carriage, but he would have none of it. While the smell of the petrol was mildly revolting and stung his nose, technology was the way of the future. And the only way of defending against the Wild.

"I do hope she's mildly attractive."

"I'm sure you'll cope. And she won't be here long," came the gruff, but amused reply from behind him. Ivan, his lead body-guard, and closest thing Raziel had to a friend. Oh, he had people he trusted—organizations like his lived and died on trust. It was the only currency that really mattered.

TP8 段

But Ivan was the second cousin to Raziel's third cousin. It made him a full-born vampire as well, but not highly ranked enough to wind up with his own region to control. Not that Ivan seemed to have the knack or the taste for being in command. The huge, tattooed bodyguard seemed perfectly content to be witness to, but not in charge of, all of their deals and goings-on.

Raziel couldn't help but linger for a moment as his driver exited the car and opened the rear door for someone he could only presume was Monica. A young woman climbed out of the back of the car with the grace of a cat—lithe and smooth.

His interest was suddenly piqued as his previous concern vanished.

It was hard to make the details out from his distance, but she was certainly not what he was expecting. Maybe he should rethink his opinion of what the outer bastions of humanity had to offer up.

He had intended her to be ushered into a lounge to wait and stew while he attended to other matters. But now, perhaps he would rather see her up close and personal.

Which would soon be *very* personal, he assumed. Yes, she wouldn't survive their honeymoon trip to their ancestral estate— but that didn't mean he couldn't have fun beforehand.

Waste not, want not, and all that.

Ivan followed after him as he left the room to head downstairs. "Mark's dead."

"Who?" Raziel tried to remember if he knew a Mark.

"Loring's cousin."

"Right." No, he still didn't remember Mark, but he pretended to just to make it go faster. "That's a shame." And no, he didn't give a shit. "How?"

"Murdered in a hotel room. Nobody knows by whom," Ivan grunted. "Judging by the wounds, it was a professional hit. I have Hank hunting it down."

Raziel shrugged. "Hazard of the job." If he didn't remember

the man's name, he certainly didn't care if he was dead. "Probably someone angry at Lana or Deniel. I vote Deniel. That simpleton is always pissing people off." He sometimes hated having a large family. It always made it difficult to know who was angry at whom and for what. "Don't waste Hank's time on it. His efforts are better served securing the grounds."

"Hrm," Ivan grunted. That was usually how he preferred to communicate.

"Fine. Just... keep an eye on it." That'd calm down his bodyguard. Ivan was always jumpy when someone dropped dead. Which, to be fair, was his job.

They reached the first-floor foyer of his home the moment the doors swung open to allow in the person he assumed—*and now perhaps hoped*—was Monica. Yes, he had seen a photo of the young woman, but it had been faded, and not of any quality to speak of. It had not done her justice.

She was taking in her surroundings with wide, green eyes filled with awe. Her dark brown hair ran along tanned skin in delicate waves and curls.

"Welcome to my home." He held his arms out at either side and bowed dramatically. "Soon to be *our* home."

"Thanks," she replied shyly. "What a beautiful place." Her slight drawl betrayed exactly how out of her element she was. Deliciously so.

He held his hand out to her. "Come. Let me give you a tour. You *are* Monica?" He smiled his best.

"Last I checked." She chuckled and placed her hand delicately in his.

"Good."

Beautiful.

That was the first thought that came to him as he studied her. The second?

I'm going to have so much fun breaking this one...

Yes. They were about to have a *great* deal of fun together.

THREE

Nadi's heart was lodged in her throat.

She hadn't ever been so close to Raziel in her life since that final night so long ago.

And she'd barely been more than a child, then.

Inches—only *inches*—separated her and the monster she'd sworn to kill over eighty years ago. He was holding her hand in his. He was slightly cool to the touch—vampires fed on the blood of others, after all, and often had lower body temperatures if they hadn't fed recently.

But when he lifted her hand to his lips and kissed the backs of her knuckles, his blood-red eyes meeting hers, her skin felt hot. She locked up.

Why? *Why?*

There was no doubt that he was a sight to behold. Sharp cheekbones, long, straight black hair, and a piercing stare that played no small part in his ability to control those around him. He was tall and built—though perhaps not by his brother's standards on either front—and dressed in a deep crimson suit that was meticulously tailored to suit his frame.

He made an imposing sight, and it was all by design.

And for the second time in her life, she was the focus of his attention.

And he had *no idea who she was.*

That was what shook her out of her frozen state. She was wearing a mask. A shield. *She* was in control of the situation, not *him.* Playing the game, she meekly tucked a strand of her hair behind her ear, and took a step closer as if drawn closer by his alluring demeanor.

Raziel let out a quiet hum of approval. "Did you have a pleasant trip?"

"I did, thank you. Never taken the train before. Didn't see any of those hideous monsters on the way. I think I might be disappointed." She chuckled. "I've never seen a real live fae before."

"Hope you never do, my dear. They would sooner eat your eyes from your skull than show you a moment of compassion. Come. Let me show you around." He released her hand to give her a brief tour of his home. He walked her from room to room, explaining what each one was along the first floor.

Nadi couldn't help but gape. She knew where the vampire lived—she knew everything she could about him, including the fact that this was one of three homes he owned—but to see it up close and personal was something else.

The center of the metropolis was densely packed with stone buildings and steel structures. But here, on the outskirts, the structures were spread out far enough to allow for some small semblance of privacy. His mansion was tucked back away from the street behind a large stone wall and iron gate, with *fake* trees and *fake* shrubberies along the edges of the property providing even more privacy.

Couldn't let anything Wild nearby, of course. What plants there were, decoratively kept in pots or the few small areas of grass, were ringed with wrought iron—to keep any magic at bay —and likely groomed back daily to keep them under control.

The building looked a hundred years old on the outside, but the interior was newly gutted and renovated. The walls were a shining, heavily lacquered wood inlaid with sharp-edged geometric patterns. Everything was made of clean lines and the detail was minimal. But the materials were where the opulence and the expense came in. Marble, gold, brass plaques depicting vampires fighting *savage fae* set into the floors.

Electric bulbs glowed from fixtures that had clearly just been wired to replace the gas ones, handmade stained glass casting contrasting light across the surfaces in various shades of red, amber, and yellow.

Everything was *expensive*. And everything was placed *just so*. It was a far cry from her clean, but cheap, little rented room and its pastel printed wallpaper.

This was the kind of luxury that most people could only dream of.

Instantly, she wanted to break something.

Namely, Raziel's smug, smirking face. It would be so easy to just take the pin from the sections of her hair she had coiled up into a bun at the back of her head and just put it right through his jugular.

Vampires were hard to kill. But if you stabbed anything enough times, it would die.

But she didn't just want him dead.

She wanted him to *suffer*.

The rest of his moons-damned family had to die *first*.

His red eyes were gleaming in amusement and hunger, like a wild animal stalking its prey. She smiled, trying to hide her sudden rush of adrenaline as shyness, and tucked a strand of her hair behind her ear. Her face was flushed, but not for the reason he probably thought.

The tour ended where it began, back at the foyer.

"You have quite the place here, Mr. Nostrom."

"You may call me Raziel." He hummed and stepped closer

to her. Towering over her easily by a foot, it was clear he was used to using his height and appearance to intimidate. Those red eyes of his burned into her—*through* her.

His fingers twisted in a coil of her own hair, wrapping the waves around his digits lazily.

She wanted to hurt him. Very, very badly. But she had to keep up the act—she had to *pretend*. She adopted the faintest look of fear on her face. There weren't many vampires in the outer cities. There was very little influence to wield out there, after all.

He smiled, reading her feigned fear exactly as she hoped he would. "That's right... you probably haven't met many of my kind."

"You're the first." She shifted a little from one foot to the other.

The slow, leisurely smile that spread over his face was that of a wolf recognizing his next meal. And it glinted with just a hint of *pleasure*. "I look forward to teaching you everything about us." Releasing her hair and crooking one of his fingers beneath her chin, he tilted her head up to him. She hadn't realized she'd fixated on his ruby-encrusted tie pin until he redirected her. "You're afraid of me, aren't you?"

"I—I heard—I heard vampires drink blood." *Easy, Nadi. Easy. Don't knee him in the nuts just yet.*

"We do. But it isn't deadly. And it certainly isn't painful. On the contrary—it can be the most exquisite, blissful experience anyone could possibly have... it can be positively addictive." When he curled his knuckle to run his finger along her cheek, her stomach churned. "But don't fret. I've promised not to mark your pretty little neck until *after* the ceremony. Otherwise, my dear mother will have my head on a pike."

Trying to look as shy and demure as possible, Nadi took a step away from him and stared down at his shoes, still faintly smiling. He smelled like sandalwood and cologne—or maybe a little like a campfire. "O—oh." What else was she supposed to say to that?

"Shame your family couldn't attend the wedding."

Good. She was right about that. She stared down at her feet. Monica would be shy. "Too risky, what with the family business to run and all."

"Mm. And Mother wasn't going to foot the travel bill. Well." Turning from her, he headed back toward the stairs. "I have business to attend to. I'm sure Hank over there will be happy to show you to your room, Miss Monica. I will return by dinner. I think it would be lovely to get to know each other, don't you?"

"Y-yeah." The stammer came easily. She didn't know what she had expected him to do, but having him simply *dismiss* her like that was a surprise. She wasn't used to being immaterial. When she was on the job, she was usually trying to be unimportant—but not like this.

Anger and frustration roiled in her before she dismissed it. *You're just a political means to an end for his family. And to him, you're just a toy to be used and discarded.* Swallowing down all her anger, she kept her voice shaky and unsure. "Sounds lovely."

He was already halfway up the stairs to the second floor. "I'm sure for you, it will be. Come along, Ivan. Oh—and Hank? Get Sarah to find the girl some proper clothes that *fit* her, will you? By the moons, she looks like she rolled out of a workhouse. Make her presentable before I eat, yes? I'd hate to lose my appetite."

"Yes, sir," the one that must be Hank replied.

It took all Nadi's strength. Everything she had. Every ounce of discipline she'd taught herself. All the patience she had earned on rooftops waiting for her target to show up after twenty or more hours of sitting perfectly still. All of that—just to keep her hands from pulling into fists.

This was normal. This was expected. This was exactly the

kind of shit that Monica would have been warned about and been coached to dismiss. She was a low-born, moderately affluent human from an outer city. He was a ridiculously wealthy, powerful vampire with extremely obvious connections to organized crime.

But *fuck* she wanted to hurt him. She *needed* to make him suffer. Swallowing it all down, she bribed herself into submission with the promise of a few hours of peace and quiet. Once Raziel was gone, she turned to Hank, who, from her sources, was Raziel's second-in-command guard next to Ivan. "Thank you—I hate to be a bother."

The man grunted. Clearly, she wasn't even worth a word. Or eye contact. He simply went toward the back of the house down a hallway and waved at her to follow.

Oh, she hated *all of them.*

Hank would be fun to kill. Leave him strung up somewhere with his own tongue shoved up his nose. Or somewhere less polite. At least he was sparing her miserable and pointless small talk. He brought her up the back stairs—like a servant—and showed her to a room at the back end of the house.

Walking in, she pretended as though she was in awe of the place. It was clear this was a spare bedroom but to Monica, it would have all been astonishing. Turning to Hank, she smiled. "Thank—"

Hank shut the door on her.

"—you." Nadi counted backward from ten. Then did it a second time. Otherwise, she would've stormed down the hallway and killed the man right then and there. Too soon. She couldn't start murdering people ten minutes after arriving. No, she'd have to take her time. Let everyone adjust to her presence. Likely, she should wait until after the wedding to start taking out his friends and employees.

Right.

The wedding.

There was no small part of her that wanted to avoid thinking about it. Not so much because she hated weddings—they were exciting, the few she had ever attended in her life—but because of what was going to follow *after* the wedding.

If Raziel even waited that long before forcing her into his bed.

Putting down Monica's luggage on a chair by the door—luggage that Hank hadn't offered to carry—she unzipped it to see exactly what the young woman had brought with her.

Clothes. A few books. And a stuffed teddy bear. It looked fairly new, so at least she hadn't accidentally stolen the real Monica's favorite childhood toy. *Poor girl. He would have chewed her up and spat her out. Sorry, Monica—you wouldn't have lasted even a single week with him.*

There was a modicum of honor in saving Monica from Raziel. Nadi hadn't set out with that in mind, and it wasn't like it was a big thing—but she supposed she could at least hold her head up high a tiny bit. Right? Some good was coming out of what she was doing in the short term. She wasn't a good person. But what she was trying to do *was* good.

Flopping down onto the bed, she let out a breath. She was exhausted. She didn't dare drop her glamor. Luckily, it stayed active in her sleep. She had to be pretty badly injured for her magic to falter. But falling asleep, unguarded, in an unfamiliar space was unwise. Even so, she was extremely tempted to say fuck all that and just take the opportunity to rest.

Getting back up off the bed with a grunt, she went to make sure the door was locked. *Don't be stupid, they have keys.* At least her room came with a private bathroom. That was a plus. She explored the space, checking every drawer and under every piece of furniture, looking for spyholes, cameras, anything.

But it seemed clean.

You're not important. They've made that very clear.

Not even important enough to spy on. Maybe she *could* take

a nap. That was certainly what Monica would do after a long day of travel. Letting down her guard felt... gross. It just felt wrong. But she had to play the part.

And she was exhausted, after all.

With a sigh, she picked up the little teddy bear—it still had a tag on the bottom of it. Maybe a going-away gift? Or something Monica had bought on the way? It didn't matter. Pulling the tag off, she climbed under the top comforter of the bed.

Even the shittiest of the shitty guest rooms Raziel had was still miles more comfortable than anything Nadi had ever owned. Using the stuffed animal as a pillow to prop her arm up on, she shut her eyes and quickly nodded off.

At least she didn't dream. That was all she'd need—his smug smile and velvety voice haunting her in her sleep.

* * *

Raziel flopped down on the sofa on the balcony of his suite, turning another one of his gold coins over on his fingers. There was no business to attend to.

But if there was one thing he'd learned to do with his toys, it was to make them wait. Make them yearn for his voice, his touch, his presence. His staff had been told to leave her alone unless otherwise directed to—she would be isolated, cut off from interaction with everyone except him.

Alone in the metropolis with no friends or family—with no one to rely on but him? He'd have her literally eating out of his hand in no time at all. An old game, but an easy one.

Ivan took his post by the door, his hands folded in front of him, as he stared ahead into the middle distance. Once, Raziel had asked his friend and guard what he thought about when he stared like that, and the man only shrugged and said he didn't really know.

Good man.

Perhaps the joke was on Raziel, and Ivan was secretly penning entire novels in his head while he stood there and blankly watched time go by.

Around the coin went again.

He had a collection of antique currency to choose from, from before the modern age of Runne, before the humans built their cities with the aid of his kind. The coins were one of the few gifts people could give him that he actually enjoyed. One of the few things he actually cherished in his life.

Little was known of life on the island those thousands of years ago. Only that it was a time of tyranny, savage cruelty, and that only by combining forces had the humans and the vampires driven the fae underground and established *some* modicum of true order and civilization to the world.

The war had never truly ended, of course. And the fae had leaked out like mold, retaking the plains. The coin in his hand was a delicate piece. Covered in filigree on both sides in almost impossible detail that must have taken a master artisan to create.

Savages. But capable of such beautiful pieces of art. A shame they couldn't be tamed.

"What do you think?" Raziel turned the coin around over on his fingers, flipping it over his knuckles. The largest moon, the one that had once been worshiped as the Father god, was just starting to rise over the tree line.

"Of?" Ivan sniffed.

"The girl, you dumb fuck." He rolled his eyes. "What did you *think* I meant?"

Ivan shrugged. Sweet man. Good friend. But the intelligence of a brick. And, just like a brick, he was very useful for bashing people's heads in. "Cute."

Brief, but accurate. Monica was, contrary to his concerns, quite attractive. His body tightened in response to the memory of seeing her, standing there in her ill-fitting clothes and with her big, innocent, green eyes. Underneath the stupid patterned dress was a body that he couldn't wait to have stretched out before him, taut, waiting—*begging*.

Her dark brown hair had hints of chestnut. And the way her eyes went just a little wide when she looked at him? The way she almost trembled when he drew near?

What a wonderful trinket. He would have so much fun breaking her, even if he suspected it would be far, *far* too easy. He wondered if he could shatter her in a night—have her licking his shoes and begging for his attention by the following dawn.

The thought made him shudder in anticipation. Picking up his wine glass of blood, he took a sip from it. Monica wouldn't last long, either by design or necessity, sadly. He had no desire to turn her, and therefore once their honeymoon was over, he'd drink her dry.

But they could have fun together before then. He idly wondered if his siblings would try to get a piece of her before she was gone. Lana, most certainly. Mael, perhaps.

His thoughts turned back to Monica. Tasty little thing. But he had the sincere suspicion that she'd be disappointing. Like ordering a plate of food from an expensive menu only to find it was a single floret of broccoli sitting in the middle of an empty plate.

All anticipation. No meat.

"I should wait until after the wedding to destroy her, I suppose." He took another sip of the blood before setting the glass down with a clink. "Bad form to have a vacant-eyed bride at the altar."

Ivan shrugged. "Doubt anybody would be shocked."

"Perhaps. But I wouldn't hear the *end* of it from Mother." He sighed. "I'll be a good boy and wait."

Ivan snorted a single, incredulous laugh.

Raziel grinned. "I will! I promise."

Adorable, innocent little Monica, sold to a monster.

Raziel's last toy had been found walking the streets of the

city, stark-raving mad, begging anyone to forgive him for his misdeeds. Begging to be punished. He'd wandered into a canal and that was the end of that.

Poor Oliver. But like all his partners, Oliver had been weak.

What Raziel needed was a challenge.

Kicking his feet up on the coffee table, he leaned his head back on the sofa, and shut his eyes. For now, he would dream of all the terrible and wonderful things he would do to Monica when she was his wife.

Though... maybe there was a *little* fun to be had before the wedding.

Maybe just a *little*.

FOUR

Nadi looked at herself in the bedroom mirror. Sarah, one of Raziel's staff, had come by to drop off "proper clothes" and makeup for her. The woman barely made eye contact before leaving and shutting the door.

It was clear how little Monica meant to these people. And that was fine—if they paid her no attention, it would be easier to dismantle them from the inside. Leaning in, she touched up the deep red lipstick that had been brought for her. It came as no surprise that she was wearing his colors—black and red.

The dress was revealing, with a plunging neckline that made wearing undergarments impossible, and thin straps on the back criss-crossing down to the waistline. But it was hardly the most scandalous thing she'd ever worn in her life. Besides, fae in the Wild usually wandered around stark naked, anyway. She was used to nudity.

The silk fabric and lack of a brand label told her it was *expensive*. The black stilettos and the makeup she had been brought were also clearly the best that money could buy.

Not because Raziel wanted to give his fiancée nice things, of course. But because he wanted her to look exclusive, like every-thing else in his life.

She was just an accessory to him.

Disgust boiled in her, but she swallowed it down. He was playing a game with her. And she was playing with him too. But they weren't playing on the same board.

Curling her hair up into an artfully messy bun, she stuck the two long, pointed pins into it to keep the knot of hair secured. They were her only weapons here.

If Raziel attacked her, they wouldn't be of much use. In her line of work, she relied on stealth and surprise. Not brute strength.

But she could at least turn them on herself if necessary. Nadi refused to become another rumor of the disgusting things Raziel did to his enemies. And his lovers. She knew only too well what he was capable of.

The sound of screams echoed in her memories.

Jaw twitching, she took a breath and let it out. The memo-ries of that night flashed back to her unbidden.

The underground caverns of the Wild were something to behold. She honestly sometimes pitied the humans and vampires who had never seen them. The darkness held wonders, if you weren't too afraid to see them.

All fae clans were nomadic, traveling in packs and wandering with the chaotic currents of the Wild. Any attempts to build *structures* and *civilizations* like the humans did would be a total waste of time and effort down there. Fields of crops would turn to forest overnight. Twisting roots and vines would tear buildings down days after they were made.

Her father had been an Iltani, a member of the few fae clans who dared to trade illicit goods with the upper world and whose ranks were more human than fae, half the time.

It had left her and her family cast out from most of the other fae in the Wild, but... it had also meant that Nadi and her family had never gone hungry, or without the finest fabrics, or really had ever wanted for anything.

So, Nadi had spent her youth gathering mushrooms from the Wild that her family would then sell to the humans, and she spent her life living closer to the surface than most—in those places where the faintly glowing vines had begun to overtake buildings and structures that the humans and vampires had surrendered to the fight against nature.

All the world was a gradient. Nothing was truly black and white. Good and evil. Life and death. Civilization and Wild. And growing up, she'd lived in those liminal places, those forgotten spaces—abandoned by humans and shunned by fae. Neither in the metropolis nor in the Wild, but in the spaces in between.

At the time, Nadi didn't understand *why* the humans were so interested in the ugly mushrooms she worked to gather. They couldn't even be turned into anything useful.

Now, she understood that they made for some *incredible hallucinogenic* drugs. It had made her clan influential, if not wealthy. But she hadn't known why. As a child, she hadn't known *why* her uncle Luciento had joked with her father that "he could really use a shapeshifter like her in his ranks when she got older." And why her father would laugh and say it'd cost him the two moons in the sky to let him recruit her. Luciento would snort and say "Sold."

They had been staying in a warehouse recently overtaken by the Wild when it had all gone wrong. Their clan had overstepped their bounds. They had grown too bold. And like the Wild, they needed to be *beaten back.*

But it was not their blades and their fire and their machines that came to destroy them. It was something much, much worse.

A vampire had come for them. But not just any vampire.

It had been *him.*

The Serpent.

Even then, she had stared at him. At his stark beauty against the natural world around him. He didn't belong there, with his long black hair, pale skin, and sharp red eyes. Her world was untamed, all tangled vines and leaves. Not pinstripes and tailored suits.

She hadn't known his real name then. Only the title. Only the legend that when the Serpent came, everyone died. She'd never seen a vampire until that moment.

Chaos had struck almost instantly. He and the other vampires had swarmed into the warehouse, coming at them from all sides. They had moved faster than she could even see. Things with wings like bats, or—things that could *become* a swarm of bats, she hadn't been quite sure.

The vampires had set fire to the warehouse, forcing her family farther out above ground, blocking any safe escape into the Wild. They'd driven them out into the street. At the time, she hadn't known where she was. Now, she could see it in her mind's eye. Somewhere deep within the metropolis, underneath an overpass of the stacked roadways that hid the undesirable world from those above.

They'd run directly into a waiting squadron of humans. The sound of gunfire had echoed in her ears. Her mother had grabbed her arm. "Hide—shift! Be one of them—" And had pushed her down behind some crates by a wall.

In her head, time and time again, she replayed that night. In her dreams, in her nightmares, in her waking moments. She imagined herself being brave. She imagined herself standing up and saying *no* and fighting alongside her family.

Instead, she had done exactly what her mother had told her to do. She'd shifted her form into that of a human, crawling along the ground in the smoke and the dirt, glad that her clan generally wore the clothing common to human women. It made it easier to blend in if she needed to.

And in that moment? She'd needed to.

She had been a coward that night.

But that was when she had heard his laugh.

The gunfire had ceased.

Nadi had stared up in awe at the overpass—at the time one of the many great twisting structures of the metropolis. Road built over road built over road built over homes and offices and workshops. A dizzying sea of twisting girders and metal that looked like madness made from straight lines and lit from stinky glowing flames in glass lamps on metal sticks.

The vampire from before—the one with the suit and the red eyes—had stood before her family. Her mother, father, brother, and two sisters. They had all been on their knees before him, bloody and covered in soot, her father already bleeding from a bullet wound in his side.

"Mm. I apologize for this. It really isn't personal." The vampire's voice had been smooth. Calm. *Friendly.* As if this were any other day. "But, unfortunately, your brother has been testing our patience—and a message must be sent. So... here I am, the messenger—and you, the message."

"You hideous, inbred bloodsucker." Her father had spat down at the vampire's expensive shoes, defiant to the last.

The vampire laughed again. "Oh, my dear, sweet *savage.* As if I could be hurt by any insults you can levy against me." He had strolled casually over to her brother and... snapped his neck with a sickening *crunch.*

Her mother's scream would replay in Nadi's mind for the rest of her life.

As would the look on her brother's face as he fell lifelessly to the ground.

"*Damn you!*" Her father's shouting had been pointless.

"It's a shame my powers are useless on your kind." The vampire had sighed. "I do hate getting my hands dirty. Though, I suppose it is nice to have the practice now and then. Now, do remember, your brother Luciento is to blame for this, not me."

Nadi's eldest sister had followed next.

Followed by the youngest.

None of the desperate pleas for mercy from her parents did any good. Nor did they do anything to change his calm, casual, *friendly*, demeanor.

The vampire had put an end to her mother's suffering next before smiling warmly down at her father and shrugging. "Luciento knew the price he would pay for acting out of turn."

Her father never had the chance to respond.

But Nadi's terror had not ended yet. Because the vampire had then turned his attention to *her*. She was still cowering there, wearing the face of a human she had seen once, crying and weeping, bunched up in the corner of some crates against what she recognized now as bricks.

His expensive shoes had echoed on the cobblestones as he approached her. The silhouette he made against the light from the gas lamps still haunted her nightmares. "Wrong place, wrong time..." He chuckled, then said one more word to her. "*Run.*"

And she had.

But she'd decided, then and there, that she would carve that word into his skull as he died.

There was a knock on the door. "*Dinner. Ready?*" Fucking Hank again.

And he was summoning her to dinner.

With Raziel Nostrom.

Shutting her eyes, she took a deep breath in, held it, and let it out. Taking in the reflection of Monica one more time in the mirror, she braced herself. Yeah. She repeated the phrase in her mind that had kept her going all those years.

I am going to kill you, Raziel Nostrom.

FIVE

For a moment, Nadi considered her approach. Raziel likely expected Monica to be a boring, idiotic, and naive country girl. She could use that—keep him off guard. He had no idea what he was dealing with.

Cracking her neck from one side to the other, she put on her best smile and opened the door. Hank was waiting for her in the hallway. He was clearly trying to appear bored, to show her she meant nothing. But the way he stared when she walked out of the room gave her a spark of pride.

Monica might look like an innocent farm girl. But that didn't mean Nadi had to wear her like one. "Lead on." She gestured down the hallway, eager to get going. And eager now for Hank to stop staring at her cleavage. Monica was an ample girl.

Hank cleared his throat and started walking. She followed him, head held high. She was glad she was practiced in heels.

This outfit was designed to put Monica on full display, but also to make her deeply uncomfortable.

Nadi was going to make everyone *else* uncomfortable, instead.

By fucking *owning* it.

Hank brought her to the balcony that overlooked the large, fenced-in back yard. The sky was lit by one half-moon and a sea of stars. There was an in-ground pool back there—*of course he has a pool*—the yard and gardens elegantly lit by pockets of glowing lamps on stanchions.

Suddenly, she very much was looking forward to going swimming, if she survived long enough. At least there would be one upside to this insane plan, besides the revenge. She couldn't remember the last time she had been able to go *swimming*. She wouldn't dare to do so in her true form, but just the idea of being fully submerged in water made her smile.

A table on the balcony was set for two, draped in a white cloth with plates and expensive silverware arranged *just so*. Raziel was already seated, a crystal wine glass perched between his fingertips and filled with crimson liquid. Nadi knew it wasn't wine.

The sound of her heels clicking on the stone of the balcony caught Raziel's attention. As he turned to look at her, she couldn't help but smile at the way his red eyes went just a little bit wide.

Keeping her head held high and her shoulders straight, she brushed past Hank to approach the table. It was clear neither of the two men were going to pull out the chair for her. Fine by her.

Raziel stared at her, eyes glued, as she walked up to the chair opposite him.

Placing her hand on the back of the chair, she smiled and leaned over just a little to pull the chair out. Monica had nice assets; she might as well use them while she was wearing them. "May I?"

Her words seemed to shake him out of something. Clearing his throat, he gestured aimlessly with his wine glass. "Help yourself."

Sitting down, she ignored Raziel's staring. "I can't thank you enough for leaving me in my room all day. That was so thoughtful of you—I was absolutely *exhausted* from the travel." There wasn't a hint of sarcasm in her voice.

He didn't seem to know what to do with that. "I... yes, I expect you would have been."

A waiter—of course he had gods-damned *waiters*—came up to pour her a glass of white wine. She thanked the man kindly and waited until he walked away to pick up her glass and take a sip of it. It was fantastic. And, as far as she could tell, not drugged.

How positively polite of him. Though, she supposed he was a renowned hypnotist. He didn't need drugs to get humans to do what he wanted. "How was your day?" It was fun, being unshakably perky in the face of what was obviously meant to be an intimidating situation. "Did you get your business done?"

"Hm?" He was staring at something else that was perky. Not exactly her fault—it was cold out and the dress didn't let her wear a brassiere or a corset or even a slip.

Stare all you like, arsehole.

Shaking his head, he turned his attention out over the back yard, clearly trying to peel himself away from her. There was that welling sense of pride in her heart. He wanted her—that was obvious. And as he shifted in his seat—it seemed he was also a little uncomfortable.

Good.

"My day was fine." He sipped his "wine." The way it stained the edges of the glass told her it was blood. Hopefully, that meant he'd keep true to his word and keep his fangs away from her neck until after the wedding. She wasn't sure what would happen when he bit her—if her glamor would hold until after he tasted her blood, or if he'd instantly know what she was —and she didn't want to find out until she had a chance to kill him first.

That was a problem for another night. She focused on the now. And right now, she was winning. Raziel didn't seem to know what to say. Or do. Her appearance and tone must have derailed his game.

"What is it that you do for work?" Reaching over the table, she picked up a tiny loaf of bread from a bowl and placed it on the porcelain plate in front of her. Tearing off a piece, she lifted it to her mouth. "Father wouldn't say."

"My family works in shipping and receiving, mostly."

That was a comically understated way of putting it, though she supposed she had to admit that it was technically true. His family shipped and received drugs, guns, people, stolen goods, contraband, corpses...

"Is it interesting work?" She made sure to chew and swallow the bread before speaking. Even ranch girls had manners.

"Sometimes, it can be fascinating. Other times, I am little more than a well-paid errand boy." He finally regained control of whatever was going on in his head, and turned those red eyes back to her. He studied her silently between sips from his glass.

Huh. She had never heard of any rift between the Nostrom siblings. From the outside they'd always looked to be a tight-knit operation. "You don't get along with your family?"

"Hardly what I said." Those red eyes stared through her. She had gone too far. That question had come from Nadi, not Monica. She'd have to be more careful next time. "Merely that my work often involves cleaning up their mistakes. But as the youngest, that is my duty."

"Oh." She paused, and recalled everything she could about the real Monica. "I have a younger sister. She usually gets away with everything, though." *Quick, idiot, change the subject!* "What's that?" She pointed at his glass. She knew the answer. She just wanted to see what he'd say about it. "Doesn't look like normal wine."

His smile was thin and wry. "Astute. It isn't."

Nadi expected him to say something foreboding, trying to intimidate her with "It's blood" or something of the like.

Instead, he held the glass out to her. "Try some."

Blinking, she took the glass from him and sniffed it. The metallic smell of the blood mixed with wine made her want to turn her head away. But Raziel was watching her with those red eyes of his, and she knew it was a test.

She felt like she was in one of those human medical auditoriums being dissected by a team of doctors. For a split second, she wondered if he could see through her glamor, she felt so exposed.

No wonder people were so afraid of him.

She had to force herself to move. After a beat, she took a sip of the substance. It was vile. It wasn't the first time she'd tasted blood. But it was certainly the first time she'd drunk it with red wine. She wrinkled her nose and handed the glass back to him. "Going to be honest, it's not my favorite thing in the world."

That seemed to impress him, if even just a little bit. He chuckled as he took the glass from her and took his own sip from it. "It is... an acquired taste."

Silence stretched between them as she munched contentedly on the bread and occasionally sipped her own, non-bloody wine. It was his turn to move the next piece on the board.

When he pushed up from his chair, it took every ounce of her willpower not to tense up. Monica might be a little jumpy, but she wouldn't be afraid to turn her back on him like Nadi was.

Which seemed to be exactly where Raziel was headed. He strolled behind her before trailing his fingers over her shoulder.

Goosebumps flooded over her in a wave. She shivered at the unexpected touch. His skin was unnaturally warm from the bloodwine. Behind her, he let out a pleased hum at her reaction.

He's mistaking it for attraction. Nadi gritted her teeth. He'd just caught her by surprise, that was all. He trailed his fingers over her shoulder, and she turned her head to watch him. "Have you ever had lovers before?"

He lifted his hand from her shoulder briefly to turn her head forward again. He didn't want her to see what he was doing. Or going to do. Her stomach twisted into a knot, but she obeyed.

She wanted to grab the knife from her plate. She wanted to drive it into the artery in his crotch. She wanted to watch him bleed out, screaming. "Are you asking me if I should be wearing white at our wedding?"

"I do not like being asked a question in exchange for a question..." His tone dropped to a low, quiet rumble, like a storm on the horizon. "So, simply answer mine, would you?"

Swallowing the lump in her throat, she took a moment. It was a threat, plain as day. She wondered if Monica would see it for what it was, but she supposed she would want to make her new fiancé happy, so that didn't really matter. And she didn't sense any vampiric magic in the statement. Not yet. "I... once or twice. Only the one guy."

"Good." He traced his fingers over the tendon of her throat, just the tips of his nails. It made her shiver again. No one had ever touched her like that. "I despise the inexperienced."

"O-oh."

He leaned in closer, one hand on the table beside her, caging her in. His other hand wandered up her throat and to her hair before pulling the two pins out, undoing the bun. Her hair fell down around her face and shoulders. "Your hair stays down from now on."

There it was. There was the Raziel she had been expecting. The one she'd heard of in the stories and rumors. It was a *command*. There was no room for argument. She felt the power in it. Like a warm blanket, surrounding her soul. If she had been human, or, by the void, if she hadn't been paying attention, his words would have been tattooed *into her very being.*

Without even making eye contact. Without even making a gesture—with only the power of his voice—he had *commanded* her to wear her hair down for the rest of her life. She had heard all the stories of people who had torn out their own eyes, had eaten their own fingers, all because he had politely asked them to.

When she didn't answer, the point of her dangerously sharp hairpin was suddenly against her throat. She tilted her head back away from it until it touched his shoulder. His lips were close to her ear, his hot breath pooling against her skin.

Heat pooled somewhere else in her, sudden and unexpected.

"I love the ones that look so sweet, so innocent, so *simple,* yet have such resilient minds." He chuckled, nuzzling close into her hair. His voice was a quiet rumble, and it sent a shudder through her that made her head spin.

The clash between that and the point of the pin against her throat made every nerve in her body feel electric. Like lightning.

Gods.

She *wanted* him.

She felt herself leaning back against him, seeking more of him, her eyes slipping shut. It was wrong. This was wrong. He was *wrong.* But it was unlike anything she'd ever felt in her life. And it had absolutely nothing to do with his failed attempt to hypnotize her.

"You cannot fight me."

Oh yes, *she* could. But Monica couldn't. She took a deep breath in and, as she exhaled, forced her shoulders to go slack.

"That's it... now. Your hair stays down from now on."

All the bizarre, warring emotions that were crashing through her were making her head spin. But she didn't have time to examine them now. She had a role to play. And if she let him trip her up now, she'd be dead. "Understood," she whispered.

"Very good." But he wasn't done with her. Not yet. He trailed the pin down her throat, following the line of the tendon, the point scratching her skin just enough to feel it, but not hard enough to leave a mark. Her heart was racing. Every nerve in her body felt like lightning.

The tip of the pin moved down her shoulder and her arm before he placed both pins on the table beside her left hand. Lowering his head just a little more, he kissed her shoulder. Slowly. Lingering. His lips searingly hot.

She didn't know what to do. Didn't know what to say or how to react. All afternoon she'd played dinner out in her head in a thousand different ways. But this wasn't one of them. This hadn't been part of her plan.

Not that she hadn't expected him to flirt with her, or to touch her. That much she'd figured would happen. No, that wasn't what had her eyes shut tight and her heart pounding in her ears. That wasn't what she had failed to anticipate.

The way she was reacting to him was *not okay*.

No, no, no, no, no! This was an anomaly. It would pass. It'd just been a long time since anybody had touched her, that was all. And the wine on a nearly empty stomach was probably going to her head.

He hummed. "You are afraid. But intrigued."

When she answered, her voice wavered. "I've—I've heard stories of vampires, but never met one, and I—"

"Do you think you are the first human who wishes to be hunted? Who wishes to feel the fangs of the beast, and know their sting? Hardly. Nor will you be the last." He kissed her shoulder again.

"I..." She trailed off, uncertain as to what to say.

After what felt like an eternity, he finally straightened up and walked back to his seat. In his absence, she realized how *warm* he had been, like standing next to a hearth. It must have been the blood he'd been drinking. His skin had been cool earlier this afternoon, and now he was throwing out heat like a coal fire.

Shivering at the sudden cold, she blinked her eyes open. He was sitting across from her with a pleased smile across those perfect features.

She might have won the first point, but he had won the second. And judging by the smug expression he wore, he knew it.

Fuck.

* * *

Raziel smiled at Monica. She had put him on the back foot for a moment when she'd walked out onto the balcony, but he had recovered and quickly showed her precisely who was leading the dance. Not that he hadn't deeply appreciated her attempt—though he knew it hadn't been intentional.

By the Father, the country girl cleaned up *nice*. He'd expected a demure, shy, trembling thing to walk out, tugging at the bottom hem of her dress or trying to close the front to keep her modesty in the scandalous outfit he'd chosen for her.

Not for her to walk out like a black cat along a fire escape railing, owning every step with pride and surety. Even the high, pointed heels he'd expected her to wobble on didn't seem to give her pause. The dress he had chosen would have shamed even the ladies his sister sold at her jazz clubs, and yet this Monica seemed to be unfazed. What did it say about him that the body underneath the dress wasn't as impressive to him as the way she wore it?

He supposed he shouldn't be surprised. Beauty only reached a certain point before it was all the same. But the unassumingly confident way she had walked up to him, smiling as though this were just a picnic in a field, had made a sudden roaring inferno of *need* nearly overcome him.

The mental image of bending her over the railing, rolling up that short hem, and burying himself in her tight flesh had struck him dumb.

This was unexpected.

This was new.

And not *entirely* welcome.

There was never anything stopping Raziel from scratching whatever itch he wanted—no matter how profane, no matter how sinful. He relished his easy access to anything and everything his twisted mind could dream up.

Especially as he could simply tell others around him to do whatever he wanted them to do, at any point, meaning very few things were ever outside of his reach. But, the sad result of that was... he found almost everything boring. Uninteresting. A waste of his time and attention.

He couldn't remember the last time in over two hundred years of life that he had ever been stunned to silence by desire. Left gawking like a schoolboy at a pretty girl.

It was only the sudden, equally powerful rush of anger that had finally shoved his lust aside. How *dare* she? How *dare* she saunter over like that? Dressed like *that*? In his home?

No. He had needed to take control of the situation back, at any cost. He needed to remind her exactly where she was and who she was dealing with. And when her cheeks had gone pink at his nearness and goosebumps had prickled her bare skin, he knew he had done just that. Wonderful little thing, she had even tried to fight his invasion of her mind.

But like all humans, she fell to his hypnotic gifts with only a moment's worth of struggle. She had put up a fairly good fight, which was surprising—most humans collapsed like a house of cards in a breeze—but soon enough, she was in his palm.

The rest of the dinner after that went along peacefully.

They barely spoke. She knew well enough to not prattle and fill the air with vapid nonsense, and only responded to him when he prompted her first. Instead, her inquisitive, spring-green eyes were taking in every detail around her as if memorizing them all.

Three very interesting things had come out of their dinner that left him pondering what his next step should be.

First—he wanted her. Very badly and in a way he hadn't experienced in *centuries*.

Two—she had the bravery to sip his bloodwine and barely flinched. It was vile to humans, but she took it in stride. She clearly had more of a backbone than he had imagined.

And three—she had no clue about the truth of his "line of work." That was the most intriguing part of all of this. Had her father really not told her? Or had she written it all off as rumor and slander?

She was about to become the wife of one of the most feared crime lords on all of Runne. He wondered how she would deal with that knowledge. Part of him was suddenly deeply interested in finding out.

One of his men approached from inside his home. "Sir?"

"What?" Raziel hated interruptions.

The man shifted nervously. "Your sister wants to speak to you."

"Tell her I'll call her back." He rolled his eyes.

"No, um—she's downstairs." The man took a step back, flinching away from expected rage. And for good reason.

Raziel's instinct was to hurl the messenger from the balcony. But he bit all that back down and let out a long, weary sigh. Some things couldn't be avoided. And Lana was definitely on that list. Forcing a mocking smile onto his face, he turned to Monica, who was watching the exchange curiously.

He knew why Lana was there. His meddling sister very likely wanted to greet the fresh meat for herself before Raziel broke her into tiny pieces. Which was fair. Standing, he gestured for her to follow. He didn't offer her a hand up.

"I'd hoped to spare you this until closer to the wedding, but Lana waits for no one. Come, my dear... time to throw you into the fire."

SIX

Whatever Nadi had been expecting from Lana, this wasn't it.

Now, she knew a lot about Raziel's sister—the so-called "Sweetheart Mistress"—since the vampire was solidly near the top of Nadi's must-kill list. Nadi had even been in the same space as her a few times, watching and learning all she could about the blonde's mannerisms and habits.

But it was a different thing entirely when she was up close, personal, *and being frantically hugged by her*.

Nadi laughed quietly, nervously, as Lana threw her arms around her and squeezed her tight like she was a raft in a storm at sea.

"My new sister-in-law!" Lana squealed, laughing far more cheerfully than Nadi. "Well, soon-to-be, anyway. Hello, hello, hello! You must be Monica. So wonderful to meet you—I am *Lana*, but I'm certain you already knew that—and moons be *damned*!" Lana took a step back, holding onto Nadi's upper arms, scanning her up and down in appreciation. "You lucked out, brother dearest! Look at *her*!"

Raziel walked over to one of the square-armed sofas in one of his many living rooms—or maybe this was a parlor. Rich people had fun names for their excess spaces. He lay down on it, grunted, and slung an arm over his eyes without responding, looking for all the world like he had a sudden insufferable headache.

He probably did.

"Thanks." Nadi kept a smile on her face, though she was fighting the urge to shove away from Lana and put some distance between them. It was easy to forget, in the face of the vampire's bright smile, exactly what Lana was infamous for.

The Nostroms, the most powerful sect of vampires in Runne, traded in *everything*. Drugs, guns, stolen goods, influence. Lana?

Her expertise was flesh.

"Pleasure to meet you." Nadi tucked a strand of her hair behind her ear.

"The pleasure's all mine, trust me." Lana chuckled and walked away from her, heading straight for the bar by the wall. "Brother, when you get bored of her—do let me know."

I'd rather stab out my eyes, thanks. Nadi kept her hands from balling into fists. Instead, she walked over to a chair and sat, purposefully avoiding the furniture that could fit two people on it. "Do you have a hand in the family business? Raziel told me he's in shipping and... What was it?"

"Receiving."

Lana snickered as she filled her glass with alcohol. "Did he, now?"

Raziel still didn't move, just lay there with his arm over his eyes.

"I do have a hand in the family business. All us ladies do," Lana continued. "I'm in automobile sales, actually."

Raziel snorted once in laughter.

"Really? How modern." It was easy to feign surprise on that one. Lana pretended she dealt in *automobiles*? How in the name of the moons did that make any sense?

"Mmhm. All manner of vehicles." Lana poured a second drink. Nadi watched carefully just in case the woman slipped anything into either glass, but it seemed fine. Lana crossed the room to offer her one of the drinks.

Nadi took it, smiling in thanks. Even if she wanted to smash the glass on the marble coffee table and ram the broken pieces into Lana's skull. "That sounds fascinating."

"It is, honestly. We offer every kind of ride. New and used. We rent, we lease, we sell. Any kind of ride you could imagine, we provide it. Cheap? Expensive? Exotic? Even the hard-to-find ones—we'll procure them for our patrons."

Ah. *There* was the joke. Nadi kept her expression smooth as if she believed it. "Is there a lot of money in it?"

"What do you think?" Lana sat down on the arm of Nadi's chair. So much for personal space. Lana reached out and stroked her hand over Nadi's hair. "We *are* one of the richest families in the metropolis." The vampire let out a rush of air. "Goodness. You came from one of the outer cities? I need to get out of the metropolis more often."

Lana was beautiful, with her long, perfect blonde hair, and her full lips painted a garish color that matched her magenta eyes, revealing what she really was. She had curves in all the right places. What Nadi hadn't expected was the seemingly genuine... brightness to the woman. Like she was about to coo over a baby rabbit.

How could she rent, lease, and sell *people*—and still smile like that?

"I just can't get over how *pretty* you are." Lana's expression was almost innocent. It was missing the cruelty, the deviousness, the inherent predatory nature that her brother had. "I'm sure Raziel has had a hard time keeping his hands off you."

Nadi blinked. "I just arrived. He's—he's been busy, and—well. He's been letting me rest from the travel."

"How... *gentlemanly*." Lana shot Raziel a withering stare.

"I'm sure his intentions are nothing but pure. He is such a chivalrous man, after all."

"Love you too." Raziel didn't even dignify Lana's obvious barbs with a gesture or eye contact. "Are you done, now? Can you leave?"

"Rude!" Lana huffed. She scooted down the arm of the chair, squishing Nadi into the other side to squeeze in next to her. She put her arm around Nadi's shoulders. "And I'm here to get to know my new sister. You can fuck off, for all I care."

Nadi went tense, trying her best to relax. But she supposed the real Monica would be a little uncomfortable with the situation, so she was still in character. She sipped the drink Lana had given her in an attempt to refocus her attention on something.

Raziel laughed dryly. "Like I would trust you with her alone? It wouldn't be five minutes before you had her legs spread and your hand buried up to your wrist in her—"

"Brother!" Lana placed her hand over her chest, gasping in horror. "What a horrid thing to say! You'll offend Monica's innocent ears."

Right. Innocent. Nadi killed people for a living. The idea that she hadn't witnessed her fair share of what people could do with each other was pretty hysterical. But, she was supposed to be a sweet, bright-eyed cattle rancher's daughter. Not an assassin who had walked in on some *fascinating* scenes in her life.

"Besides." Lana rested her head on Nadi's shoulder. "I would never do something so crass before your wedding. Now... *after* the wedding? That's another story."

Nadi had to bite back a genuine laugh.

Lana's coarse joke earned her a reaction from Raziel. Namely, he lifted his other hand to idly flip her the bird. Nadi just sat there, pretending like she wasn't a part of the conversation. Because she really wasn't.

Lana noticed her silence and, lifting her head from Nadi's shoulder, kissed her cheek. "I'm joking, of course."

"I figured." Nadi smiled at her, feigning nervousness. "Sibling banter." Sure. Because normal siblings talked about shoving their fist up the other's fiancée. Vampires...

"Raz and I have a special rapport." Lana wiped away what was probably a magenta smudge on Nadi's cheek. "And he is heinously inappropriate. You'll learn soon enough."

"Don't you have somewhere to be? *Cars* to sell?" Raziel sounded both bored and annoyed. Listening to them dance around Lana's real profession was half insulting and half hysterical.

How dumb did they really think Monica was? Pretty fucking dumb, by the sound of it.

Lana snuggled in closer to Nadi. "I want to hang out with my new best friend!" She snapped her fingers. "Oh! We should go out! Have you ever been to a jazz club? Of course not. They're all the rage out here now. They don't have clubs out where you're from. Do they?"

"N—no." Nadi honestly didn't know. They probably did, but not the kind Lana was talking about.

"Then we *must* bring you to one of the ones downtown. It'll be your bachelorette party! I'll get all my friends, and we'll hit the scene. Really welcome you to your new home in style."

"No." Raziel's single word was firm. "She stays here. *Alone.*"

Lana stuck her tongue out at her brother, whose arm over his eyes meant that he couldn't see the expression. "She's not your pet, Raz. She's basically your wife already. You wouldn't treat your wife like *property*, now would you?"

Yes. Yes, he would.

And so would Lana, if given the chance.

But it was a pretty clever ploy by the vampiric mistress, Nadi had to admit. It forced "Raz" to either assert that yes, he was going to make decisions for Monica, or say no, and let her go out on the town.

Of course, neither of them had consulted Monica at any point.

"I do not want her to get dragged off, hopped up on powder, fed too much alcohol, and then who-knows-what-else done to her, and have you roll her out on my doorstep like a used prophylactic." Raziel grimaced as he bit out the words.

"You have such a beautiful way with words, brother. Truly a poet." Lana rolled her eyes. "Monica deserves to celebrate. To meet her new friends and family. To have *fun*. Not be kept locked up in a proverbial cage."

Knowing Raziel's proclivities, a literal cage wasn't out of the question.

Finally, Lana turned her attention to Nadi. "What do you want to do, Monica? Stay here, bored out of your mind, and then get shuffled to the wedding and back without a single moment of fun, or go out on the town? Really cut loose? Meet your new family?"

Oh, gee. How sweet. They were finally asking her opinion on something. For the first fucking time since she'd arrived. But only to put her in an impossible situation. By the void, they were *obnoxious*. "I'd hate to upset him."

"Smarter than she looks." Raziel huffed a single laugh.

She wanted to stab him *very, very badly*.

"Hmph." Lana sighed. "I suppose that's smart. He does have a terrible temper. Well, then. That settles it." She stood, downed her drink, and set the glass down on the coffee table with a clink. "We'll have the party here, instead."

"*What?*" Raziel sat up for that one. "No. Absolutely not."

"I'm not giving you a choice, brother. If you won't let her go have fun, I'll bring the fun here." Lana giggled sweetly. "You're right! It's a much better idea. I'd hate for anything terrible to happen to our wonderful little Monica."

Raziel growled, a sound that was not human. His canine teeth were longer than they were a moment prior. "I will not let you take over my home and—"

Lana didn't let him finish. "Well, it's a good thing you won't be here for it. It's a *bachelorette* party, after all. No boys allowed. Well. No *you* allowed, anyway. There'll be plenty of boys." She waved her hand dismissively at Raziel as she headed for the door. "Anyway, I'm off! I have a party to plan. Bye now!"

The expression that Raziel wore was one of pure, unadulterated, and seething rage. He glowered at the back of his sister's head as she left.

All right, maybe Lana wasn't *all* bad. Anybody who could piss him off that badly had at least one redeeming factor.

With a snarl, Raziel pushed up from the sofa and stormed upstairs. Nadi sat there, watching the whole scene unfold. An echoing *slam* of a door told her that he wasn't going to be bothering her anymore that night.

Smiling, she sat back in the chair and finished her drink.

This was a suicide mission—she was going to die, no matter if she succeeded or failed. But before that happened, she was going to take every possible opportunity to ruin Raziel's life.

And damn it if she wasn't going to have a little bit of fun in the process.

* * *

Monica was his. *His!*

How dare his sister breeze in and make designs on *his* home and *his* things! Raziel paced back and forth in his room, his muscles taut as he fisted his hair in his hands, yanking on the strands.

Lana always acted like the perfect princess and Mother's favorite—namely because she *was*. Mael was the firstborn son and the heir to the throne. Lana was her mother's joy.

Raziel?

He was the *spare*.

And at the moment, he wanted to hurt something. He wanted to watch something *bleed*. He wanted to watch something *suffer*. That was the only way to calm down his anger—to eke out his revenge on anything within range. Part of him wanted to drag Monica into his bed by the hair and show her who she should be taking orders from.

But this wasn't Monica's fault. There was no stopping Lana when she got something into her head. And he knew, no matter what he said or did, Lana would be showing up the next night with a caravan of people for her "party."

Now, that wasn't to say he didn't want to drag Monica into his bed for *other* reasons. Lana wasn't wrong. The young woman who had stumbled into their family was a treat and a half. He wanted to taste her. To make her taste him. To show her exactly who and what he was.

But he had to wait.

He wanted to make Monica *want it* first. It was no fun to seize what he wanted—that particular game bored him now. He liked his playthings to crawl to his feet, begging for more.

Walking up to a wall, Raziel smacked his forehead on the hard surface. He needed to do something. He wouldn't be able to sleep like this. If he couldn't loose himself on Monica, he'd have to find something else to distract him.

His fangs were pricking the inside of his lower lip. He needed to *kill*.

Taking a deep breath, he cracked his neck from one side to the other and changed into a different outfit. Something a little more appropriate to cause mayhem in. A heavier wool peacoat that reached his ankles, and an all-black suit that he wouldn't mind ruining when it became soaked in blood.

Throwing open the doors to the balcony off his bedroom, he stepped out onto the landing and took a deep breath of the chill night air. The stars were beautiful, framed by the two moons. The larger white one—the Father—was high in the sky, giving him plenty of light by which to see.

And hunt.

Tonight, he'd rip someone's throat out and drain them dry. It was considered *bad form* for a vampire to murder a human for blood. Mael would have to smooth it out with the mayor and the police force when they found the body. Not that anything about the kill would tie Raziel to the scene. Even if Mael suspected Raziel, nothing would come of it.

For vampires were the superior species in the metropolis, and the humans knew it was because of the vampires that they were safe from the fae. Without them, the humans would still be pets and servants to the hideous savages beneath the ground. So, it was the least the humans could do to serve as food from time to time. The least they could do was give up a spare life now and then. They *did* breed like rabbits, it seemed. Always so many of them underfoot.

Spreading his arms, he dissolved his form into bats and took to the night sky.

Tonight, someone would die.

Tonight, he would drink his fill.

Even if, when he shut his eyes, it was *her* throat beneath his fangs.

SEVEN

Nadi left her room around lunchtime when nobody had come by to get her. Not that she particularly wanted to interact with anybody—she was just hungry. And once it was clear she was going to be largely ignored by the staff—and Raziel, it seemed—she didn't feel bad throwing on a much more casual set of clothes and heading down to the kitchen to make herself a sandwich.

A few of the staff and the guards stationed around the house gave her odd looks, but other than that, it seemed they weren't going to stop her. Great. She made herself a grilled cheese with what she could find in the fridge, poured herself a cup of coffee —cream no sugar—before making the trek back toward her room.

As she passed one of the doors leading out to the back yard, she stopped. Sitting out there, lounging on an elegant piece of outdoor furniture, was Raziel. He was staring into the shim-mering waters of the pool from under a patio umbrella, his expression drawn tight. His eyes were hidden behind dark sunglasses. Vampires were sensitive to light—it weakened their powers to almost nothing—but they weren't hurt by it.

He looked... upset. Not angry. Just *upset.*

In his hand he had a coin. He walked it over his fingers to his thumb, then back again. It was an almost hypnotic pattern he kept repeating again and again.

Her curiosity drove her outside, approaching him a little cautiously. What was upsetting him? Likely still Lana. But she had to know.

Ivan, Raziel's chief bodyguard, turned his head to look at her as she approached. He nodded once in greeting. "Miss."

I'm going to love murdering you. Even if it's going to take me eighty-two stabs to do it. She smiled at him sweetly. "Mornin'. Though I guess it's afternoon, now."

Raziel looked a little surprised as she sat down near him, placing the plate on her lap with her grilled cheese.

"Want half?" She motioned to the plate.

There was the faintest, quizzical smile on his face as he turned his attention back to the pool. "No. Thank you." He paused for a moment. "You kept your hair down today. Good."

Shrugging, she started eating in silence. She wasn't sure whether the people in his service were under his hypnotic command or not. He made it sound like doing his bidding was a willing choice on the part of his victims. That made sense. She supposed it was a lot more problematic if his victims knew they were dancing on puppet strings.

Still, the coin danced effortlessly across his fingers.

"That's a fun trick. Where'd you learn to do that?" Nadi smiled at him cheerfully.

"I taught myself. I have had many years to learn." He caught the coin between the fingertips of his pointer and middle fingers and held it there for a moment. Then, flicking his wrist, he made the coin vanish. Another flick, and it was back again. A street magician's illusion.

Smiling, she applauded quietly. She knew it wasn't real

magic, but simple dexterity and practice—which somehow made it more impressive. "That's wonderful. How old are you, if you don't mind my asking?"

"Over two hundred years old."

"Oh. Wow." She let out a whistle. "How old do vampires get?"

"We don't age." Raziel's expression fell flat. "My mother is well over five hundred, and my grandmother... well, she does not speak of her age. And no one knows how old she is."

Grandmother Lilivra. The great-grand matriarch of not only the Nostrom clan, but of most of the vampire sects. She was a mysterious figure that Nadi knew next to nothing about. No one had seen or heard from her in centuries—rumor was that she was long dead, or in hiding, or had been murdered by one of her own children and overthrown. Nadi didn't quite know what to think of the whole thing. And honestly, she didn't care.

Her interests were much closer to home and far more mundane on the scale of things than vampire demigods and elder creatures that were probably legends.

"Oh," was all she really had to say in response. They fell into silence again for a long stretch as she finished her sandwich and put down the plate with a clink. Watching his expression, she saw he seemed a thousand miles away.

There was a bit of a choice in front of her. She could either say "Have a good one," and go hide in her room until she was forced to attend the party that Lana was throwing. Or, she could pretend she cared and ask him what was wrong. The first option was her preference, though she was deeply curious what could be bothering him. The second was probably pointless. He wouldn't tell her the truth, he didn't trust her. She was just some twit from the farmlands who he assumed wouldn't live long enough to grow wise to his real business dealings.

But if she wanted to get close enough to hurt him and take down everybody around him, she'd need his trust. Even just a little bit of it. Somehow, some way, she had to get him to *like* her. As stupid as it sounded. But she had no idea how to actually go about doing that. She'd memorized every single detail about his life, but it wasn't the same thing.

The coin danced over his fingers. It was fascinating to watch.

Smirking, she sipped her coffee. "How many coins do you think you'll get as wedding gifts?"

That earned her a glance of surprise followed by a laugh. He hadn't expected that. "The answer is too many. It's the thing *everybody* gets me." He rolled his eyes. "It's one of the few things I appreciate, I suppose. But it's the easiest and only option."

"At least you'll never run out." She shrugged. "What else do you like? Besides, you know, coins?" It was a mundane line of questioning, but it'd do. "I figure I should know something about my future husband other than that he drinks blood mixed with wine and owns too many antique coins."

Reaching out his arms to both sides of him, Raziel propped his feet up on the glass-topped coffee table in front of him and crossed his legs at the ankles. "I have the curse of being that person you just can't buy anything for because I have everything already. I wouldn't worry about it, if I were you."

"Hm. Handmade gifts, then." She sipped her coffee again. Thank the Mother moon for coffee. "Something you can't buy."

He furrowed his brow for a moment. Something crossed over his face like a cloud over a moon before it was just as quickly gone again. Maybe nobody had ever made him anything in his life, and he was just realizing that.

Because nobody loves you, you heinous piece of shit.

She opted not to say that bit out loud. But any bit of pain

she could bring him by pointing out the yawning emptiness in his life was more than fine by her.

Part of her wondered who he really was, deep down. Behind the veneer of arrogance. If there was anything at all. Maybe he was like a mannequin—pretty on the outside, hollow in the middle. Just wearing clothes and pretending to exist.

"I'm sorry your sister is going to ruin your house tonight." She let her legitimate disdain for having to go to this so-called party show through. "It's honestly the last thing I want to deal with."

"Not a party girl?"

"No, I like them well enough. Just not when I don't have a choice in the matter." Her smile faded a little. "I should get used to that, though. Not having a choice in things."

Raziel finally turned his attention fully toward her and away from the pool, red eyes regarding her thoughtfully from behind his dark sunglasses. Almost curious. "I assume you wanted nothing to do with this marriage."

"Leave my family, my friends, my home—and be forced to marry a man I don't know?" Shaking her head, she let out a sigh. "Not a lot of people would willingly sign up for that. I assume you want nothing to do with me either."

"Hm. I wouldn't say that." His smile turned a little fiendish as his voice dropped, becoming husky and sensual. "I think there's plenty of fun we can have together, don't you?"

Something in her twisted in reaction to his words. Then embarrassment flooded her at her response. She hated him. Despised him. *Loathed* him. But his words *did* something to her.

This was getting more and more complicated.

Maybe she should just stab him and be done with it. Throw out her plan of killing the rest of his family first to make him suffer and just cut him to ribbons instead.

Maybe she should have thought this all through before

throwing herself into the middle of things. But she hadn't had much time to react. She'd seen her opportunity and gone for it without really considering all of the details.

Never mind the fact that he wasn't telling "Monica" the whole truth about what the arrangement was with the wedding. That Monica was doomed to either be turned or be killed. But she had to play her part, either way.

"There has to be more to you than shipping and receiving, and, well, *that*." She looked down at her lap. Monica was likely a little shy, and it gave Nadi an excuse to hide her turmoil.

"Hm." That was all he was willing to give her at first. But a moment later, he got up to sit closer, his thigh against hers. When he draped an arm over her shoulders, she fought the urge to punch him in the face. "Tomorrow, you have a dress fitting appointment with my mother that you need to attend. She'll know if you're hungover. You cannot be hungover."

It wasn't a question. He wasn't giving her a choice. That much wasn't lost on her. But she smiled at him brightly, all the same. "Noted." After a pause, she frowned. "Your sister isn't going to be mad if I refuse the powder, is she?"

"You have an issue with drugs?"

"No, I just don't like what it does to me." She wrinkled her nose. That wasn't a lie. "I prefer the natural stuff. The chemicals make me feel itchy."

Laughing, he leaned in closer to her and kissed her temple. "I didn't even know they had powder out your way."

She almost flinched away from his lips. They were too hot, and he was too close. He must have fed recently. And a lot, by the feel of it. "You'd be surprised. Not much else to do out there, except get drunk and high."

"Well, I'll let her know. She'll bring a selection, I'm sure." He began to run his thumb back and forth over her shirt on her shoulder. The heat was still there, even through the extra layer.

"Should I worry about you going too far with anyone? She does love to bring all of her pretty friends along."

"I—I mean. I did warn you I wasn't a virgin, if that's what you're asking—"

He barked a laugh, squeezing her closer to him briefly. "No, no... trust me. I do not do well with breakable things."

The knot in her stomach cinched tighter at his insinuation.

"But I would very much rather you not get in the mix with Lana or any of her *associates* if you can help it. I'm sure you understand why I'd rather my future wife not have a history with anyone too close." Those red eyes were watching her again. "It just gets needlessly dramatic."

"Another good reason to stay off the powder." She smiled, though it was wavering and didn't last long. "And I'll do my best."

"What, no promise?"

"I don't know what I'm up against." Chuckling, she tucked a strand of hair behind her ear. "I can't very well promise if I'm not certain. But I promise to try my best."

"Smart girl." Her fingers were replaced by his in her hair. "Because if you break your promises to me, I *will* have to punish you..."

There was that knot in her stomach again, twisting and turning like a bag of snakes. She knew exactly what he was threatening her with. She had a choice—play shy or surprise him. Resting her hand on his thigh, she shot him a wry smile of her own. "Something tells me, you'll find a reason to punish me no matter what I do."

The look on his face made her heart skip a beat for a reason she couldn't understand. It was equal parts shock and like a wild dog being shown a platter of fresh, raw meat. The sudden hunger in his expression made her want to shrink away from him. She'd just thrown gasoline on a fire.

"Pretty, tasty thing..." He cupped her chin in his hand. His lips were hovering close to hers. "Teaching me to adjust my expectations for what cattle country has to offer."

The heat of his nearness, the feeling of his breath against her skin, gave her goosebumps and a shiver of cold despite the warmth of him. She had no response. No words she could form. Nothing she could think of to say. She had made an unexpected move on the board—but he was still winning.

"I suppose..." His voice was a dark, dusky purr. "I could make sure I get to have you first... I've been trying to be a good boy—trying to keep my hands off you until we're married. But, *fuck* if you aren't testing me to my limits."

He wanted her. The realization sent another roll of electricity through her body. He *wanted* her. Her. A fae whose life he ruined.

Nadi had spent her life being invisible. Unknown. Someone else. Literally and figuratively.

To have those red eyes boring into her, seeing through her, with such starving need? She didn't know what to do with that. Didn't know how to respond.

She didn't know how to contend with her own smoldering fire.

This was wrong.

This was dangerous.

This was going to get her into a *lot* of trouble.

Of all the things she expected to have happen to her... She knew she'd likely have to fuck him—or more aptly, let him fuck her—she wasn't a moron. But she had expected to suffer through it. Go through the motions. Fake it the best she could.

This?

This wasn't okay.

Her hand tightened on his thigh reflexively. She needed something to hold onto for dear life. Even if it was the source of all her problems.

"Careful..." He tilted her head back, exposing her throat.

He bent his head down to kiss the line of the tendon in her neck. It was almost scalding, it was so hot. "I don't do well being teased, pretty thing."

Her eyes slid shut of their own accord. The words that left her were almost a breathless whisper. "Ivan's right there."

"He's seen much, much more than this," Raziel murmured. His hand slid into her hair to cradle the back of her head, as he slowly kissed her throat. His teeth grazed her skin before he nipped her with his fangs, causing her to jolt in surprise. His chuckle was... well, there was only one word for it. *Evil.* "I'd ask if you want him to join in, but I don't like to share my toys until I'm done breaking them in."

"Is that what I am to you?" She meant it to sound strong. Instead, it came out just the same as before—heavy with need and confusion.

"Everyone is a toy to me, pretty thing." He lifted his head to meet her gaze, his red eyes seeming to flicker like firelight. "Everyone."

"A breakable toy."

"Precisely." His hand in her hair tightened into a fist, pulling the strands just enough to make her hiss from the sudden sting.

But she didn't push him away. Her hand tensed on his thigh, digging her fingers into his skin. She needed to keep his attention. She needed to earn his trust—his respect. And there was only one way to do it. Fixing him with as defiant a stare as she could manage, she smiled, with just a hint of her own wickedness. "You can do better than that."

* * *

"You can do better than that."

The words ran through him like molten lava. Lit every

nerve of Raziel's body on *fire*. Her bright green eyes regarded him with something he had never, ever experienced before.

Contempt.

Daring.

And almost, perhaps, a little bit of arrogance. But painted over with such sweet and beautiful lust.

She wanted him.

Desperately.

He knew that. He knew he was beautiful. He knew people desired him for his looks. But very few ever wanted him for everything *else* he brought to the table. A few whose curiosities got the better of them would come to him, begging to experience a night or three with him. But no one stayed.

No one lasted.

No one ever looked at him and *challenged* him in such a foolhardy way. The pretty thing was out of her league. Likely doing her best to flirt with a man whose darkness ran far, far deeper than she could possibly know.

It was that realization that shook him loose. That snapped the moment like an icicle. She didn't mean her words—she didn't know what she was talking about. She was goading on a wild stallion thinking he was some tame, neutered workhorse.

She thought she was playing with matches.

He was an inferno.

"Hm. I can. But not today." He let go of her and stood. She looked stunned at his absence. He had to shift himself slightly with his back to her to keep from making an obvious and embarrassing display of just how riled up she had made him.

Which, points to her, he supposed. That didn't happen much. Well, not from something so *benign*, at any rate. There was something to be said for teasing, for not scratching every itch and fulfilling every urge right away.

"You should get some rest. You're going to have a very long

night." He walked away from her without a second glance. "And do try not to fuck my sister, will you?"

"Y—yeah," came her uncertain reply.

Heading indoors, he waved Ivan away as his bodyguard went to follow him. He wanted to be alone. He needed a moment to think. Damn her. *Damn* this Monica to the void. His arousal would not go away. It wouldn't stop. And it was getting downright painful.

Locking the door to his room behind him, he stripped naked and headed into the bathroom. Starting the shower, he set the water to as hot as his boiler could manage—and he had it set ridiculously high. The steam filled the room with a fog by the time he stepped into the stream. The walls were made of dark, river rock tiles in uneven shades and patterns. The texture of them bit into his hands as he pressed his palms against the surface, lowering his head to let the hot water pour over him.

Get a hold of yourself.

But his mind flashed to an image of her on her knees in his shower, gazing up at him with those beautiful green eyes. He didn't picture a woman begging for his attention. He didn't dream of a broken thing, desperate for his touch.

No.

He saw that challenge. That *dare.* That sheer *contempt* mixed with a need as great as his own.

"You can do better than that."

Gripping his length in his hand, he surrendered to it. He imagined it was her, touching him. Her, fawning over him, goading him on. Taunting him and begging for him. Challenging his dominion. His control. His power.

Where did she get the nerve? The *balls?* She didn't understand who she was dealing with. But he was going to show her soon enough. Just a few short days, and she would learn precisely who she had been tormenting.

Growling low, he quickened his strokes, his body tingling in ecstasy. She wouldn't last a night with him. She wouldn't last an hour. She was mistaking a tiger for a house cat.

This was temporary.

"You can do better than that."

Letting out a muffled, furious roar of release, he pounded his fist into the wall, not caring for how the edges dug into his skin.

Yes, Monica. I can do better than that.

And you're going to wish you'd kept your pretty mouth shut.

EIGHT

The day was shaping up to be a real whirlwind. Nadi went back to her room, confused and uncertain after Raziel had abruptly abandoned her by the pool. She would have bet any amount of money on him kissing her in that moment.

Not just... storming off.

What had *happened*? What had she done?

Even Ivan had looked bewildered by his boss's actions. He had simply shrugged at her before going back inside.

She wanted to scream. Just flip the coffee table and *scream.* But she kept her composure, and decided she'd lock herself in her room to prepare for her bachelorette party.

Thrown by her most hated enemy's sister.

An enemy that had just been about to kiss her.

An enemy that she... had wanted to kiss her.

Fuck. Fuck, fuck, fuck! This wasn't part of the plan. Okay, fine, she hadn't gone into the whole scenario with a plan, not really—but if she had, this certainly wouldn't have been on it. Pressing the heels of her hands into her cheekbones, she sat on the edge of the bed and let out a long, ragged sigh.

It'd be fine. It'd absolutely be fine. She could get through this. And, hey, maybe it was a good thing that she was attracted to the man that she would soon need to have sex with. Never mind the fact that it was *Raziel*. The man who had killed her family and countless others.

Sighing, she ran her hands through her hair.

"I can use this." She took a deep breath. And it was true—this was an upside. Fine, sure, it was putting her whole set of so-called moral values up for debate. But if she was actually going to enjoy fucking him, then... it made things a lot easier.

It felt like she was making lousy excuses, but whatever. Tonight was going to be exhausting—she should focus on survival. Keeping her veins away from all the hungry vampires in the room wasn't a task she was looking forward to.

Lying down for a nap before the party, she tossed and turned for a while before finally finding a comfortable position. But as she tried to sleep, her mind stayed locked on one moment. The feeling of his hand in her hair. The heat of his presence—like sitting near a roaring fire. The smell of his sharp cologne.

She wanted him.

That much was painfully clear.

Don't worry. He only sees you as a piece of meat. Inter-changeable with all the others. You're nothing special to him.

She repeated that to herself as a mantra as she drifted to sleep.

Nadi decided that "sexy but understated" was going to be her vibe for the evening. It was easier said than done, considering the clothing options that Raziel provided for her were... less than modest.

A red lace blouse that cut down past her cleavage and a pair of too-tight black pants that draped over boots were what she wound up choosing. For a few reasons—one, the pants were *incredibly* hard to get on, so hopefully anybody who slipped drugs into her drinks would find them *incredibly* hard to get off. Pants were a working woman's clothes—she expected everyone else would be wearing dresses, but she couldn't care less.

Two, she could slip her hairpins into her boots. Never go into an unknown situation with known enemies unarmed.

Three, she was wearing Raziel's colors—a reminder to all those at the party exactly who she "belonged" to, as sickening as it was.

And four, she rather liked how she looked in blood red. It was a good reminder of why she was there.

She was going to murder them all.

Every. Last. One.

Taking a breath, she adjusted her hair in the mirror one final time before heading out of her room for the first time that evening. She'd heard the commotion in the house and knew that she was arriving "fashionably late" to her own party.

But seeing as nobody had come to fucking *fetch* her, it seemed fair.

The thump of the live jazz music reverberated through the floors as she headed down the hallway and then the stairs to where the rabble was the loudest. About thirty or forty people had come to attend—a mix of vampires and humans.

The grand dining room had been decorated and rearranged for a party, the brass inlay in the walls polished, and no elegance was spared. An ice sculpture of a large, bat-winged creature glinted in the amber light of the electric fixtures where it stood surrounded by food and alcohol. Everyone was dressed to the nines, sequins and jewels sparkling like the ice as they moved.

And there was Lana—draped over a man next to her that Nadi recognized as Azazel. A third cousin to the family, and, according to Nadi's research, Lana's favorite... pet, for lack of a better word.

He was slim and almost painfully beautiful—with sharp

features and bright orange eyes that seemed to catch the light like that of a wolf in the darkness. When he laughed, revealing his fangs, it only made the comparison more apt.

He was dressed in a pair of skin-tight pants, a thin white shirt that was mostly unbuttoned, revealing his various tattoos, and what could be mistaken for ritualistic scars.

Cruelty ran in the family.

Nadi walked up to them, smiling shyly, and lifted her hand in a slight wave. "Hey, Lana."

"*There* you are!" Lana leapt from the sofa to throw her arms around Nadi in a hug. "I was wondering if my brother had tied you to his bed to make sure you couldn't attend. Everyone! Meet Monica—our soon-to-be sister-in-law!"

The group that had been sitting around Lana—all business partners of the family—half-heartedly greeted her. It was clear they weren't interested in her in the slightest, save for the lingering stares at her... assets.

Making small talk with a bunch of vampiric mobsters wasn't high on her list of shit to do that evening, anyway.

"You weren't kidding." Azazel smiled at her, crimson-painted lips pulling into a faint, sardonic curl. "The bastard got lucky with this one."

"Let me get you a drink. What would you like?" Lana was already heading toward the bar. "Talk fast or I choose for you!"

"Uh—old fashioned," Nadi called after her. "And no drugs."

"Pah! No fun." Lana huffed in fake indignation. "But *fine*. Since you're the *bride*."

"Not a fan?" Azazel asked as he scooted over on the sofa and patted the spot next to him.

There wasn't a point in pretending it wasn't inevitable. Nadi sat down next to him, smiling cheerfully and shrugging. "The chemical stuff isn't for me. I prefer natural."

"I'm sure Lana brought everything." He chuckled and draped his arms over the back of the sofa—right behind her.

When he started to curl a strand of her hair around her finger, she couldn't help but go a little tense. "Afraid? Of little old me? You're sweet."

"I'm engaged, is all." She brushed his hand away from her.

He laughed as if that was the cutest thing in the world she could have said. Like a child insisting they knew how the world worked. "You'll learn."

Lana came back carrying two drinks. "One *boring* old fashioned," she teased as she handed one of the glasses to Nadi. Lana sat down on the other side of Azazel. "I see you two are already getting acquainted."

"Someone was very keen to remind me that she's getting married." Azazel was grinning like the cat who ate the canary.

"Well... can you blame her? She's not from here, and she's a human. I'm sure she doesn't know what our customs are." There was a wicked glint in Lana's eyes. The Sweetheart Mistress was plotting something, that much was painfully clear.

"Oh?" Nadi played dumb. She had a sense of where the conversation was going.

"In our family, it's tradition for a bride-to-be to sleep with a stranger before their wedding. A last hurrah." Lana reached out and stroked some of Azazel's chin-length, curly blond hair away from his face to tuck it behind his ear. "It's rude not to."

Bullshit. "Is that a vampire thing? Or a... Nostrom thing?" She sipped her drink. Seemed like Lana had stayed true to her word—there wasn't the usual tang of chemical drugs.

"Does it matter?" Azazel asked.

"I don't want to be rude, but... also, Raziel asked me not to—y'know, get into the mix with anybody tonight. That's all."

"Well, what Raziel doesn't know about won't hurt him." Lana leaned forward, showing off her own "assets" that were squeezed into a sparkling pink and black sequined dress. "I bet you could have the pick of any man—or woman—here, but I figured Raziel would cause a fuss, so... I found you someone discreet." She placed her hand on Azazel's inner thigh.

The man didn't flinch, just kept those orange eyes on Nadi.

"I—I mean—I'm sorry, but—" She played up the scared-girl-from-the-farm routine. She didn't want to have to kill Azazel so early into her game. There was no way she could think of to make it look like an accident. *Oops, he fell and landed on that lamp. Repeatedly. Until it bashed in his skull.*

"Don't worry, baby—I'm good at keeping things a secret." Azazel stood, and took her hand, pulling her up to her feet. "Come on. Before someone else gets a hold of you."

"I—"

He started pulling her off into the rest of the building. He wasn't giving her a choice. She could cause a scene, but that would complicate matters. *Fine. So he dies tonight.* She'd have to think fast and come up with a way to hide his corpse. But it wouldn't be the first time she'd had to do that in her life.

She was plotting her way forward and out of the situation as Azazel pulled her into one of Raziel's guest rooms. He shut the door behind them, threw the lock, and let out a long, exaggerated sigh. *"Fuck, I hate her."*

Nadi blinked.

Azazel walked to the bed and threw himself down onto it on his back. He stretched his arms out at his sides before letting out a long groan and shutting his eyes. Hardly the actions of a man trying to seduce a nervous bachelorette.

Something about his actions felt... familiar. Tired. Just a weary soul doing their job. And tonight was one night too many. Or perhaps that day had come and gone years ago. Studying him, Nadi stood by the door and leaned against the wall. "Lana told me she deals in cars."

"Did she, now." He sounded so bored.

"You must be the company car."

That surprised him. He lifted his head to look at her in

disbelief for a moment before howling in laughter and flopping his head back down on the bed. "Oh, thank *fuck* you aren't an idiot."

"I'm glad they think I am, though." She sipped her drink. "Makes it easier."

"Ain't that right."

"I'd rather not fuck you, if it's all the same to you."

"Usually, I'm the one doing the fucking, but either way I get your meaning. And that is fine by me." He sat up with a grunt, watching her with renewed curiosity. "Lana will assume we did the dirty, which gets her what she wants. You can go back to Raziel with a clean conscience."

"It wasn't my conscience I'm worried about. If he finds out —or even hears a rumor—he'll probably kill me. Or you. Or both." Nadi sighed.

"Hm. Nah. He'll be able to smell it on you. Or rather, the *lack* of me on you. We'll rumple up your clothes and hair and get you off to bed before anyone else figures out that you're *unspoiled*." He snorted.

She laughed. If he only knew.

He patted the bed next to him. "Sit. Let's talk. You seem... interesting. And I don't remember the last night I didn't spend either ass up or ass down." He flopped back on the bed, eyes shut. He looked exhausted. "Oh. And call me Aza."

She sat down next to him, sipping her drink still. It was good. She really hoped it wasn't laced with something she couldn't detect. "Do you have a choice?"

"Nope. Same as you. I'm under a contract someone else signed."

That detail was new to her. She frowned. "I'm sorry to hear that." She wasn't lying. Nobody needed to have their body pimped out because of somebody else's decisions.

"Eh. I'm good at what I do. And most nights I enjoy it. But

I'm just so fucking sick of her games. Oh, and that line about 'customs'?"

"Total bullshit?" She smirked.

"Total bullshit." He stretched like a cat before rolling onto his stomach. Through the thin fabric of his shirt, she could see that his back was an array of criss-crossing scars put there by hand. Lana's hand, no doubt. Or maybe one of her more frequent clients. "She just wants to mess with Raziel."

"I heard the family was close."

"Oh, they're close all right. Nobody from the outside can *ever* fuck with Momma Volencia's children. They would *never* suffer an attack from outside the family. But internal drama? Messing with the other siblings' toys? Fair fucking game."

"Huh." Nadi paused. "Do you want a drink?"

"I would *love* someone to make me a drink."

Standing, she headed over to the bar by the wall. "You seem like a gin guy."

"Smart girl."

She mixed the gin and the vermouth, put in a couple of olives, and brought it back to him. "A dirty gin guy."

He took the glass with that fiendish grin of his and sipped it. "Ah, fuck, and you mix *good* drinks. Yeah, I'm sad Raziel's going to kill you."

"What do you mean?" Now she wanted to see how much Aza would tell her.

Aza stared at her and his expression went thin. "You don't know."

"I suspect. But I want to see what you'll tell me."

He sighed, his expression one of pity. "Do you really wanna know?"

Nodding silently, she waited for him to continue.

"Here's... the thing about vampires. We're... a picky bunch." He grimaced. "At least about who we let into our little club. Lana only turned me because she wanted to make sure the 'company car' didn't need to be brought out for so many repairs. We don't just... blindly get married and turn somebody. This so-called marriage tradition you're stuck in is—well, it's based on an old tradition, from—from like *the before times.*"

She arched an eyebrow. "Before the metropolis?"

"Yeah. When vampires and humans were just starting to work together. Before civilization beat back those ugly fucks down into the Wild."

She tried not to take that personally.

Aza shrugged and kept talking. "It's based on some stupid story. The first of our kind went to a human village and said to the town elder, 'Give me your daughter as my bride as a sign of your devotion and I'll keep you safe.' Well, the elder did. And the vampire..."

"Killed her."

"Drank her dry, like a bottle of shit champagne." He took a deep swig from his glass. "Took her to his ancestral lair. They were wedded in blood, whatever, highfalutin bullshit. The vampire kept his word, and that was the start of the partnership between our people. So..."

"I've been offered up as sacrifice. I'll be carted off to the Nostrom family home and popped like a bottle of shit champagne." Nadi shut her eyes. She had to play this off like this was new information. Walking to the edge of the bed, she sat down. Hanging her head, she let out a breath. "My father knew."

"I can guarantee it."

"I guess you and I have that in common, then."

"What?" He moved to sit next to her, sipping his gin.

"We were both bought and sold like cattle."

He huffed a sad laugh. "Cheers to that." He held his glass out. She clinked hers against it, and they each took a drink in silence for a moment before he spoke. "Can we be friends? Well, for as long as you're alive, anyway."

That legitimately surprised her. "Why?" Monica was

already as good as dead in his eyes. And in hers too. Void, she was also as good as dead in reality. "If what you say is true, a few days after the wedding I'll be shuttled off to some abandoned estate and murdered."

"All mortal lives are short. I appreciate them no matter how long they last. Or don't." He shrugged. "You're smart. You seem like you care. And you make a *fuck* of a good drink." He paused as he stared down into his glass. "I like being seen as a person."

"Yeah. We can be friends." She paused. No harm in having an ally, even if they were a fake one. "Thanks for being the first person here to tell me the truth about anything."

"The truth won't do you any favors around here. Remember that." He stood, downed the rest of his drink, and set the glass down on the top of the bar. "All right, let's ruffle up your hair. I'll tell Lana you pulled a muscle with me and want to go soak in your tub."

"And what'll you do for the rest of the night?"

"Wrong question." He grabbed a bottle of whiskey and uncorked it. He took a chug before walking up to her with it. There was an emptiness in his eyes when he finished his thought. "The question is 'who' will I be doing. And how many."

It was then that she made up her mind. Azazel would survive her murder-spree. Lana, however... would *suffer*. And the best part was, Aza would be a wonderful tool in getting to the vampire mistress. Azazel had her confidence—and therefore, he was her weakness.

And in exchange? Maybe, just maybe, she'd let Aza watch.

That's what "friends" were for, after all.

Right?

NINE

Nadi was a light sleeper.

It was part of the job.

Nobody had ever come after her—she was careful at covering her tracks and generally stayed away from any targets that would warrant a revenge-kill of a hired gun. But it was always a real, and serious, possibility.

So, when someone crawled into bed on top of her, their hands on either side of her body... she reacted *very* poorly.

Before she could even process what she was doing, she'd grabbed the hairpin she'd stuffed underneath her pillow, rammed her elbow into the attacker's jawline, and used their recoil of pain and shock to roll them both over.

It wasn't until she was straddling the man beneath her, hairpin digging into his skin hard enough to make him bleed, that she realized who he was.

Raziel.

Oh.

Shit.

She blinked down at him, at a total loss for words. He had

his head tilted back, baring his throat, his red eyes burning like coals.

Lips curling into a slow, lazy smile, he let his hands rest on her bare thighs. It wasn't until he touched her, his hot skin on hers, that she remembered that she slept naked. "I was right—that was why you were keeping your hair up. You wanted a weapon close by."

Her heart was pounding in her ears. Swallowing the rock in her throat, she debated what to do. She could kill him here, now —just put the pin through his eye and into his brain and be done with him. She'd lose on any chance to witness his suffering, but he'd be gone.

Vampires were hard to kill, but they weren't truly immortal.

She'd just tried to attack him. If she let him live, how would he respond? And if he was suspicious that her hairpins were her weapons... did he just figure her out? Had she just given herself away?

His hands trailed up her thighs to her waist, slowly caressing her. She shivered, her skin breaking out in goose-bumps. "You like to be touched..."

She did. It wasn't something she experienced often. But now wasn't the time.

"Usually, *I'm* the one wielding the weapon but... I have to say this is... strangely enjoyable." He shifted, and that was when she felt his desire pressing into her core where she was strad-dling him. With a grunt, his eyes slid half-shut. "I was so very much trying to be a good boy until after the wedding. Stay just like that a moment, will you?"

It was their closeness—the presence of him grinding against her—that finally drove her to climb off of him and the bed in one swift movement. She grabbed a silk dressing gown from the chair by the dresser and threw it on, tying the belt around her waist. "I'm—I'm sorry. You startled me."

Letting out a disappointed sigh, he stood from the bed like

nothing had happened, smoothing out his clothes and straightening his tie. "I wasn't expecting my cowgirl to have such a violent streak. Nor for her to be hiding weapons beneath her pillow."

His knuckles were bloodied.

Her stomach sank. "Whatever Lana told you—"

"That is why I'm here. Come. Since you're *up*, let's do this properly." He opened the door to the room and left her standing there, confused and shaking, hairpin still in her hand.

She didn't like being on the back foot. Glancing at the clock, it was three in the morning. What the fuck was Raziel doing in her room at three in the morning? Why had he been in her bed?

Putting the hairpin down on her dresser, she debated her next actions. She could disappear. Get dressed, jump the fence, and be gone. But she'd given Monica all the money she'd had in the bank. All her things were gone. She'd destroyed her life to come here to ruin him. There was no going back.

And, even worse than that?

Curiosity burned in her.

She needed to know what was going on here.

The feeling of him against her, of his body so close—his touch. She shut her eyes, let out a wavering breath, and combed her hands through her hair.

Fine. *Fine!* This was a one-way trip for her, she'd known that going in. Whether she succeeded or failed, this was how she died. Quickly pulling on her clothes, she squared her shoulders, and followed after Raziel.

He hadn't waited for her, but she found him on the balcony that overlooked his pool. It seemed to be one of his favorite places to be. He was already sipping a glass of ice and amber alcohol, and a second one was resting on the railing next to him.

He glanced at her from the corner of his eye. "Aw. You got dressed."

That actually made her laugh. Not a lot, and not loudly, but it was a genuine laugh. "I'm sorry about the hairpin."

"No, you're not. Don't lie to me." He placed his drink down on the railing.

Something struck her—an urge. She didn't know what it meant, but she followed it. "You're right. I'm not." Walking to the bar, she picked up a container of vodka and a cloth. Pouring some of the alcohol onto the fabric, she headed back to him.

Raziel was watching her now, curious and dubious in equal measure. Picking up his hand, she studied the blood on his knuckles. "How much of this is yours?"

The dark chuckle that left him sent another shiver down her spine. "None."

Chewing on her lower lip, she started to clean the blood off his skin. When she reached one part, he hissed and jolted, but didn't recoil. She shot him a raised eyebrow.

"Okay, maybe some." Shrugging dismissively, he looked off into the city, his expression unreadable.

Finishing his first hand, she went to the second, cleaning him up as best as possible before folding the cloth and putting it on the railing. It was an action she'd done to her own hands many times—cleaning someone else's blood from her skin. She picked up her drink and faced the city, finding that she really needed the benefit of alcohol at the moment. "I heard rumors. Rumors that I think are confirmed now."

A hum left him, but nothing more.

"I didn't fuck anybody. And they didn't fuck me. No matter what Lana—"

"She told me you and Azazel just chatted. That you were both more than happy to pretend he ran you ragged and went to bed ridden hard. I heard the same from him." He sneered. "Though he thinks Lana is none the wiser."

"I..."

"She's my sister, Monica." He reached into his coat pocket

and fished out a silver cigarette holder that had a decorative "R" etched into the surface. Picking one out, he tucked the cigarette between his lips, clicked the case shut, and slid it into his pocket.

Click-click. That was why he sometimes smelled of smoke. But it wasn't tobacco that she smelled in the air, it was more like... woodsmoke or incense. Vampires were strange. His face was illuminated by the glow of his lighter as he lit the cigarette. He took a heavy drag before exhaling a cloud of smoke into the air above them.

She'd seen a million people light cigarettes in her life.

But something about the way he moved was *distracting.*

"Then why did you sneak into my room if you believed me?"

"It's my room, Monica. You're merely using it. This is my house." He gestured aimlessly at the building around them.

Rolling her eyes, she sighed. "Why'd you sneak into *the* room, then?"

"Tell me about these rumors that you've heard." Another slow drag from his cigarette.

By the great deep lords of the deepest caverns, she wanted to throw him over the balcony. Not like she could budge him, she was a third his size—but the mental image made her happy all the same. She ran a hand over her face. "I'm sure you've heard them."

"I want to know what *you* think I am."

"Your sister deals in flesh, not cars. It's painfully obvious, even if I hadn't heard the stories. Your brother deals in drugs and uses the fact that he's the senior advisor to the mayor to move things in and out."

"And me?"

"You... kill people." She gestured to his hand, still a little stained with red, which was resting on the railing.

"I do."

Sipping her drink, she pondered the metropolis at night, just as he was doing. There were always lights, blinking in the distance, even though nobody in their right mind was awake or working. Cities were always awake.

Whatever inspired her to ask her next question, she didn't know. But it left her lips before she could stop it. "You're going to kill me on the night of the wedding, aren't you? I was given to you as a sacrifice."

The next few seconds were a blur of motion. He was just *too fast*. He grabbed her by her hair, fisting it in his hand, yanking her away from the railing so quickly that her drink clattered to the floor, the thick glass somehow surviving the fall.

Before she could do anything more than squeak, he threw her forward. Up became down then up again as she landed on something surprisingly soft. One of the pieces of furniture on the balcony.

He was on top of her again, straddling her thighs, pinning her down. She took a wild swing at him, but he caught her wrists easily and pinned them over her head with one of his hands. He was a silhouette against the starry night above him.

Raziel was smiling, watching her struggling to kick him off with all the amusement of a tiger that had just pinned its prey.

Letting out a ragged, frustrated sigh, she glowered up at him. "What the *fuck* was *that* for?"

"See... this is the thing. This is what I don't understand about you." He slipped his other hand around her throat and squeezed. "This. Right here."

Gagging, she kicked uselessly, trying to wriggle away. But there was no use. He was going to choke the life out of her. She was going to die. This was it.

Helpless, she watched as he lowered himself closer to her, resting his weight on his elbow, even as his grasp around her throat never wavered. He wanted to watch her die. Wanted to watch the spark of life leave her eyes. There was a keen fascination in those red orbs.

My glamor will fall the moment I die. He'll see me for what I really am. What a wonderful little mystery he'll have to deal with, then.

"Cowgirl from the outer cities. The daughter of a wannabe gangster who got on the wrong side of my mother. Sacrificial lamb sold off to make amends and pay a debt." He hummed, moving his lips closer to her ear, his voice dropping low even as he was slowly killing her. "You're supposed to be small. Immaterial. Uninteresting at best."

Fuck you.

Lips ghosted against her cheek, just at the corner of her mouth, a faint impression of a kiss, but nothing real. He lifted his head to watch her eyes.

Fuck. You. Her vision was going spotty at the edges. She didn't have long.

"A little mortal human, lost in the metropolis, surrounded by politics she can't possibly understand... engaged to the most dangerous murderer in all of Runne. And yet? When you look at me?" Brow furrowing slightly, he was looking at her like she was the most intriguing puzzle he'd ever seen. "Your eyes hold no fear. None at all."

All at once, he let go of her throat and sat back, releasing her wrists. He stayed straddling her legs as she coughed and wheezed, turning her head to try to desperately fill her aching lungs with air. Her head was spinning.

"You aren't afraid of me. Just there, you looked at me with nothing but defiance. I could kill you in a thousand ways, a thousand times over, every second you're near me." He caught her chin in his hand and forced her to look at him, even as she was wheezing. "Why?"

When she felt like she could speak without coughing, she

answered him, her voice quiet and hoarse. "Because I'm already dead."

* * *

Raziel sat back on his heels, watching the girl beneath him.

Because I'm already dead.

He laughed. *Oh, pretty thing.* There were far more things to fear in this world than death. But even as he had been slowly robbing her of life, there was nothing in her eyes but sheer *contempt*.

The image of her atop him, naked in the moonlight, hairpin pressing into his throat, flashed into his mind. By the two moons, he had never been aroused so quickly and so intensely as he had been right then.

In her eyes in that moment, in that honest place between sleep and awake, he had seen that same contempt—but he had also seen *desire*.

"I snuck into *your* bed tonight to see if I could scare you." Reaching down a hand, he stroked his knuckles along her cheek. To her credit, she didn't pull away. Just watched him, wavering, angry, and uncertain.

"Why"—she stopped to cough—"do you want me to be afraid of you?"

He lowered himself down to her again, loving the smell of her. Not the shampoo and the soap, but the scent that went deeper than that—*her* smell. Monica. She smelled like the sea, of salt spray, and something he couldn't name. He placed a slow, gentle kiss against her cheek before climbing off the sofa and letting her up. "You should be. Because everyone else is."

Fetching his cigarette from the floor near the railing, he leaned back against the stone balustrade. Would she stay? Or would she go back to her room and sulk? Monica crouched to pick up the glass that had once contained her drink. Kicking an ice cube off the balcony, she headed to the bar and made herself another. A double, by the looks of things.

"I'm not an idiot," she snapped at him. "You can stop treating me like one *right now*."

Her anger was somehow a relief. "No. That much is becoming very clear." He stretched, cracking his neck. "What sob story did Azazel give you? Who sold him into the flesh trade this time? Was it his aunt, his big brother, or his lover? I can never keep his lies straight."

"Hm." She leaned up against the railing, some two feet away from him. Not close, but still within arm's reach. "He spared me the details."

"Did you believe him?"

"I wanted to." Pausing, she stared down into her drink. "And I suppose I did. This world is full of enough tragedies like that." That was an honest answer from her. "Which means I'm not as smart as I claimed I was."

Curious cowgirl. Curious, strange, fascinating, *infuriating* cowgirl. Far more interesting than he could ever have expected. He watched her for a moment. "Aza is a manipulator. That's what he does."

"I guess you're right." She sipped her drink.

"Did he give you some 'let's be friends' line?"

The flinch of pain that crossed her features was almost a visceral slap. It was as much of an answer as he needed.

"Word of advice, lost, pretty thing." Facing her, he stepped in close. She held her ground and didn't turn to meet him. Stroking a hand over her hair, he decided he liked the feel of it. It was so very soft. "You may be smart. You may be more capable with a blade than I had expected. But in this, you are a novice. The games we play... Trust no one in my family. Trust no one who works with us or for us."

"Including you."

"Especially me." Leaning down, he kissed her temple. "Good night."

"Not much left of it," she grumbled under her breath.

Laughing, he headed for the stairs. "Don't disturb your sleep, lest it make you cranky. Noted. Well, sleep in. One more day until the big day. Oh. Don't worry about your throat for the dress fitting tomorrow. I know how to not leave a bruise."

She kept from rolling her eyes at how cocky he sounded. "You never answered my question."

One foot on the stairs, he paused. "Which one?"

"You're going to kill me on the night of the wedding, aren't you? How long until it's my blood on your knuckles and staining your teeth?"

Studying his hand for a moment, he pondered her question. He hadn't cut himself. His flinch had been simply for humor. He wondered if she'd noticed. "It depends entirely on how breakable you turn out to be."

With that, he left her to her own devices.

He had enough to think about.

TEN

Nadi wasn't quite sure what to do with herself the following day. She had an appointment to get her dress fitted. Neither of which—the appointment nor the dress—she had been consulted about.

There was absolutely no point in getting upset over it. This wasn't her wedding. This wasn't her body. This wasn't her name. This wasn't her face. This wasn't *her*. She was exactly just another luxury object to Raziel and his family—something to be purchased and put wherever and immediately disregarded.

Well, that much was at least clear when it came to everyone else in the house. As for Raziel?

Their exchange only seven hours earlier was the reason why she was pacing around her room, fidgeting with the sleeve of her blouse.

Raziel.

Shutting her eyes, she forced herself to recall the horror. The gunfire. And the sound of his laughter. The sound of her mother's screams. "*Run.*"

Holding onto that moment was the only chance she had in

the world. Otherwise... otherwise, she'd have to come to terms with the fact that she was *attracted* to him. In a way that she hadn't ever felt with another person in her *life*.

Maybe it was because he was the person she hated more than anyone else in the world? Maybe that was a part of it? It had to be. It made no sense, otherwise. But even when he had been about to end her life... something in her craved him. *Needed* him, in some deep and twisted way.

Sitting down on the edge of the bed, she put her head in her hands and tried to think. Tried to reason with herself.

He was a murderer.

And so was she.

He had killed her family.

And soon, I'll do the same to his.

But he had made her laugh.

A *real* laugh.

And the look in his eyes when she had cleaned the blood off his knuckles was so confused as if nobody had ever done that for him in his life. As if nobody had ever cared. He was like a junk-yard dog shown affection for the first time in its life.

Rubbing her hand over her face, she sighed. No. This was all just a game to him. She wasn't special to him—she wasn't unique. She was just a puzzle. A curiosity. The moment he had sex with her, the mystery and allure would be gone, and she'd be tossed away with all the rest.

Right now, she was just teasing him, dancing outside his reach until the moment they said their so-called vows. Then he'd take her to his ancestral home, as was tradition, and slaughter her.

That also meant she would have to work quickly to dismantle everything around him. She hoped she could prove useful—or at least inoffensive—enough to be kept alive for a little while after the wedding. She assumed she wouldn't be shuttled onto a boat the morning after—she'd have a *little* time to work her "magic" before their bloody honeymoon. Maybe she could convince him to stall and keep on a seemingly human wife for a little while.

It depends entirely on how breakable you turn out to be. Maybe if she proved entertaining and useful, he'd postpone the trip long enough for her to complete her mission.

We'll see which one of us breaks first, buddy-boy.

"Oh, no, no, no. We can't have that *hideous* birthmark of hers visible. Are you *insane?*"

Nadi decided she very much disliked Volencia Nostrom.

"Ugh. And do something about her *nails*," the vampire matriarch scoffed.

Yep. Raziel's mother was instantly and firmly on Nadi's shit-list. Not like she wasn't already there, to be fair. It was more about the order that she was going to murder them all in.

Volencia was just starting to show her years. Although vampires and fae didn't age, they did still somehow *show* age, like old furniture. How they held themselves, how they dressed, how they acted. She had also been turned later in her life. Her skin was creased at the eyes and at the corners of her mouth, but she was beautiful all the same. None of the gray hairs that were mixed with her black strands were hidden or dyed. All were simply tucked into the carefully braided bun.

Pride.

That was what this woman was. *Pride.*

Volencia would be a difficult target to kill. She was *old.* Easily five hundred years or more. And, if the stories were true, she'd dismantled her husband, the father of her children, into tiny pieces and walled him up in the family estate in separate buildings to ensure he *never* came back.

That kind of deranged bloodlust would be dangerous to take

on. And, it explained a great deal about Raziel. The apple didn't fall far from that particularly rotted-out tree.

Volencia also never went far without all her bodyguards. She was always flanked by at *least* two big, burly, vampiric men the size of Ivan who were likely loyal to the death.

But where there was *pride*, there was a way. Pride was one of the easiest emotions to use against a person, second only to greed. Nadi just had to wait for her opportunity and be clever about it, that was all.

The vampiric woman's unnatural amber eyes watched her with a mix of disgust and haughty disdain. Like Monica was a cow patty in the fields of her father's ranch. But Nadi held her head up high and kept her gaze fixed firmly on the three mirrors in front of her, ignoring the red, iron glare of the older woman.

Nor did she argue with any of the vampire matriarch's orders.

The dress was a beautiful champagne color. She was very glad it wasn't stark white. That would be as comedic as it would be hideous, in her opinion. It was a lacy, off-the-shoulder number that could be easily edited to cover her *hideous* birthmark.

It took everything in her power not to roll her eyes or pick up the shoes on display and dig the pointed heel directly into Volencia's eye socket. No. Now wasn't the time. Once the wedding was done and Raziel's guard was just a little lower, she could begin dismantling the family.

"Give her—something for that thing. We can't have our guests losing their appetite. A shawl." Volencia gestured, her long nails painted pitch-black and sharpened to points.

Volencia had just bumped everyone else off the top of her main family to-do list, however. The woman was *definitely* going to die painfully.

The attendants around her muttered apologies and affirmations as they bustled around Nadi, pinning things or rushing off to find various shawls that would work with the lace dress.

"Does she *speak*?" Volencia finally addressed her.

"I wasn't aware I was welcome to." Nadi shrugged idly. "You've been treating me like a prop this whole time, I figured that was what you wanted."

The vampire huffed, a faint twinge of a smile to her darkly painted lips. The dark crimson velvet suit dress that the woman was wearing was expensive, custom-made, and was clearly advertising that fact. "So you aren't an idiot. How charming."

"Everyone keeps acting surprised that I'm not."

"You don't come from the brightest stock in the world."

Nadi let out a hum. "That's fair."

Volencia laughed dryly. "I cannot imagine how it must feel to be sold to us by your father without even any consultation."

"I'm used to being treated like a possession by him. He's never much thought about what I've wanted." Nadi didn't know if that was true. But she figured it fit the narrative well enough.

"At least you seem to have some fight in you." Volencia moved to sit down on the edge of a round velvet ottoman. A few of them were scattered about, clearly meant for giggling bridesmaids. "And you wear it well enough."

Nadi wasn't sure if Volencia meant she wore the dress well, or acting the part of a prop well—or both. She settled on both. Staring at a stranger's reflection in the mirror, she couldn't help but feel just the slightest bit of pang in her heart.

She would never get to stand in the mirror as herself. Never wearing her own face, let alone her own shape. She would never have her mother beside her, smiling as she tried on a dress.

Her mother was dead.

That woman in the mirror wasn't real.

It was a lie. A ghost of a future that she would never, ever have.

Because Raziel, Volencia, and all the rest of their miserable family had taken it from her.

It wasn't new information. It was what she had carried for over eighty years since that fateful night. But it was rare that she saw such a perfect example in front of her of... exactly what her future could have been.

She could have danced around a fire with a boy from another fae clan. She could have been wed under the glow of the *yubi* bugs.

"Raziel told me you have become... acquainted with our business practices."

Nadi watched the older woman in the mirror for a moment before turning her gaze away. "I have."

"And what is your opinion of the family venture?"

"I wasn't aware I was expected to have an opinion. Same as the dress. Same as everything else."

Volencia smiled. "Very smart girl. Well. I will rephrase. What do you plan to *do* about it?"

"Stay out of it, best I can. Unless I need to act in any way, in which case... life has chosen a side for me." Nadi shook her head. "For as long as I survive, Raziel will be my husband. My loyalty is to him and his family. I will support him in any way I can until he decides I'm no longer of use to him."

"The rumors do travel far, don't they?" Volencia crossed one leg over the other as she pulled a cigarette out of her purse. "Tomorrow will be a very important day, girl. My youngest is getting married for the first time."

Nadi overcame the urge to say "Probably not the last time" and let Volencia keep speaking.

"Everyone who is anyone, or wishes to be anyone, will be in attendance. You are—exactly as you've stated—a prop. Smile. Shake hands. Be gracious. Defer to Raziel and the rest of us in all things. Be beautiful and charming. Do not drink too much and do not eat too much." Volencia stood, smoothing a hand down her dress before lighting her cigarette, taking a lazy drag from it, and exhaling the smoke. "Do all this, and I will see that Raziel is... as kind to you as he is capable of being."

"Yes, ma'am." Nadi kept her gaze on the mirror as the attendants kept buzzing about her. "I will do my best."

"See that you do, girl." With that, the older woman was gone.

Nadi shut her eyes and let out a wavering breath the moment Volencia had exited the room and she heard the door click shut.

"I fucking *hate* that bitch," one of the attendants said, looking up at her from where she was kneeling, pinning the hem of the train. "She is the absolute *worst*."

Nadi laughed. "I'm not gonna disagree."

"I'm sorry you just have to stand there and take it. And—and it's so sad—your father sold you to them? The Nostroms?" The woman frowned as she went back to pinning the hem. "I don't know how you can do it."

"I've dealt with worse, believe it or not."

And that much was true. She had dealt with worse. But something told her, that little unsettled feeling at the back of her neck... that it might not be true for much longer.

Nadi had hoped to spend the night hiding in "her" room. The following day was the wedding, and she had little desire to interact with anybody. But when one of Raziel's minions came to fetch her for dinner, she knew it wasn't a request—it was an order.

She changed into something that she could fight in if necessary, touched up her makeup, and, with a sigh, headed out of her room.

Not like she stood a chance against Raziel in a fight. That much was painfully clear with how they had left things the previous night. He was right—he hadn't left a bruise on her throat. But the feeling of his fingers wrapped around her neck lingered, and she found herself absentmindedly rubbing where he had gripped her.

She found him sitting alone at a table by the railing that overlooked his back yard. He was toying with another golden coin, and she watched as it flickered in the light of the two moons. The Father and Mother were both out, one bright and white and the other black. Most people couldn't see the light it gave out. But she was fae—she could see it as clear as the sun. And it broke her heart that vampires and humans missed how beautiful it really was.

Approaching the table, she hesitated before pulling out her own chair to sit. His red eyes were gazing out to the darkened city beyond the walls of fake paper and metal shrubbery that kept his home as private as possible. He looked so lost in thought, she wondered if he even knew she had sat down.

They sat in silence for a long moment before she couldn't take it anymore. "I figured you'd be out partying."

A huff that could have been mistaken for a single, silent laugh was all she got in response at first. One of his staff came up a second later to serve them. Steak—and basically raw, by the look of it—with a side of roasted potatoes and green beans. Red wine accompanied it—poured from two bottles, as his was likely the bloodwine mixture that he preferred.

"Your mother is insisting I wear a shawl to hide my birthmark." She picked up the fork and knife and sliced off a piece of the steak. The middle was almost blue, it was so undercooked. But she didn't mind. Fae had no problem eating meat. "But I did win the debate with the stylist about leaving my hair down tomorrow."

Another long stretch of silence. He had still failed to even look at her. Finally, he spoke. "What do you think of my mother?"

She had a choice. Honesty or a lie. A lie would be seen as just pandering. But was that what he wanted? With a breath, she picked up her red wine to sip it, glad it was missing the tang of blood. "Between us? I think she hates me. And I believe it might be mutual."

That earned her another half-laugh. "She is protective of her children."

"I will do everything I can not to get on her bad side." Right until the moment she stuck a knife between the woman's ribs.

"That is wise." He finally reached for his own glass of wine and sipped it.

Silence.

Maybe it was curiosity that drove her forward.

Maybe it was a need to end the awkward silence.

The third option was unthinkable.

"What's wrong?"

He laughed for real that time, though it was empty and mirthless. It was then that he finally looked at her, those red eyes regarding her with a haughty kind of disinterest. "Don't insult me by pretending you care."

"You're right. I don't. Because I don't know you. Nothing more than rumors and our few interactions that have been... uh... mixed." She rubbed her throat.

His smile was that of a shark smiling at his prey. Too smooth for its own good.

"But whether we like it or not, tomorrow we're going to be married. And while I'm *fairly* sure you're planning on me not lasting longer than a month, I'd like to try." She went back to her steak, cutting off another cube.

"Try what?"

She gestured between the two of them with her fork. "This."

"Why?" He arched an eyebrow.

It was her turn to huff a laugh. She smiled at him as if *he* were the idiot this time. "Because while I'm not afraid to die, Raziel—I don't *want* to. I'd like to keep living. And... this whole lifestyle you and your family have. It's fascinating. And maybe I don't... know if I want to be turned. But I certainly don't like the alternative. Being brought to your ancestral home as a sacrifice is... not on my to-do list."

"I wish you understood what you were saying." He leaned back in his chair to sip his wine. He had yet to touch his meal.

"I know more than you might think." She had to get him to trust her—maybe even like her, just a little. Without that, there was no way she'd live long enough, or get close enough, to complete her mission. "My father, while he can't hold a candle to the lot of you, had plenty of shady deals. Yours aren't the first knuckles I've cleaned blood from. And if that's what it takes to survive, so be it."

Raziel leaned forward then, resting his elbows on the table, his crimson gaze boring into her like she were a butterfly beneath pins in a collection. "Knowing about it and being capable of it are two different things."

Picking up her steak knife, she gestured at Hank where he was standing some ten feet away. Raziel was rarely without at least one of his bodyguards. Ivan must have the night off. "Where do you want me to stab him?"

His laugh this time was finally genuine. "You're playing a game for adults, child."

Standing, she smiled at him sweetly. "I've been putting down cattle in the slaughterhouse since the moment I was old enough to walk. And these were creatures that I raised—that I named. That I *loved*. You don't think I have it in me to put a knife in your friend?"

"Boss?" Hank clearly wasn't a fan of this. "You really gonna let this bitch stab me?"

Raziel ignored Hank and spoke only to her. "I don't think you have what it takes, girl." He leaned back in his chair, picking up his wine glass and swirling the liquid thoughtfully. "But go ahead and try."

"Boss." Hank shook his head. "I don't—"

Walking up to Hank, Nadi kept her approach casual until she reached a few feet from him. Hank shifted his stance, ready to defend himself.

He was so much bigger than her. But she was fast. She lunged as if she were going to slash his arm, and he moved to block her—which let her sink the knife into his side. Not far— only a half an inch—but far enough.

"*Fuck!*" Hank jumped back. Touching his side in disbelief, his hand came back with that inky, black-red blood that was the telltale sign of a vampire. "Shit, you stupid little—"

Raziel was howling in laughter. He slapped the table before standing and approaching the scene. "That was better entertainment than any strip club you could have planned for a bachelor party. Go get yourself fixed up, Hank."

"But she—" Hank argued.

"Oh, come on. You've had worse scuffles after a few too many drinks with Ivan." Raziel rolled his eyes. "You're just mad because she got you fair and square. Go on."

"Yeah, boss." Hank grunted and walked away, muttering to himself as he left the room, shutting the door behind him.

Raziel approached Nadi, holding out his hand for the knife. She handed it to him, handle forward, and wondered if he was going to slash her throat open in retribution.

Instead, he lifted the knife to his lips and slowly, sensually, licked the gore from the blade. All the while, he kept his red eyes on her. He tossed the knife aside, and it clattered to the floor.

He took a step toward her.

She held her ground, staring at him in defiance. "I told you."

"Stabbing a man is different than making them suffer—than taking their life. But I'll admit... that was a thing of beauty." He crooked a finger underneath her chin, tilting her head up to his as he took another step forward, closing the distance between them.

"Don't underestimate me."

"Yes... I admit I might have done just that." He lowered his head toward hers, his breath hot as it pooled against her cheek. His other hand snaked around her lower back and pulled her flush against him. He grunted.

She felt his desire pressing against her. He had deeply enjoyed the show, it seemed.

"But there is something you have to know, my violent little thing..."

Resting her hands on his chest, she couldn't help but shiver at the sound of his voice as it went low like gravel.

His lips brushed against her ear as he whispered to her. "I don't just kill people. I murder people, Monica. Innocent people. People who don't deserve it. I murder them and I *like* it. I love the smell of their blood. People call me the Serpent for a reason. Even my brother and sister fear me. That is who I am. That is who you are marrying."

"You don't scare me."

"But I should, Monica—I *should*." He lowered his head farther, kissing her throat, before scraping her skin with his sharp, dangerous fangs.

She jolted, pulling in a sharp breath through her nose at the sting. But it wasn't a sound of pain. She didn't recoil. Without intending to, she was leaning her head away from him, giving him room. *Welcoming* him.

"Tempting... so very tempting." His tongue ran along her throat, along the vein. "But Mother would have my head." Trailing slow kisses back up her throat to her ear, he nipped the lobe before whispering to her again. "But tomorrow night? Tomorrow night, we teach you the meaning of *fear*."

Instinct took over.

She turned her face to his and kissed him.

She kissed him *hard*.

With all the hate and all the desire she felt for him. They mixed together into a cyclone. Threading her hand into his hair, she fisted it and deepened the embrace, going up on her tiptoes.

The sound of surprise he made was like music to her ears. His hand slid from her lower back to her ass, grasping it hard enough that her eyes watered. He returned the kiss just as roughly as she was giving it—like a desperate and wild creature.

But who was out of control, she wondered.

Both of them? Or neither?

Finally, he broke the kiss, pulling his head back. She was breathless as she blinked her eyes open. By the moons and stars in the sky, by the lords of the deep Wild, she *needed* him. He tasted like a winter hearth—like spices and wood mixed with the coppery tang of blood.

It was addictive.

"Impatient... I like it." He placed his hand to her cheek, resting his thumb on the hollow of her chin, his nail just grazing her lower lip that was swollen from the intensity of the kiss. "Twenty-four hours and you will learn just what kind of a monster you think you want to dance with."

He pushed away, and she was quite proud of the state she had left him in. "Now, if you'll excuse me, I have something to tend to." He plucked the bottle of bloodwine from the table and headed to the door. "Good night, Monica. Good luck tomorrow. You're going to need it."

In his absence, the chill night air was free to wake her up out of her daze. Shaking her head, she combed her hands through her hair.

What was getting into her? Why did she kiss him?

Because she had wanted to.

No, because she had *needed* to.

Tomorrow night, he'll show you exactly the kind of monster he truly is, by his own words. Then, this lust of yours will shatter. Twenty-four hours and everything would be different.

But damn it all, if she didn't want to follow him to his room.

"No, no, *no*." She growled.

Storming back to her own room, she locked the door behind herself and decided she was going to have a hot bath in pitch darkness. It reminded her of her home before it had been taken from her. It was her favorite way to unwind. Sinking into the liquid in the dark let her pretend she was somewhere else.

Twenty-four hours, and she would have the real chance to prove to Raziel that she could keep up with him.

And they would see exactly which one of them broke first.

"Save your luck for yourself, Raziel," she murmured to herself. "I think you'll need it more than me."

ELEVEN

If she lived to see the dawn, she'd call it a win.

Nadi felt like she was having an out of body experience throughout the entirety of the so-called "wedding." Wearing a dress meant for someone else. Wearing a persona that wasn't hers.

Marrying the man she had vowed revenge upon.

Carrying a bouquet of flowers the color of blood.

Smiling. Shaking hands. Posing for photos. Forcing herself to look demure as she stood at the altar, saying the vows in front of the human priest. It didn't feel real. It was all happening to someone else. It was the only way she could go through it all, like she was watching someone else go through the actions. She was playing a part on a grand stage—reading lines from someone else's script.

The vows had been the most surreal.

Listening to Raziel say the words as he placed a ring on her finger. Repeating them back to him as she did the same. Lines in a play.

None of it was real. To either of them. A gesture of a motion of a feeling.

Only the kiss had any attachment to reality. It was chaste —they were in front of a crowd, after all—but that was the first time Raziel looked at her and truly seemed to *see* her. The first time those red eyes hadn't been glassy, faraway, and utterly *bored*. She wasn't the only one going through the motions.

What a fucking mess.

When she finally had a moment to sit down at the head table in the reception hall, she could actually take a moment to assess the situation. They were in a giant, expensive hotel that matched the same kind of hyper-modern elegance of his home. It looked extremely fancy, yet somehow devoid of detail—so foreign to the way she grew up in the Wild. It seemed... somehow austere to her. Cold. Unwelcoming. Too fancy.

Insincere.

That was it. The whole damn thing. The hotel. The decor. The food. The feelings. The people. The smiles. The friendship. The family. The love. It was all fucking *insincere.*

The humans mingling among the guests were fascinating to her. Most of them seemed to orbit one or other of the vampires —serving as thralls, or toys, or temporary playthings. Just as Monica was expected to do for Raziel.

But she was *not* Monica. She was Nadi. And the people around her *weren't* her new family. They were her victims. Each one could have had a name tag on them that had a number etched to it.

Ezekiel Nostrom, third cousin, drug runner. Number eighty-seven. She could kill him in the back stairwell and make it look like an overdose. Make him eat all the powder he was peddling to people from his coat pocket and trying—and failing—to make it look subtle.

Timothy Verrik, human, slave trader. Number thirty-four. That one, she'd bludgeon to death in his hotel room. Make it look like the women he was just introducing into the market had turned on him in a fit of desperation.

Mael Nostrom, older brother, kingpin. Number one. There he was, sitting at the head table to her right, with all the other immediate Nostrom family. He was smiling and laughing, telling some grandiose story that had the table in rapt attention. He was charismatic, handsome, and always the center of attention. By the pit, he even had the mayor of the metropolis sitting at the table with him, smiling and laughing at his jokes.

Mael was the smiling face of the vampiric influence upon the human race. The constant, benign protector who had long since vowed to shield the humans from the Wild in the name of his ancestors who had done the same.

The sun to Raziel's moon. No one would guess by looking at him that he was the mastermind of an entire drug empire and the one who made sure that all of the mayor's problems quietly disappeared—and therefore the most powerful person in all of the isle of Runne.

Vampires were an obnoxious bunch. Each one was "blessed" with their own version of their blood-gifts. No two seemed to have the exact same powers, though there were definite patterns that formed in families. Turning to bats, or into mist, or rats—those seemed to be common.

Raziel's gift of hypnotism? That was truly unique. But it didn't make him any more or less durable than the standard vampire. Whereas Mael and his father seemed to share the trait of being *exceptionally* difficult to murder.

Yeah. Nadi had *no* clue how to kill *him*.

She'd heard stories of people who had tried. Poison hadn't done it. Stabbing hadn't done it. Setting him on fire hadn't done it.

No, it'd require something more permanent to take him out.

Then it hit her.

Like father, like son.

Dismemberment. She'd have to knock him out, saw his limbs off, and... she looked down at the plate of food in front of her, and found she suddenly wasn't at all hungry.

Raziel leaned close, whispering in her ear. "Eat something. You'll need it."

The meaning was clear. *We can't have you passing out when I drink your blood and make you regret teasing me for the past few days.*

Gods below, she prayed her glamor would hold on her blood long enough for him not to detect what she was. Otherwise, her revenge plan wouldn't last until morning, and she wouldn't have to worry about convincing him to delay the sacrificial honeymoon.

Nodding once, she picked up the fork and knife and forced herself to eat as much of the roast beef as she could.

"Nice of your father to provide the beef for tonight." Raziel was clearly unimpressed. "I hope he will enjoy the photographs we'll send him. A reminder of the daughter he dismissed from his life."

"I'm sure he'll be thrilled." The sarcasm was thick in her voice as she took a sip of her champagne. Fuck, she hated champagne. Somehow too bitter and too sweet at exactly the same damn time. How it managed that, she had no idea. But it was a moment for celebration, so... here she was. Eating overcooked roast beef and drinking champagne.

Next to the man she hated. Who had killed her family.

Who she was now married to.

Who she was extremely attracted to.

Who was going to kill her if she didn't beat him to it and kill him first.

The whole situation was so farcical it was hard to be upset by it, really. That was probably why it was easier to smile over the whole ordeal than she would have expected.

Raziel sat back in his chair and watched the crowd in front

of them. Laughing, sharing drinks, clearly having more fun than they were. "Parasites." The single word was said with such disdain—such *hate*—that she was taken aback by it.

"These are your family and friends."

"Are they? Look at them. Do you know how many of these humans I've even *met* before? Let alone even *care* about?"

"No?"

"None of them." He sneered. "They circle about us like vultures. No. Worse than that. They are hyenas, waiting for the lions to make a kill so they can lick the bones clean. They're weak, powerless, insignificant little *things* and if it weren't for us, the savages would have rendered them all extinct long ago."

If the Nostroms were lions, Raziel wasn't even the king of the pride. Mael was the brother with the most influence, the most standing in the family. Even Lana outranked him. She opted not to point that out to him.

Shaking her head, she went back to her food and drink. "If you aren't a fan of humans, why have us around at all in the first place?"

He was silent for a long time. "Isn't it obvious? We can't feed on each other. And we *certainly* can't feed on the fae." He gestured vaguely at the scene in front of him. "So, we protect the meat."

"Why can't you feed on the fae?" Oh, now this was interesting.

"They're vermin. They taste *utterly vile.*" He took a sip of his wine. "Unmistakably so."

Was that true...? Well, *fuck.* She had no idea if it was true or not. Would Raziel know the moment he sank his teeth into her neck? She could only continue to pray that her glamor held out.

She downed her glass of champagne and poured herself another. If he noticed her sudden exasperated and slightly panicked expression, it didn't stop him from continuing his rant.

"Look at them. Celebrating like this is some kind of momentous occasion. They all know this is just as fake as we do. They don't *care* about me. They don't *know* me. They're simply hiding in the safety of our power." He grimaced, revealing his dangerous fangs. The fangs he planned to sink into her throat— or elsewhere—before the morning. "But they celebrate the death of one of their own, don't they? They know the moment we leave for our ancestral home, only I'm coming back. Yet they have the *gall* to toast you. You might as well be on the plate with the *fucking* beef." He almost sounded offended on her behalf. How... oddly sweet.

She huffed. "I'm almost flattered that you rank me on par with what the chefs did to this poor slab of meat." She poked the steak in front of her. "They really didn't need to kill the cow a second time, I wonder if they knew that when they cooked it. At what point do I graduate to 'properly cooked dinner'? Or is that never going to happen?"

"You've turned out to be more than I expected, I'll give you that much." He trailed his hand over her shoulder, tracing the line of the shawl she was wearing. "But if you think a pretty face and a willingness to stab Hank is going to win me over, I have terrible news."

She laughed. She didn't know why. The farce of the situation finally caught up to her. Or maybe it was the champagne. She turned her focus to the crowd in front of them. Tables upon tables of people, many who were known to her—but not a single one of them his *friend.*

Ivan and anyone else Raziel might actually consider friends were working, after all. The bull in question was standing nearby, arms folded.

As for Hank, the other guard? He was watching the rear entrance. She'd apologized for the gash on his side, and he'd just simply shrugged and said he'd gotten worse going to brunch.

No one who knew the real Monica was present. No one who cared about the girl whose life had been given away. Sold to a monster who planned to chew up and spit out the little human.

"But I will say this much, sweetheart." Raziel picked up her hand, lacing his fingers into hers. The warmth of his skin was fascinating. It came and went so quickly when he drank blood—like someone experiencing a fever. Lifting her hand to his lips, he kissed her knuckles before turning her hand over to place another kiss, slower, against her wrist. Over the veins that pulsed there. "I am enjoying having you around more than I expected."

There was a rumble in his chest that she could barely hear over the chatter of guests and the clinking of dinnerware. But she could *feel* it. Like the vibration of an engine. He kissed her wrist again, his lips parted. It sent a shiver through her, goose-bumps exploding onto her arms, as he slowly ran his tongue along the vein.

Everything in her went tense, watching him in fascinated horror as he kissed her wrist a third time, scraping her skin with his fangs.

What would it be like, to be bitten by a vampire?

Would it hurt? She had seen humans become addicted to it, worse than powder—throwing themselves at the feet of their vampiric masters, begging to be emptied like a bottle of wine. Worse were those who had been hooked and then discarded—those poor souls would beg *any* vampire to open their veins.

But that was how it felt for humans.

She was *fae*.

There were no stories she'd ever heard or anything she'd witnessed that would explain what was coming. Would it hurt her? Would it be bliss? Would he taste it, or would her glamor hold on, and she would taste human in his mouth long enough to fool him?

Why was the idea of it so *exciting*?

It should be revolting. Terrifying. He could discover her

secret. There was no *way* she'd taste the same as a human to him. He could bite her and her ruse would be over in the single beat of a heart.

Instead, she shifted in her chair, unable to fight the fire that it lit in her. The *need*.

Why did she need him to take her? To consume her?

When was the last time she had ever needed something that badly in her life?

His crimson eyes were darkened with lust, as he rolled his tongue over her vein again. The grip of his hand in hers tightened as if he was about to lose control. She couldn't help but picture him sinking his fangs into her skin, snarling like the lion he compared himself to, as he drank her dry at their wedding table. She could picture a bloom of her blood spraying out over the white linen tablecloth like so many rose petals.

It should be a horrifying image.

Instead, she squeezed his hand back. Her face felt like it was on fire. Everything felt like it was ablaze, only a shade cooler than his tongue.

"Congratulations, brother!"

Nadi jolted. She had been so caught up in the moment she had entirely missed the fact that someone was walking up to her. Blinking, she turned her attention up to the mountain of a man now standing in front of their table, smiling. It was clear he knew exactly what he'd just interrupted.

Raziel sighed. "Mael, I was *busy*."

"I noticed." Mael sniffed, dismissively, his broad smile unflinching. "That's why Mother sent me over here. Didn't want you bending the girl over your table and rutting her in front of the guests."

Mael was his brother's opposite in almost every way. Long blond hair that seemed to want to curl into little ringlets that seemed far too innocent for someone like him. Golden eyes that were rare for a vampire. He was built like a tank, standing inches over Raziel's already towering form. But like Ivan, Mael added to his presence with girth, his perfectly tailored suit clearly working hard to contain the musculature underneath.

He was beautiful, with squared features that were quick to smile. Where everyone feared Raziel, and even the humans seemed to distrust and shun him—everyone *loved* Mael. He was welcome at every level of society. He was invited to shake hands. Hold human babies.

Raziel was left to deal with matters better left unspoken and unseen.

"I would hardly do anything so crude, dear brother." Raziel released Nadi's hand. "I was merely enjoying myself for the first time in this ridiculous day."

"Mm. Yes, that was exactly what we were worried about." Mael chuckled. He smiled at her gently. "I apologize for my brother. He's such a moody bastard. Welcome to the family, Monica." He held out his hand to her. "I hope he hasn't been too unbearable."

Nadi took it, smiling. "It's all right. This is all very lovely."

"As are you." Mael bent down to kiss her knuckles like a gentleman.

She didn't miss Raziel's growl from her side. Deciding it would be a great deal of fun needling her new *husband*—the thought almost made her burst out in laughter again—she decided to play along. "You'll make me blush, Mael. Don't make me sad that I didn't get to marry the charismatic one."

Mael laughed, warm and genuine, revealing his own set of fangs. "Brother, I like her. Let me know if you get bored with her before you make your decision."

It was clearly meant as a joke, but Nadi had no doubt in her mind that he was also incredibly serious.

"We shall see." Raziel's reply was curt. Cold. "Your mission has been accomplished, brother, now *go away*."

"All right, all right." Mael put up his hands in a show of

harmlessness and took a step back. "Have a wonderful night. And congratulations to you both again."

Nadi waited for Mael to walk away before turning to Raziel with a sweet and innocent smile. "He seems nice."

By all the gods, the look of sheer *misery* on his face was like sprinkles on an enormous ice cream sundae. It was the best wedding gift she could ask for. Tilting her head to the side slightly, she regarded him with more false innocence. "What's wrong?"

He shut his eyes, and she imagined him counting to ten to calm his nerves. When he finally reopened his eyes, he sighed in defeat. "He is simply my older brother."

"I know what it's like. Mine ribs me all the time." She had at least been smart enough to look up how many relatives Monica had before she decided to go into this insanity. "It's clear he loves you, though."

"In a fashion that only brothers can, yes."

"Can I ask... have you made your decision yet? Whether or not you plan on..." She trailed off. Monica wouldn't want to put it into words. *Whether or not you plan on murdering me or turning me into a vampire like you?*

Raziel picked up his wine glass—he was drinking blood, not champagne, lucky bastard—and downed the liquid in one go. "Come." He held his hand out to her. "Let's get this idiotic stage production of ours over with. I hunger for what will happen once the curtains close."

Weirdly, she didn't disagree with him.

Placing her hand in his, she let him lead her to the dance floor. The musicians, who had been playing inoffensive music throughout the meal, wound down their piece and prepared to play the accompaniment to what she assumed would be their first dance.

The chatter and clamor of the crowd went silent.

Raziel placed one hand on her side. She placed hers against his chest by his shoulder.

"Do you know the waltz?" His smile was clearly fake. "Or can you only line dance?"

She didn't let her own false smile break. "Do you know how to lead, or should I?"

His laugh was genuine, if edged in darkness. His voice was quiet and low. "You will see soon enough precisely how well I lead a dance..."

The obvious innuendo twisted the knot in her stomach that was already threatening to make her nauseous. Or maybe that was the champagne. "I—"

She never got to finish her return jab.

Something clattered across the floor with a *tink, tink, tink*. It spun idly where it came to a stop, some five feet away.

The knot in her stomach instantly switched to terror. Raziel grabbed her arm. They were suddenly moving.

The explosion of the grenade echoed in her ears. Everything went white.

Then dark.

TWELVE

The ringing in Raziel's ears deafened all other noise.

There hadn't been much time to react to the grenade. He barely had a second to process before he had grabbed Monica by the upper arm and half flown, half run with her toward safety.

The heat at his back and the sudden percussion had sent him tumbling and crashing through a table and into a pack of panicking guests. It took him a few precious seconds to recover. Bullets were already flying—volleys both toward him and return fire from his guards and those of his guests who had been packing.

He suddenly regretted not carrying his own gun.

It looks so tacky under the suit, his mother had scolded him. *No one would dare come for you at your own wedding! Besides... vampires have their own methods of defense, should someone be so foolish.*

Yes, if he lived through this, he would enjoy wielding this moment against Volencia in the future. He loved his mother dearly, but all was fair in love and politics. He bared his fangs and readied himself to shred his nails through the flesh of anyone who got in his way.

Someone would *bleed* for this.

He managed to get to his feet just as the smoke began to clear enough to see what was going on. Bodies lay strewn about, blood pooling from wounds. It was only a moment later that Ivan and Hank were at his side, with Ivan handing Raziel his secondary firearm. There were no words exchanged. There was no need.

It seemed the invaders had achieved their goal. The attackers had come, done their damage, and fled. There was only one body on the ground that was not dressed in formal wedding attire. One of the attackers.

Walking up to the single corpse, Raziel ignored the rest of the chaos as his guards did their jobs of chasing—and hopefully capturing—the bastards who'd dared do this. Nudging the body with his foot, he rolled it over onto its back. A human man, dressed in a green, simple linen shirt underneath a black wool vest. His eyes were open, locked on a view he would never see again.

Hank grunted. "Lee Iltani."

"*Fuck.*" Raziel shut his eyes. Of course. Of *course* the Iltani gang were to blame for this. "Of course. *Of course!*" Snarling, he clenched his fist at his side. He warned his brother—didn't he? That damned fool—fae and the humans who bred with them were all *animals.* Rabid things, meant to be put down, not kept as *pets.*

One of the wedding attendants rushed up to them, trembling, her eyes wide in a panic. Her hands were clutched in front of her, and she was trying to make herself seem as small as possible, clearly fearing his wrath. "Sir! Sir!"

"What?" He barked the word at her, baring his fangs. He had more important things to deal with than the fact that the dessert course was ruined. "Spit it out!"

"It's—your bride, sir—she's... they took her."

Raziel turned on his heel, surveying the scene. Sure enough, Monica was nowhere to be found. "She might have run." It would have been the sensible thing to do, after all. Run and hide.

"No. I—I saw—I saw them carrying her out. A few of us did, sir."

Raziel shut his eyes and began to laugh. Oh, how absolutely *wonderful*. Here he stood, married to a woman he did not wish to wed, who he was meant to *kill*, and who his enemies had just *dared* to steal from him?

"You are going after her." Volencia stormed up to him, not a blessed hair out of place. How that woman managed to get through an explosion without a smudge, he would never know, yet he was somehow not surprised.

"It's likely too late for her, she's probably dead already. It's not worth risking the men." Raziel tucked the gun into the back of his belt.

His mother took two steps closer to him, pulled back a hand, and *slapped him*. The sound was more jarring than the blow itself, but his head moved with the gesture, all the same.

Rage boiled in him. His jaw ticked. But he held perfectly still.

His mother was not to be trifled with.

"You *idiot boy*," she hissed. "She is a *sacrifice*. These are the *old ways*. You do not piss on family traditions like one of your rented whores. Do you understand me? You will fetch her, and you will complete what must be done!"

Several of his more loyal foot soldiers had gathered in front of him. Mael was there as well, soot from the blast smeared across his forehead, his lips thin and his jaw fixed in anger. This was now a full-on family matter.

Even Lana stood prepared for the fight.

Raziel laughed quietly, shutting his eyes. What a farce.

What an abomination. "This is your fault, Mael—your pet dogs have grown rabid. You're coming with me to fetch *my* wife."

His brother wordlessly nodded, knowing not to get in the middle of the mess in front of him.

Cracking his neck from one side to the other, Raziel let out a breath. "Tonight, we hunt the Iltanis. Tonight, we end their miserable bloodline."

* * *

Was it ever okay to murder someone?

That was the thought that ran through Nadi's head as she went in and out of consciousness. It was hard to remember what had happened. She was wearing someone else's face and marrying her worst enemy. They were about to dance, and then...

A grenade?

Was murder ever acceptable?

Not killing. Murdering. Two different words for two different reasons. *Killing* and *murder*. Though the line between the two was usually up for debate depending on one's point of view. One could kill a cow for meat or consider it murder to take an animal's life.

She remembered the first time she ever *murdered*. It was the second time she had *killed* anybody. The first time she took a man's life it had been in self-defense. He had dragged her into an alleyway after she left a bar. And no matter how she cried out for help, people had only glanced into the alley and kept walking.

No one would help her.

They all decided to abandon her with the monster who planned to rape her and then likely *murder* her. When she stopped struggling, though, he let down his guard. And before he could defile her, she snatched the knife from his hand and drove it up into his skull from under his jaw.

She would never, ever forget that moment. The look of panic and pain in his eyes that slowly turned glossy and dim as the life fled his body. The way his blood poured from the wound and covered her hand, her arm, and her clothes.

The warmth of it felt almost like an embrace.

It... hadn't bothered her.

Oh, she was upset that she'd been attacked.

But the death? The killing? The blood? She expected to feel something—to cry, to weep, to panic—anything. But it... was *nothing*. If anything, she found it vaguely fascinating.

She felt far worse when she had to kill a *jibba* beast on a hunting trip with her father. She still didn't know what that said about her. But it had been an innocent animal, it had just been trying to live. The man had been a bastard.

But that had been her first *killing*. Not her first *murder*. That came several years later. Generally, one doesn't decide to go into being an assassin outright. Generally, one starts by getting good at murder and *then* making a career of it.

In her case, it was all Betty's fault. Betty also ran a bar in the slums in the lower areas of the metropolis, which was a front for all of her... extracurricular work. And Nadi had taken a job waiting tables and pouring drinks. She was good at her job, and she got along with the regulars.

But, like all seedy places, there was competition. And Betty's extracurricular work—like smuggling drugs, gambling, or the like—had drawn notice from rival gangs. When one of the boys from a rival gang had taken a shine to Nadi, Betty had paid her to quietly dispose of the lad in the canal.

Nadi couldn't remember the young man's name. But she remembered his face. His kind smile. Never mind the fact that he had also killed or murdered dozens of people in his life. She had taken her knife and stabbed him to death before rolling his corpse into the canal.

Betty had paid her handsomely. Nadi saw more money in one night of work than she had in a *year* tending bar or waiting tables. So, when Betty wanted to hire her again? She said yes.

And again, became again, became again. The deaths blurred together. She couldn't remember them all. Only the ones that went really smoothly, paid really well, or went absolutely to shit.

But, slowly, little by little, it became... normal.

Was it ever okay to murder someone?

Was it ever *righteous*? Was it ever *justice*? Sure, the people Nadi killed were usually murderers and monsters in their own right.

But how bad did a person have to be, to make the *murder* just a *killing*? When did it become an execution of a convict, and not a black mark on the person delivering death?

Where was the line?

Was there one?

The thoughts and memories swirled as she started to come to. She was lying on her side, curled half into a ball. There was movement underneath her. Her hands were tied behind her back with something scratchy—probably cheap rope.

She couldn't see anything. Her breath was hot and close, and she smelled something musty and a little like straw, maybe? She had a bag over her head. And she believed she was in the trunk of an automobile.

Great.

Just fucking great.

Whoever it was who had crashed the party had taken "Monica" hostage. Either to get Raziel to *do* something, or to start carving pieces of her off and sending them to him in the post.

There was no point in trying to pay attention to which way the car was going. She had been out for long enough that she couldn't track the movements of the vehicle if she tried. So, she lay there, and stayed calm. Besides, the metropolis was gigantic. Not only was it enormous in footprint, but it was layers of buildings stacked on top of each other, with roadways on top of roadways on top of roadways. There was no way in the void of knowing where they were.

The car drove for what seemed like an hour before it finally came to a stop. When the trunk opened, Nadi could hear that wherever they were, the walls were close by the way the sound of the click bounced off the walls. Interesting. She couldn't smell anything through the hood she was wearing, so any other hints were useless.

Hands grabbed her under the armpits and hefted her out of the trunk, setting her onto her bare feet. Her shoes were gone—also interesting. The floor beneath her was smooth gravel. Her hands were still lashed behind her back, and if it weren't for whoever it was standing next to her, she likely would have eaten said gravel.

"Can you walk?" a man next to her asked.

Testing her ankles with an experimental roll, she nodded. "Yeah."

"Good." The man wasn't much for small talk, but neither was he particularly rough with her. He could be shoving her around or barking orders. Instead, he had *asked* her the question, and had waited for her to test her joints and give him an answer before urging her to walk forward.

More clues. More bits and pieces of a puzzle to start sorting into some kind of order in her head.

It was all she had to go on. She was unarmed. Defenseless. And alone. While she could probably change her shape into somebody two or three times Monica's size and snap the ropes that had her wrists bound behind her back—the key bit there was *probably*.

And the moment she revealed herself as a fae, they'd open fire, and it was all over. No, that was a bullet you only got to fire once. And she wanted to make sure she didn't waste her chance. She needed better intelligence on her situation before she acted.

Who were these people? What did they want? And how were they planning on using her to get it?

There were at least two others, judging by the heaviness of their movements. Men, she figured, by the sound of the shoes. No one was speaking. Wherever they were, it was close quarters but vacant, like a long hallway or a series of corridors.

For now, she was content to walk quietly at the direction of the man who had a grasp of her upper arm. He wasn't harsh with her. In fact, he muttered "Left" or "Right" to her when they were going to turn to keep from yanking her abruptly.

When he pulled her to a stop, she turned her head toward him.

"Stairs," he explained.

"You can either carry me or be patient." She smiled underneath the hood. "Your call."

"Just fuckin' pick her up, John. We're wasting time." That would be one of the other men present. By the sounds of it, someone loosely in charge. Or at least, more in charge than John, the polite one that was guiding her along.

Because of her arms behind her back, that meant only one thing. Fireman's carry. Oh well. Letting out a sigh, she shrugged and turned toward John. "I'll try not to puke on you."

"Thanks, miss," John muttered. He seemed like a nice boy. Shame she'd probably have to kill him by the time all this was over.

Sure enough, her world upended as he put his shoulder to her midsection and hefted her up. Keeping her wisecracks to herself about how this was hardly how she expected her wedding night to go, she stayed quiet and didn't struggle as they brought her wherever it was they were taking her.

They walked for another ten minutes, faster now that she wasn't slowing them down, before one of the other men knocked on what sounded like a very large and heavy set of metal doors. A creak and a slide, and they were allowed entry.

She heard more people in the room this time, muttering to each other. Oh good, a *crowd*. That made things far more complicated. But while "complicated" meant more variables, more variables could be either good or bad. They meant more rolls of the dice. And right now, she could use all the rolls she could get.

Her world tilted again as she was put down into a chair. She felt John move behind her to tie her arms to it. Damn. Well, she shouldn't be surprised.

"Raziel has already broken her spirit, eh?" A man's voice in front of her broke through the quiet murmuring. His accent was thick. Dread started to build in her, creeping up her spine—but she pushed it away. No. She wouldn't assume the worst. That accent could have another explanation. "Just like those vampire *hrippaiid*."

No.

No, no, no!

Shit. Shit, shit, *shit*!

This wasn't part of the plan. Adrenaline coursed through her like electricity.

Focus, Nadi. Focus. If she let it all disintegrate now, she was going to die here. Or worse, everything she'd worked for would fall apart into cinders and nothingness. She struggled to breathe. After a brief moment, she managed to speak. "No. There's just no point in screaming, crying, or making a fuss. I don't know where I am, who you are, or what my odds of survival are. Only thing I'll get by making John's life miserable is a fist to the skull. I'm not in the position to make enemies right now."

The male voice huffed a laugh. "Smart girl. Heard you were

from the outer posts. Had to grow up with a brain in your head. Take the bag off."

Somebody grabbed the sack over her head and yanked it away. Blinking at the light, she groaned and shook her head, trying to blow her hair out of her eyes.

Part of her wished they'd left the bag on, though.

Because the moment she looked up, she received confirmation that her life had just become far, far more complicated, which was something she had no idea was even possible at this point.

Sitting on a table across from her, perched with one bare foot up on the wooden lip and the other dangling down, was her captor. Or at least, the one who was clearly in charge of the human men who had done the deed. He was watching her keenly, the creases around the corners of his eyes hinting toward his true age. The beads that were carefully woven into his hair were one of the ways she knew his clan counted the decades. It revealed not only his *centuries* of age... but the places in the underground Wild he had called his home. Each one marked off somewhere he had been. Somewhere he had claim to.

Pointed, pale-green ears jutted from dark green hair that ran down almost to his waist.

Fae.

Luciento Iltani.

Her uncle.

Fuck.

THIRTEEN

Nadi could not stop swearing in her head.

And thanked the moons above and the great lords of the deep Wild that she was a shapeshifter currently wearing someone else's face. Because the fear and panic in her expression could easily be explained as that of a human's first time meeting a fae. Rather than the truth, which was that Nadi recognized the fae she was staring at.

She knew him very, very well.

All the jokes about her joining his ranks... how much he'd have to pay her father for her to join the human Iltani foot soldiers. *The price of two moons*, her father would always reply. Her father. *His brother*.

Fae were rare in the Iltani clan. Most of them were humans, cast out from society for choosing to live on the fringes of the Wild. Her father and her family were the only kin Luciento had that she knew of.

And Luciento had been the reason her whole family had died. It had been Luciento's mistakes that had cost everyone she loved their lives. And for a short time, Nadi had hated Luciento for that. But... when she'd been forced to quickly come to realize

how hard life was living on the outskirts of the human civilization? She'd soon forgiven him.

No, she didn't blame him.

But that didn't mean he wasn't about to *fucking ruin everything for her*.

Thank the moons for her glamor being impervious even to
other fae.

"Never seen a fae before?" Luciento chuckled.

No. That was very much not the problem. "My father kept
me inside the town walls."

The others in the room were all part of the Iltani clan.
Humans, all of them. Nadi didn't recognize any of them from
back in the day—it had been so long, the ones she would recognize were likely all long dead.

"I'm sure you've heard all sorts of stories of how we eat the
flesh of pretty little *ligas* like you." Luciento grinned wide,
flashing his slightly pointed canines.

"I have. I never really believed them, though." She
shrugged, trying to play up the game. Trying to tamp down her
panic. Raziel and the others might send a force to rescue her to
salvage some of his dignity. That meant Luciento was in danger.
And no matter how long she'd spent separated from him and his
clan, they were still her family.

"Oh?" The Iltani patriarch shifted, dropping his foot from
the table to lean forward. Despite his age—he was nearly four
thousand years old, if Nadi could remember correctly—he was
still limber and could beat anyone in a brawl. "And why is
that?"

"Because we'd have a lot more dead cows if that were the
case. I've heard humans taste terrible." She smiled.

Luciento blinked in surprise, then cackled in laughter, slapping his thigh. He pointed at her and looked over at the three
men who had brought her in. "I *like* this one. Shame she'll have
to die, eh?"

Shit.

Her shoulders slumped.

The older fae clicked his tongue. "Bah. Don't give me that look, *liga*. It's nothing personal. We just know an opportunity when we see one, and you are a fantastic opportunity."

"What're you going to do to me?" She kept swearing in her head. This was going to get ugly, and ugly quick.

"Nothing worse than that bastard was going to do, trust me, *liga*." Luciento hopped off the table, his beads jingling as he moved. He walked up to her and crouched down at her feet, smiling up at her with genuine kindness. "You'll die fast. Painless as we can make it. Sorry to say you're just the bit of cheese in the trap."

Ah. She watched the fae's iridescent green-blue-yellow eyes for a moment, and her heart cinched in the memory of him from her childhood. Those days of happiness were so far gone that they were little more than ghosts. Yet there was one, right in front of her, as bright as day. "Are you after Raziel or the whole family?"

"We'll take as many of them as we can get." He patted her knee and stood before walking over to a pack of his people who were gathered by the wall. He clicked his tongue and jerked his thumb, gesturing at them to get their things and go. "But I'll settle for that one *fuck* and be happy with it. *I na'h ha. Ish iba baleha.*"

He was getting his people out the door and fast. But she wanted more answers, first. "What did he do to you?"

"Oh, sweetie." Luciento laughed sadly. "What hasn't he done?" He picked up a canvas bag by the wall and slung it over his shoulder.

Yeah. She knew how he felt.

Luciento paused by the door as he headed out of the room to glance back at her. John and the two men who brought her in were staying behind. His smile was sad. Kind. "May your ances-tors come for you quickly, *liga*."

It was an old blessing, given to those who were destined to die. Because sometimes the best fate was a quick and painless death. Luciento didn't want to kill her. She was just bait, like he had said.

Lords of the deep, how many people had she killed in the name of a so-called greater good? All in the name of trying to stop the same bastard that Luciento was hunting?

She smiled at him. "I understand. And I forgive you." *For more than you know, old man.*

He put his hand over his heart and bowed his head before leaving the room with his clan.

Letting out a breath, she shut her eyes. Great. Fantastic. She wanted to scream. She wanted to tip the chair over, in an attempt to knock herself unconscious. Or maybe split her skull open and end the misery.

Because she had a serious moons-damned problem ahead of her.

The three people holding her hostage were part of her own *clan*. They were her *people*. Sure, she had left them behind ages ago, but that wasn't their fault. And while these humans were strangers to her, they were family. *Family!*

It had been her own bitterness about Luciento's decisions that had kept her from running to him after her family's death. And then... it'd simply been too late to change course. For all they knew, she was dead. She'd decided she was going to kill the Nostroms, and that was that.

And that was still her mission in life. Wasn't it?

That meant the right thing to do was to be bait. To sit in the trap, and willingly die. Or, honestly, to tell her captors every-thing—who she was, what she was doing—get Luciento back into the room, confess her secret, and tell them that she would sacrifice her life for him if it meant she took Raziel down with her.

That was what she *should* do.

She should shout "*saestren!*" after Luciento. Calling him *uncle* in fae would get his attention *real* fast. The scene played out in her head perfectly. She'd have a tearful reunion with him. Embrace and forgive him for getting his family killed. She would play the bait as Monica. Luciento would lay his trap for Raziel as planned.

But there was a problem.

She didn't trust Luciento.

She hadn't known him for *decades*.

How careful was the fae patriarch's plan? How trustworthy were his people? How many of them were secretly working for the Nostroms or any rival families? How many of them had already reported her location to the human authorities?

The scheme could already be doomed to fail for a thousand reasons. Maybe Raziel wouldn't come in the first place. Maybe he'd laugh in the face of whatever scheme Luciento had planned and send him a "thanks for dealing with my marriage situation for me" card and a bouquet of flowers.

Or maybe Raziel had paid Luciento to do it in the first place.

She knew that if she were left to her own devices, she had a decent chance at killing Raziel. But whatever the Iltanis had planned?

It just wasn't something she could risk her life on.

Literally.

Fuck.

Fuck!

Squeezing her eyes tight, she lowered her head and let out a frustrated sigh. She didn't want any of this. Killing vampires or their human goons was one thing. Killing fae... was it worth it? Was it really honestly worth it?

Raziel would keep killing her kind. The Nostroms were responsible for hundreds of fae deaths. And would be responsible for hundreds or thousands more if they weren't stopped.

She just needed time. Time to dismantle the Nostroms, one by one, from within. This wasn't a war that could be won quickly. She needed to act carefully, decisively, and plan out each murder with precision. And this? This wasn't precise. This was a flash grenade thrown into a black powder storehouse.

There were only three Iltanis in the room with her. She only had to take down three of them. Just three. What were three more souls on her conscience? Her ancestors weren't coming for her when she died. No, she was going straight to the void, and she knew it. Besides—she had no family to watch over. No one to care for. Why would her soul ever need to linger?

Opening her eyes, she stared down at the grimy tile between her feet. Her stockings had been champagne-colored but were now splotchy with dirt and soot. The tile looked like it hadn't fared much better in its life. It had once been white, but now was caked with dirt and what looked like a mix of... dried blood? It had that rusty and ruddy reddish-brown color she recognized a little too easily.

Where *was* she?

"Sorry, miss." John was standing by one wall, frowning at her.

"Thanks. But I know it's not your fault. We're only what the world makes of us, after all." Letting out a breath, she looked up at him and cast him a weary smile. She didn't know who she was trying to make feel better—her or him. Both. "The world kills, and so do we."

Finally, she had the chance to take in a little bit of her surroundings. Oh. That explained the blood. They were in what looked like an old, abandoned slaughterhouse. It must be down in the depths of the metropolis, close to the Wild and near enough to the caves for the Iltanis to feel comfortable moving in and out so easily. But not in their base of operations.

The walls were the same dingy and disgusting white tile as the floor. Whoever decided to put white tile in an abattoir suffered from catastrophic optimism. And it hadn't done them, or the room, any favors in the end. Chains, rusted and likely useless by this point, hung from the ceiling in loops and were latched out of the way with vicious, angry-looking hooks.

She hoped nobody planned on using those on her, but she doubted it.

Only three men had been left behind to watch her, everybody else had left. Which meant they likely weren't planning on a full, all-out war. Smart. Vampires were fast, vicious fighters. And they had them outnumbered and outgunned. The Iltanis would also have no element of surprise. Raziel was a lot of things, but he wasn't stupid.

What were the Iltanis up to?

Letting out another breath, she looked over at John and figured—when in doubt? Ask. "So. I'm curious. How's this all supposed to work?"

"What do you mean?" He blinked.

One of the other men shook his head, clearly not liking the prisoner getting chatty. He was standing by the door they must have come through to get into the room, staring down the long hallway, his hand on his gun. He looked twitchy. She dubbed him the Nervous One.

"Well, you abducted me from my wedding. The fae said I wasn't going to be tortured, so I don't think you plan on cutting off pieces of me and mailing them to Raziel in the post. Besides, he... I'm going to be blunt—he wouldn't care. He'd just be annoyed that you'd be making a mess of his mailbox."

The third one, who she nicknamed Smiley, as he seemed to do so easily, snickered at her joke. She instantly felt bad for the fact that she was going to have to kill him. She hated that she was going to have to kill any of them. She really hoped she wouldn't have to. But she didn't see a way around it.

The only way she could get out of here was if she used her magic. And if they saw her magic, they'd know she was fae. And if they knew she was fae, that was valuable intelligence. And if her theory that any one of them was in the pocket of another family was right...

Down went her house of cards.

Why did life have to be complicated?

I really should have listened to Betty and retired last year. I really should.

"So," she continued, preferring the conversation to her raging internal debate, "if it isn't slow torture, it's what he said—bait in a trap. But Raziel has a *lot* of goons and a *lot* of guns and if he's coming at all, he's going to be *very* pissed and he's going to know he's walking into a trap."

The three men were watching her, various shades of confusion on their faces. Apparently, they had expected her to just sit there and weep. Not treat the situation like a thought experiment. *Sorry, boyos. This is kind of what I do for a living.*

"Which means you're probably not planning to just... gun them all down. I expect—especially considering how quiet it's grown since everybody left—we're the only ones in here now." She paused. Nobody spoke. They weren't going to give her anything.

She shifted in the chair. From their point of view, she was probably just trying to stretch her arms. From her point of view, she was testing the tightness of the ropes. They were actually pretty well tied. Damn. She wasn't going to be able to just shift shapes and snap out of them. She'd need another plan.

Looking off thoughtfully, she debated what she'd do in this situation. If she didn't have manpower, what else could she use? "Oh!" She grinned. "Explosives!"

"*Fuck.*" John's eyes went wide.

"Hah! I'm right." She actually felt quite proud of herself. That'd been kind of a fun puzzle, even if she was now sitting in the middle of a literal powder keg. "You're going to lure him and as many others as you can inside, run out the back, and while they're trying to untie me, blow this place to the void, collapse it into the underground."

"Fuck!" John swore again, pacing away from where he'd been standing. He took off his wool cap and ran his hand over his short dark hair. "Mick, if *she* can figure it out that fast, that means—"

"Shut up," Mick snapped. Mick was the Nervous One. Nadi preferred "Nervous One." It suited him better. "We have our orders. You want to go back to the boss and tell him that you're too much of a coward to go through with this?"

"N—no. But—" John grimaced.

"By the time the vampires make it down that corridor, it'll be too late. We blow the chamber behind them, then blow this one. If they come, they die. If they don't? They don't." Mick shrugged. "The end. We get out alive, either way. We'll never even see them. We just wait for the call."

Clever. Very clever. She'd give the Iltanis that. They were flipping one of Raziel's proverbial coins. Heads, his ego would send him in after his abducted "wife" and straight into a known trap. Tails, he stayed away, and the Iltanis didn't lose any more lives.

But then came another very important question.

One Nadi wasn't fully certain she really wanted to know the answer to. "What happens to me if he doesn't show up?"

Mick walked in front of her, holding his gun down at his side. He was older than John and Smiley by a few years but might be related to them both. A brother, maybe? He also looked like he had seen some serious shit. A scar ran down over his cheek and into his lip, and when he talked, he was missing a few teeth on one side.

"You want to know so badly? Fine. We've put in the call to the Nostroms. They have until midnight tonight to walk in here to negotiate cash for your safe release, or else they can come get you in a black bag. They come, and we blow them to the ancestors. But if they *don't*? Well... something you ought to know 'bout us Iltanis, whether we're fae or human."

Mick lifted the pistol and placed the end of it squarely into the middle of her forehead.

"We don't make idle threats."

Nadi sighed.

No.

That was something the Iltanis very much did not do.

It was settled.

Either she died. Or they died. Now, she just had to figure out the small matter of *how* she was going to get out alive. No pressure. "What time is it?"

Mick dropped the gun, snorting in a half-laugh at her dismissal of the gun against her forehead. "Eleven thirty."

No pressure at all.

FOURTEEN

It had taken Nadi twenty minutes to come up with a plan.

It was a *shitty plan.*

But it was the only one she had.

The reason it was an awful plan was because it relied on her three captors being both nice *and* kind of stupid. They seemed decent enough, for underworld types, but as to whether they were stupid... she was about to find out.

"Excuse me?" She shifted in her chair. "I know this is—I know this really doesn't matter right now, given the state of things, and all, but I really need to pee."

Mick groaned.

"Look, I know! I'm about to die, one way or another, and I'm *sorry*, but—today has been really terrible, and I really have to pee, and I've been holding it for *hours*, and I've been trying to be polite and understanding about this whole thing—" Rambling on purpose, she shifted again and let out a whine.

"Mick," John muttered. "C'mon. Let her have some dignity. She hasn't done nothing to be a pain."

I promise I'll kill you quickly, John. Poor boy.

"Fine! Fine." Mick threw his hands up in the air. "Take her around the corner. Let her piss in the sewer hole."

Oh, thank the deep gods! Relief and hope flooded Nadi, and she let out a breath. Luckily, the men in the room just took it as a woman thankful she was going to be able to empty her bladder. Not someone who was going to make a break for freedom.

John walked up behind her and undid the ropes around her wrists. Bringing her hands around in front of her, she rubbed them and smiled up at him in honest-to-goodness thanks. She'd have nasty bruises in the morning if she lived that long.

The Iltani had a pistol in his hand and gestured with it for her to get up and start walking. She did so without complaint and glanced back at him a few times to ensure that she was going in the right direction. He directed her out of the room and around a corner to a smaller area where they must once have hung pigs to cut their throats. There was a large sewer grate in the center of the floor where all the gore and muck would drain into the underground and into the Wild below. Humans loved to throw their garbage into the abyss and forget about those who had to live with it.

"Go on, then." John gestured at her with his gun.

She frowned at him. "Do you mind turning your back?" Curling her shoulders in a little, she tried to make herself look as small and helpless as possible. Just a bride, abducted on her wedding day. Torn, scratched, and bloody from a cut on her arm and her leg. Harmless. Weak.

The Iltani blinked, sighed, and shook his head. "Yeah, yeah. Sorry."

Cracking her neck from one side to the other, she changed shape. She picked the largest, toughest, meanest person she'd met in recent memory.

Ivan.

Raziel's chief bodyguard.

Walking up behind John silently, she tapped him on the shoulder.

"Wh—" John turned. But didn't get the whole word out. His eyes went as big as saucers as he suddenly looked up at a man twice his size.

"Sorry 'bout this," she mumbled in Ivan's voice as she rammed her new train-sized fist into John's head. His head snapped back and, just like that, he was out cold.

She grabbed him by the front of the shirt to stop his fall, not wanting the other men to be alerted by the sound. Catching the gun before it clattered to the ground, she set John down to the tile and debated her next steps.

A gunshot would warn Mick and Smiley.

She could snap John's neck.

Guilt stabbed at her. He'd been nice to her. He was a human in a fae clan. *Her* fae clan. He didn't deserve to die. He must hate the Nostroms as much as she did. They were on the same fucking *side*.

This was idiocy. Sheer idiocy. She should kill him. That was the smart decision.

She couldn't do it.

But the others... If Raziel was going to believe her story, the others needed to die.

With a quiet, bass growl from a set of lungs that weren't her own, she checked the number of bullets in the gun. Then she stepped over John's unconscious body and went to find Mick and Smiley.

* * *

"It's probably a trap."

Raziel checked the clip in his pistol. Full. Good. "Of course it's a *fucking* trap, Deniel." His cousin wasn't the brightest vampire in the clan, but when one was up against an unknown number of armed fae-loving idiot humans, every additional ally was useful.

A call had come into Raziel's home, not long after the abduction. The Iltanis had given them an address and a deadline—meet by midnight to discuss a cash settlement in exchange for Monica's life, or she would be returned to them in a bag.

The place in question was an abandoned abattoir deep in the pits of the metropolis near the docks—where no one would care what would happen. It was a decrepit place, the windows shattered and dark, the brick exterior covered in moss and creeping vines. The Wild didn't wait long to start reclaiming whatever structures were left to their own devices without anyone there to constantly beat back the encroaching corruption.

At the end of all this, Raziel would send a team to this place to have it burned to a crisp. Purified back to a state of pure stone.

The building looked even bleaker in the stark light from the round headlamps of his car. The metal double doors were half fallen off their hinges, rusted, and ajar, revealing nothing of the inside other than a gaping black hole.

It seemed fitting that a place built as a slaughterhouse would see bloodshed once more.

Mael was loading the drum of a machine gun into its receiver, clearly preparing for a heavy firefight. Raziel preferred handguns—Mael wasn't a fan of subtlety. "I'll take Remmy, Tooks, and Valiart. It's a long, straight corridor into the depths of that building, and that likely means they plan to block you off from any sort of escape. We'll need to find another way in from above or around the sides. But they have another way in, and so we'll f—" His older brother broke short as a figure emerged from the darkness of the front door. "What the *fuck*?"

Raziel could not believe his eyes.

Looking like a nightmare, like something from a pulp horror novel, a woman stepped out from the gloom of the meat factory.

Or, perhaps to him, a dream.

It was Monica.

Her brown hair was tangled and hung around her face in loose strands. Her wedding dress was torn, charred black with soot in areas, and soaked in blood. Her face was spattered with it, streaked in gore. A deep gash on her arm was oozing crimson. She had no shoes, her champagne-colored stockings stained with dirt.

And in her right hand, held loosely down at her side, was a pistol.

Her expression was blank. Not troubled, not afraid—simply devoid of anything.

It was the most beautiful thing he had ever seen in his life.

Raziel was moving before he thought about it, rushing to her. He placed his hands on her shoulders. "Monica?"

"Three of them. Two are dead. The last one ran. There were others, but they're long gone." She wasn't even looking at him, she was simply staring *through* him. "The whole structure is wired with explosives. Don't go in."

Raziel stroked some of her hair away from her face. "Are you hurt?"

She furrowed her brow as if she honestly didn't know. She looked down as if she needed to check.

Gods below, he wanted her.

"Oh. Huh." She glanced down at herself. She touched her hip, and grimaced. "Oh, yeah. I need stitches."

Yes, he wanted her *very* badly. "How did you get free?"

"They were idiots." She paused for a moment. "I also hit my head on the tile. I might have a mild concussion? Either that, or the champagne picked an interesting time to catch up with me."

It wasn't much of an answer, but given what she had been

through, he wasn't surprised. He took the pistol from her, which she gave him without resistance. He tucked it into his belt. Scooping her up in his arms, he held her like, well, his bride.

She leaned her forehead against his shoulder and said nothing as he carried her back to his car.

Everyone was watching them in shock.

Mael was the first to speak. "We'll... disarm the explosives."

Raziel nodded as he approached his car. Remmy opened the door for him as he climbed into the back. "I'm going to take her home. If you find any of those fae-fucking bastards, make them hurt. For me." He paused. "For both of us."

He didn't miss Mael's faint smile. "You got it."

Remmy shut the door. The driver didn't need to be told what to do. The engine roared to life as he headed back toward Raziel's home.

Raziel wasn't concerned in the slightest about Mael and the others. Now that the Iltanis' plans had been upended, they were like rats running to ground. They would be hard to catch—but harmless to hunt.

It wasn't until he was in the small, enclosed space with Monica that he realized a potential problem.

She was covered in blood. And she smelled *divine*.

Wincing, he had to bite his tongue to keep his fangs from extending in instant, instinctual hunger. He could smell the blood of the two people she had killed mingling with hers. And there was no question which one belonged to his Monica.

His Monica?

When had that started?

A thought for another time.

He could tell which scent was hers. It was... hard to describe. He had never smelled anything similar. It was entirely new to him. Instinctively, he leaned in closer, trying to come up with anything it could even be compared to.

Blinking, he pulled his head back. Without realizing it, his fangs had extended. What had come over him? He had never lost control like that before. Perhaps the alcohol had also gone to his head. It had been a long day. He was tired. That was all. "I have a doctor on staff at the house. He's human. He'll stitch you up."

"Great." She sounded exhausted. Beyond exhausted.

"Stay awake, Monica."

"I know, I know." She sighed. "Stupid *fucking* Iltanis."

"They told you who they were?" Odd.

"Like I said. Stupid."

"I suppose so." That was intriguing. But he let it go. Something to consider another time, when he was not struggling to contain his bloodlust in front of his new wife. He wanted to lick her clean—every inch of her.

But there would be a time and place for that another day.

He kissed the top of her head. "I am... glad you're all right."

Silence for a beat, and then, "Me too."

Curious creature.

But perhaps, just perhaps, she might have a place in his family, after all.

* * *

Raziel was holding her as she was seated in his lap. He went quiet, staring out the window periodically, but he seemed to keep being drawn back to her, though she couldn't figure out why at first.

Then, it happened.

Before Nadi's eyes, his fangs extended, growing longer as he prepared to bite her.

Oh.

It must be the smell of the blood she was covered in—she didn't even think about that. She wasn't used to being near a vampire.

But that wasn't all.

He was... purring.

She almost hadn't heard it over the bass rumble of the engine—the noises were so similar. The sound coming from him was that deep. There was only one word for it. *Primal.* And by all the moons, it did something horrible to her.

Suddenly, she had the overwhelming need to lean closer to him, to feel his fangs pierce her throat, to feel him drink from her. It lit a fire in her, and in her mind's eye she could see herself, straddling his lap, riding him as he drained her dry. Filling her as he took from her.

It was wrong.

All of it was *wrong*.

His eyes were heavily lidded and dark—lost in his own lust and desire for blood. He might not even know what he was doing. It took everything she had to place her hand on his lips and stop him from doing what they both wanted. It might actually kill her, for one. And two, she had no idea if that would reveal her secret to him.

She wanted to postpone that moment for as long as she feasibly could.

He blinked as if waking from a dream, and pulled his head back. Grimacing, his fangs slid back into his jaw. "It's the blood." If she wasn't mistaken, he looked a little embarrassed.

"I know." Frowning, she glanced out the window. It was impossible to know how close they were. She had no idea where they were. "Should I sit on the other side of the car?"

"No. I'll be fine. Just... stab me if I get too lost in it again." He smirked. "You do seem to have a penchant for bloodshed. You were right."

"I'm... I really didn't have a choice." It was true. But that didn't mean he was wrong. "It was either I kill them or I die in an explosion."

"I see. Purely out of a sense for self-preservation. You

weren't worried about your new husband." He huffed, though the twist to his lips told her he was teasing her. "I see how it is."

"You can take care of yourself." She poked him in the chest. If she hadn't felt like such utter garbage, she might even have smiled.

"Hm. I suppose." He turned his attention down to her side, where the bullet had hit her.

She had been pressing a part of her dress to it to slow the bleeding, but she let him nudge her hand away to inspect the wound. The bullet hadn't gone out the other side. But it didn't seem to have hit anything important either.

It was bleeding steadily, but not bad enough that she was worried she was going to bleed out too quickly. It was right at the spot where her thigh met her hip, which was going to be obnoxious to let heal. She healed quickly as a fae. Which she'd have to watch out for—she'd heal *too* quickly for a human. Shit. It was little things like that, that were going to trip her up.

His brow creased in the center as he looked down at the wound. Was he... concerned?

"I'll need the bullet pulled out and then some stitches." She moved his hand away and pressed the fabric to the wound. "Sorry that I'm not going to die on you so soon."

"It must hurt."

"I have a high pain tolerance."

"Hm." He chuckled once. "We'll see about that."

There was the Raziel she knew. She shot him a look. "You're going to have to wait. Sorry for the inconvenience."

Lifting his hand, his fingers were stained with her blood. Smirking, he licked them clean.

For a moment, her heart lurched in her chest as she watched.

One by one, like someone savoring the bits of a bowl after making brownie dough. Would he know? Could he *tell*?

Was this the moment it all fell apart?

In her mind's eye, Nadi could picture him grimacing in disgust as he tasted her fae blood before ripping her throat open and murdering her right then and there.

But he merely groaned as his pupils went wide. His voice was suddenly breathy. "Oh, Monica... I'm not so sure how long I can be patient."

A knot twisted in her stomach. Well. It... seemed her theory about her glamor lasting long enough to make it past his taste-buds was right. At least in small doses.

He leaned his head back against the rear window of the car. "If all girls out in the outer cities taste like you do, we city vampires have been missing out."

"Must be all the fresh air." She smiled nervously. At least he'd write it off as being because she was afraid of being bitten—which she was, but not for the reasons he'd expect. "And the grass."

"You do taste a bit like how the Wild smells. That must be it." He wiped his hand off on his pants—she'd already ruined his tuxedo, anyway—before smiling at her almost lazily. "Somehow, you keep finding more ways to tease me."

She was struck by how handsome he was. The light from outside cut his sharp features in light and shadow. She couldn't help herself. She just couldn't. Leaning forward, she kissed him.

He tasted coppery and bitter—her own blood. It wasn't the first time she'd tasted it.

Threading his hand into her hair, he held her closer, deepening the embrace. When he growled deep in his chest, her eyes slipped shut.

It was a long moment before he finally broke away. She was breathless—from the concussion, the champagne, and now the kiss.

"Careful, farm girl. You're playing with fire."

"You think I don't know that?" He smelled like cologne and

woodsmoke. She wanted to nuzzle closer to him. "That's the *point*."

He chuckled darkly before leaning his head back again. "I think you and I are going to get along *just* fine."

Good. Even if he didn't trust her yet, he was starting to like her.

And that was going to make it much easier to kill him.

FIFTEEN

Raziel stood at the far end of the room, his arms folded across his chest, as he watched his doctor work on Monica. His jaw twitched. It took every ounce of willpower he owned not to leap across the room and sink his fangs into her throat and drink her dry.

No, her death at his hands had to wait until their honeymoon. But by the moons, he needed to drink of her before then.

The smell of her blood was thick in the air. He had tasted just the barest drop of it in the car and it had been a terrible mistake on his part. Now that he knew what he was missing, it was doubly hard to resist.

It'd been unlike anything he'd ever had before in his *life*. It had threatened every ounce of control he owned not to rip her apart.

But his wife of only a few hours was stretched thin enough as it was.

She was lying on her side on a metal table that the doctor used for surgeries. Because of her concussion, which was thankfully deemed mild, she wasn't given any painkillers nor was the doctor able to put her under to remove the bullet. So Monica lay there, staring at a point on the far wall, as the doctor cleaned the wound with rubbing alcohol.

Her hand twitched in pain, but she didn't make a sound.

"This will hurt," the doctor muttered to Monica. His name was Bartholomew Williams—a brilliant young man who had been cast out from the local hospitals due to an... *eccentric* fascination with attempting to resurrect the dead.

"It already hurts." Monica shot the doctor a flat stare. "Just shut up and do your *fucking* job, will you?"

Raziel chuckled. His new bride had claws. He found that he enjoyed it a great deal. Far more than when she was playing timid. And now he was *fully* convinced that the timid routine was entirely an act, which was fascinating to him.

Who was she? *Really?*

Every moment he spent around his new wife, he found something that felt like a new piece to a puzzle.

A puzzle that was forming an unexpected picture.

A picture that he was starting to find a little too enchanting for his comfort.

Bartholomew shook his head, picked up the forceps, and shifted his stool closer to begin the process of removing the bullet. He paused before pressing the steel ends into the wound on Monica's side, just above her hip. Luckily, the bullet had not gone in terribly deep, nor had it hit any organs or arteries. She would be fine once the stitches healed.

The doctor turned his attention to Raziel. "You may wish to leave the room."

"Why?" He arched his eyebrow back at the doctor. Monica's wedding dress was already mostly cut away, leaving her in bloody shreds of what remained of the lacy gown and her undergarments. The maids had brought some sheets to drape over her for modesty. "It isn't anything I haven't already seen."

"The blood, sir. You already seem... affected." Bartholomew's eyes flicked down to Raziel's teeth.

Ah. Yes. Raziel's fangs had extended without his noticing. He grimaced, forcing them to withdraw back into his jaw. "Continue."

"Sir—"

It was Monica who settled the argument. "It's fine. He can stay."

He couldn't help but feel a bit surprised at that. It looked like the doctor was equally shocked.

Briefly, she shut her eyes and laid her head down on the thin pillow that had been provided to her. She looked miserable, a thin layer of sweat on her forehead mixing with the dirt and blood that she'd gathered from the day's misadventures. She blinked her eyes back open, likely remembering she wasn't allowed to sleep with her concussion just yet. "He'll control himself."

What an oddly charming vote of confidence. Leaning against the wall, he watched her with a faint smile. "Listen to your new boss, doctor, and do your job. Get to work."

"Excuse me?" The doctor did not seem so keen on that statement. "I still don't think it's best if you are here, with your current—"

"She is my wife. You answer to her now, same as me. That is how marriage works, isn't it?" Raziel huffed a laugh. "Or was I mistaken? Tell me, how would you prefer I structure this situation?"

"I—well—" The doctor didn't seem to know what to say to that.

"If you don't fucking pull this bullet out of my side *right now*, I'm going to take those forceps and do it myself," Monica snapped. "Stop. Wasting. Time."

Bartholomew stared at her. Then looked to Raziel.

He merely gestured to the wound as if to ask the doctor what he was waiting for.

With a sigh, the doctor turned to the wound and put the tips of the forceps into the seeping wound.

Monica snarled low in her throat. Her hands were curled by her face. Both of them clenched tight into fists, but she otherwise didn't move. She knew—either from experience or intuition—to keep still and try not to tense up as the doctor fished around in the wound as he searched for the spent lead inside of her.

Raziel would have to ask her about that later. If his new wife had taken a bullet before... he would have a *lot* of questions.

Bartholomew stayed quiet as he worked. Monica squeezed her eyes shut, her face twitching in pain, the only sign that she was suffering at all from what was happening as the doctor did his job.

Raziel had seen many of his human soldiers reduced to tears from similar wounds. Ones who had purported themselves to be *toughest of the tough.* Monsters and killers of the worst sort, reduced to whimpering children when the needle met skin and wounds were stitched shut.

Yet, here was Monica.

His arranged wife from an irritating upstart family from some obscure city on the edge of Runne. One he had been looking forward to ridding himself of quickly. Who he had seen as nothing more than a nuisance at worst, or at best, a brief and amusing distraction.

But by the time the bullet clinked into the metal tray and Bartholomew picked up the thread to begin stitching the wound shut, Monica had made no sound through the entire ordeal past the occasional grunt. And as the doctor went to work closing the wound, Raziel wondered exactly what they did to their young women out in the outposts to give them such a level of pain tolerance.

Indeed, if it weren't for the fact that her eyes were open and she was blinking, he would assume she had fainted. Monica was studying objects on the far wall of the room with all the passive disinterest of someone sitting in the waiting room of a legal proceeding reading a plaque for the lack of anything better to do.

Only the occasional twitch of pain or a hiss through her teeth told him that she felt anything at all.

It kept him in rapt fascination. What a puzzle she was. Who *was* this Monica Valan? His wife? This cowgirl from the outpost farming city? Certainly nothing he had expected.

One thing was quickly becoming very certain, however.

He was *not* going to let her die until he had solved this particular mystery. The honeymoon would have to wait until he had his answers. He would unravel her.

Whoever you are, Monica Valan.

You're mine now.

* * *

Nadi's head was still spinning, and though her concussion was slowly starting to fade, her thoughts remained a jumbled mess.

The doctor had told her she could sleep in four-hour shifts once she got back to her room, as long as someone was around to wake her up and make sure she still knew what day it was. Fun.

Unfortunately, that meant she had to get the bullet pulled with no painkillers. But it wasn't the first time she'd had that done—and Dr. Williams was better at it than Betty ever was. Betty was a good friend but a shit surgeon. Nadi was pretty certain she had cigarette ash permanently sewn into her leg.

But that was neither here nor there at this point.

The doctor had finished sewing her up and cleaning the wound. That meant she was finally clear to go back to her room and take a sponge bath to get the dirt, sweat, and blood off her. She felt disgusting. She was exhausted. And her head was still reeling.

And she still had the whole issue of what had happened to deal with.

Raziel hadn't left her side since she had walked out of that abattoir. And he'd barely taken his eyes off her the entire time. Part of that was probably due to the fact that she was covered in blood, but there was something else going on behind those red eyes of his. Curiosity? No.

It was deeper than that.

But she couldn't quite put a name to it.

When she went to stand, Raziel tutted and scooped her up in his arms before she could protest. She didn't struggle and just let out a breath as he walked out of the room with her. "Just... no teeth, please."

"Only when you're properly mended." He smiled with the faintest glint of mischief in his eyes.

"Right." Grunting, she put her head against his shoulder. Not because she particularly wanted to cuddle with her worst enemy, but because she just really needed something to lean against. "I need a hot bath."

"I certainly wasn't going to allow you in my bed in this state."

That had her lifting her head to look at him in confusion.

"What?" He eyed her in equal bemusement as they climbed the stairs up to what must be his room. "Did you think you were going to still be sleeping downstairs? Now that you're my *wife*?"

She blinked. "I didn't think about it. I guess it was a stupid assumption."

"Yes." He chuckled. "It was."

A moment later and they were at his room. He shifted his grip to open the door, bringing her inside before setting her gently on her feet and shutting it behind her.

The room wasn't what she had been expecting.

Oh, it was just as expensive and beautiful as she imagined the room of someone with his amount of wealth and means would be. But she had expected something *ostentatious*. Something that was humungous and screamed power. Perhaps something even with a giant bed with columns, resplendent with chains and straps hanging from the ceiling.

Instead, what was in front of her was the picture of elegance. It was refined. And while it was dramatic in its shades of black and crimson, it was... comfortable. Cozy. The bed had a heavy velvet blanket on it that spilled off the edges and onto the floor and made her want to burrow into it and never come back out.

The curtains were half drawn, casting the dim morning light of the dawn across the warm oak floor through the haze of the sheer shades underneath, showing off the black lacquered furniture scattered about the room. A large black casket was against the wall, inlaid in brass. She wondered why he had both a bed and a box. But even the coffin seemed tastefully done, and... somehow *homey*.

The whole room seemed designed for curling up in front of the fireplace that dominated one wall with a drink in one hand and a book in the other.

Raziel had left her there to take in the space while he opened the door to another room and flicked on a light.

After staring at the room for another moment in surprise, she followed him. The bathroom was just as tasteful and moody as the bedroom, this time done entirely in tones of black, gray, and copper.

While Nadi couldn't get the stitches wet, that wasn't going to stop her from sitting in the tub and scrubbing everything else. And washing her gods-damned hair. "Where's the soap? I can handle this."

"Turn around so I can get that mess off you." By his tone, it was clear he wasn't answering her question. No, he was issuing an order. He folded a few washcloths and dropped them on the edge of the tub.

"What?" She shot him a look.

He straightened up to his full height, towering over her. The change in his demeanor was instant and unforgiving. "Turn. Around."

She swallowed. Instinct warred in her. Two halves wanted two very separate things. One very primal part of her wanted to obey instantly—to do what he asked without question. *Yes.* The other part of her wanted to claw his face off with her fingernails. To hiss and show him just what kind of feral beast he thought he had tamed.

Reason won out.

This wasn't worth a fight. She was already wounded, and her head was still spinning.

She turned her back to him.

"Good." He smoothed her hair out of the way, tangled mess that it was. "You and I will have to come to a... very complex understanding of each other, I feel."

"I'm starting to get that sense." She kept still as she felt him unzip the back of her dress. It had been mostly cut to pieces by the doctor, but he hadn't removed it all to stitch up her wound. He had only opened the part of it that he'd needed to. Naturally, the zipper stuck halfway down. Raziel didn't hesitate to rip it open. The dress was entirely trash, anyway. "For as long as it lasts, at any rate."

He hummed. "Indeed. Tell me what you've heard of my reputation with my lovers. The harsh truth of it." He slipped the shoulders of the dress off, careful to avoid the cut on her left arm that was now bandaged. It wasn't bad enough to need stitches, but it was yet another thing that couldn't get wet.

"You break them."

"Be more specific." He crouched down, urging her to step one leg out of the dress, then the other. It was nothing more than dirty, sliced-up bloody rags at this point. She was in stockings, her corset, garter belt, and underwear.

"You find a man or woman you like—then you use and abuse them, mentally and physically, until they're shattered and broken. Sometimes, they're found dead. Sometimes, they're found worse than that." She wasn't sure where he was going with this, but if he wanted the truth, she'd follow along.

"Hm." He unclipped her stockings. They were torn and in the same state as her dress. "Well, that's mostly true. But it's missing a key component, my dear." He rolled them down her legs, and had her step out of them one at a time before tossing them aside, into the pile with her dress.

"I'm sure it's the part of this that secretly makes you the good guy." She smirked down at him.

He snorted in laughter, and shot her a sarcastic smile. "Naturally." His smile faded as he stood back up before he began to unlace her corset from the back. "No, what you say I do to them is accurate. What the stories are lacking is the simple fact that what I do to them, they *ask* for."

She furrowed her brow. That made no sense. She twisted her head to look at him. "What?"

"Some people wish to be broken. Some people want to feel as though they match how they believe their soul was formed, perhaps. I honestly do not know. I... do not fully understand it myself." His expression fell flat.

Lords below.

He was telling the truth.

"My partners have always been willing. They climbed into my bed knowing their next destination would be either a casket or a madhouse." Glancing at him, she saw his cruel and vicious sneer. And in a sudden epiphany, she realized... it was directed entirely at himself. "Mother always told me I was the creative one in the family."

When he removed her corset and tossed it aside, she turned to face him. He watched her, the same guarded, cruel smile on his face. But she wasn't buying it. "And what about the lovers you've had who *don't* want to be broken?"

"Oh, my dear. Everyone wants to be broken..." He took her jaw in his hand, placing his thumb against the hollow of her chin, his nail just gently resting against her lower lip. He leaned in closer as if he were going to kiss her. "It's all just a matter of degrees. And whether or not, in the end... they wish to be rebuilt."

Her reply was little more than a whisper. "We'll see about that."

"Yes. I very much think we will, my little murderer." He smiled, settling his hands on her hips. He slid her underwear down her thighs, dropping them to the floor. "Now." He pointed to the tub. "Sit."

She wanted to strangle him with the hose that ran to the removable shower head.

But she refrained.

Letting out a long, ragged sigh, she did as she was told.

Raziel sat on the edge of the tub and began to bathe her. Yet somehow, despite the fact that he was the one tending to her, playing nursemaid, shampooing her hair and tending to her like she were his princess, she couldn't help but feel like this was a warning shot.

As he gave her a satin slip to wear and tucked her into sleep, kissing her gently and vowing to wake her in four hours to ensure that her concussion wouldn't trouble her...

She still somehow *knew*.

That Raziel Nostrom had just declared war.

And now the game was truly on.

SIXTEEN

When Raziel went to wake his new wife around two in the afternoon the next day, she let out a whine and shoved her head under the pillow.

It was so adorable, he had to chuckle. The creature he had found himself wed to was a fascinating contradiction in terms. Capable of such violence, yet strangely innocent at times.

And there was nothing in this world he enjoyed more than a good puzzle.

Picking up the pillow, he laughed as she whined again.

"Come, now. Get dressed, little murderer. The family is having a meeting, and Mother has insisted that you attend."

She groaned. "Why? She hates me."

A good question. One he had asked his mother himself. "Because word has already spread through the boys how you walked yourself out of that abattoir. I believe she wants to hear the story for herself. And she feels you might want to hear what is about to happen."

His wife lifted her head and looked up at him, bleary-eyed. It was clear she wasn't entertained by the idea and had likely been looking forward to sleeping for another ten hours. But with a heavy sigh, she rubbed her hands over her face, grunted, and rolled over onto her side to climb out of bed without another complaint.

Standing from the edge of the bed, he went to the bathroom to finish brushing out his hair. He was already dressed. "Clothes are in the wardrobe for you, there." He gestured at the piece of furniture in question. He had it stocked with clothing for her the day prior.

It was only a few minutes before she was dressed and ready, and though she was still clearly exhausted, her expression was set into one of quiet determination. Her stomach growled loud enough that he heard it from across the room.

He smirked. "Yes, there will be food."

"Don't look at me like that, *I* wasn't the one who asked." She smirked back at him. "But thank the moons. I don't think I managed to actually eat anything yesterday."

"I was warned that one generally doesn't at one's wedding." He opened his door to the hallway, letting her step out first before following her out. "I admit I did not quite believe them." He led her through the corridor and down the stairs. He could hear his family already gathered in his parlor.

He, too, was starving. But as he would likely be doing most of the talking, he knew he would have to wait to fill his stomach. And sadly, what he truly wished to fill it with—his little murderer's blood—was still off the menu for a couple of days. Or at least, that was what Dr. Williams had insisted upon.

Whether or not he could actually wait that long remained to be seen.

Raziel noticed that his new wife hung back as they approached the dining room, likely not wanting to stride in first. He didn't say as he blamed her. His family was a bit *much*, even for him.

Perhaps especially for him.

Bracing himself for what was about to follow, he squared his shoulders, and walked in.

* * *

Lords, Nadi was cranky. She ached like she'd been in a train accident. She was starving. Her concussion had faded to a dull headache. And the stitches in her side were starting to *itch* as they began to heal. Luckily, fae healed quickly. Unfortunately, that meant she'd have to keep going into the bathroom to reopen the wound to hide the fact that she wasn't human. She wasn't sure if the creepy doctor would check her wound for infections, but she was certain Raziel would notice if it healed too fast.

Explaining away the quickly healing bruises was one thing. That, she could just shrug away and blame on luck and genetics. But a bullet wound being gone in days instead of weeks? And leaving no scar? That would raise instant suspicion.

And another thing that was making her cranky in no small part was the fact that she was having to walk into the lion's den first thing upon waking up. At least Raziel went in first. She used him as a shield as he led the way into his parlor. There was food on a table set up along one wall—sandwiches, finger foods, things like that.

Ignoring the stares from the gathered vampires, she went straight for the table. Everyone was in attendance.

Mael was standing by one wall, arms folded across his massive chest, his handsome features fixed into a scowl.

Lana was sitting in a chair, prim and perfect as ever, with Azazel perched on the arm next to her.

Volencia was sitting in a different chair, smoking a cigarette set into the end of a long, delicate brass holder.

Several others who Nadi recognized were scattered around, drinking from brown glass bottles or sipping hard alcohol. Some she kind of thought she had seen the night before.

"Well, now you can ask Red Lace herself."

Red Lace? Nadi blinked and turned her head to look over at Mael, who had been the one who had spoken. "Excuse me?"

The giant vampire's smile was both amused and beleaguered. "Rumors travel fast. And you were quite the sight walking out of that cesspit last night."

"Huh." She'd never had a nickname before. Or was that a title? She shrugged and went back to stacking up her plate. "Hardly impressive. Most of the blood was probably mine."

Someone snickered. It might have been Azazel. She didn't particularly care.

"Do you care to explain *precisely* what happened? Start from the very beginning, if you would. And walk us through, very specifically, how an *idiot child* like you managed to get away from three armed men?" Volencia sounded less than impressed.

What Nadi would have *cared* to do in that moment was eat some food, then break the neck off one of the bottles of beer and grind it into Volencia's smug-ass face.

However.

That would probably get her into a bit of trouble at the moment.

Instead, she plucked a bottle of beer from the ice and sat down on the sofa, taking her sweet time in silence. Raziel had his back to his mother where he stood at his bar, pouring himself a large glass of bloodwine. Volencia might not be able to see, but Nadi didn't miss the amused expression on his face.

He enjoyed the slight amount of shit she was giving his mother.

Perhaps the bond there wasn't as tight as she had thought.

That was something she could use.

"Well," Nadi finally began after the very long pause. "If you're insinuating I spread my legs to get out of there, I'm sorry to disappoint you. I'm not surprised that was the solution that sprang to mind for you, but there are other ways of solving problems."

This time, Azazel cackled in laughter.

Volencia's expression darkened in rage. "Mind yourself..."

Nadi met the older vampire woman's angry gaze. "I've had an absolutely *shit* twenty-four hours. I've been nearly blown up, kidnapped, shoved in a trunk, dragged through an abandoned slaughterhouse, threatened, and shot. I'm starving, healing from a concussion, and I'm exhausted. I killed three men yesterday. I'm sorry if I'm not handling your attitude very well."

Volencia leaned back in her chair and stared at her as if trying to murder her with her gaze alone. Fortunately, that wasn't a power that vampires had. At least, not that Nadi was aware of.

Nadi sipped her beer and felt instant relief as the cold liquid touched her tongue.

Raziel sat down next to her. "I believe what my mother so very tactlessly attempted to ask you was what happened after the Iltanis took you hostage."

Nodding, she took a breath, held it, and let it out in a rush. "They brought me down to a room where I met an... older fae man. Long green hair and pale green skin. Lots of beads."

"Luciento," Mael grunted, then swore under his breath.

"He told me it wasn't personal, that I was just bait in a trap." Nadi shook her head. "I managed to figure out, once everyone left except for the three human men left behind to guard me, that the building was rigged with explosives. The three men talked too much and thought I was harmless."

Volencia scoffed. Nadi opted to ignore it.

Lana was watching her with large, worried doe eyes, but was listening in silence.

"I asked one of the men if I could relieve myself." Picking up some kind of sliced vegetable from a platter, Nadi dipped it into a sauce they had placed near it. She didn't really care what it was. It was food. "They were polite enough to oblige. I asked the man who took me to a private spot to turn around. When he did, I stole his gun and shot him."

"Clever." Lana smiled. "Nobody wants to listen to a woman whine about a full bladder."

"Hear hear," Azazel muttered into the neck of his beer bottle.

"The other two men heard the gunshot and I tried to run, but they caught me." This was when her lying skills had to come in handy. Sometimes, there were upsides to living one's entire life as a fabrication. "They still wanted me alive, even though their friend was dead. That's the only reason I'm still here. Otherwise, they would've shot me dead in a split second."

Volencia was staring at her, studying her for any crack in her facade, any possible flaw in her story. Any piece that didn't line up.

But there wasn't one.

"I shot the other two." Nadi sighed, and shrugged before sticking another piece of food in her mouth. She chewed and swallowed before finishing her thought. "It was me or them. In the fight, I fell over and knocked my head on the tile, which is how I got the concussion." The story was so close to the truth it might as well have been real. The only difference was that she had left John alive.

Raziel reached out and tucked a strand of her hair behind her ear. She almost jolted at the sudden touch, she was so unaccustomed to it.

"I suppose resourcefulness is a necessary trait when one grows up in the outpost cities." He combed his fingers through the strands of her hair before settling his hand on her shoulder. "It might come in handy in this family, depending on my final choice."

"Hopefully, people don't lob grenades at you too often." She smiled at him half-heartedly.

"Only now and then." His expression split into a grin.

That got a small laugh out of her. She shook her head as she went back to eating.

Mael took over the conversation at that point, thankfully. "The problem remains, that this likely means war. If we can't convince them to leave the metropolis, the fae scum need to be exterminated once and for all. They clearly cannot be trusted."

Raziel's expression darkened. "I will not pass up this opportunity to tell you that I warned you, brother."

"I know. I know." Mael sighed. "But I thought even the fae had more honor than this. Clearly, I was wrong."

It took everything in Nadi—every ounce of self-control—not to visibly react. She focused on the food on her plate and the cold beer in her hand. She had spent her life in the upper world of the metropolis listening to humans and vampires insult her people and spit on the fae. But to hear her worst enemies talk like that made her fantasize about the room covered in their dead corpses, blood splattered all over the walls.

Keeping her head down, she focused on eating her food. Her hunger had been turning to nausea, and now that she was placating the beast, it seemed to be settling down.

"Attacking them will only send them scurrying underground." Lana shifted in her chair to lean against Azazel's side. "Do you think they've already gone into hiding?"

"No." Mael cracked his neck. "They won't give up the caves. Not even when they know we're coming for them. They've worked too hard for what they've got there. But with the mayoral election coming up, I *really* don't have time to be covering up a mass slaughter in the warehouses."

Raziel tapped his fingernails on the edge of his wine glass in slow succession. "I'll do it. I'll offer them an opportunity to leave peacefully with only a few lives lost. If they say no..."

"Then do what you do best, brother." Mael smirked.

Raziel huffed a half-hearted laugh. "As always." He paused. "I'm going alone, and I'll need a few cases of Deniel's weapons."

She watched him curiously, seeing the wheels spinning in his head. Whatever he was scheming, she had no idea. The cave mouths that the Iltanis controlled were attached to the network of tunnels that ran deep into the underground, both of the metropolis and the Wild. It made it a veritable maze, and fae like Luciento knew it like the backs of their hands. It made the odds of cornering them slim at best.

"You're talking about trying to catch a roach with a tooth-pick from across the room." Lana huffed, giving voice to something that Nadi had wondered about, albeit in a much more aggressive and insulting way.

"Exactly. All I will need is precision, which is why I'm going alone." Raziel shook his head. "Luciento and his entire gang of fae-loving humans will be exterminated by my hand alone."

"Absolutely not." Volencia sat forward, slapping her hand on the arm of the chair. "Are you a *fool*?"

Raziel rolled his eyes. "Charging in with twenty men will be precisely what they expect and are prepared for. There will be a gun battle, likely more explosives, and a body count. If you want to avoid newspaper attention, this must be done quietly. Carefully. And surgically. By the time I'm in, I'll have them under my control. I'll attempt to make a deal with them in good faith. If they refuse to leave? They will all die."

Nadi hated to admit it... but it was a good plan.

Mael seemed to agree, judging by his heavy, weary sigh. He wiped a hand down over his face before throwing both his hands up into the air in surrender. "Fine. The Iltanis came for you. We'll do this your way."

Fuck. Shit, shit, *shit*. Her worst enemy was going to charge in to kill her uncle and her old clan. Either Raziel was going to die or Luciento would. Raziel was *her* kill, not Luciento's. And she still felt loyalty toward her uncle, despite recent events.

Fuck. *Fuck!* Nadi realized she didn't have a choice. Taking a swig from her beer, she let out a sigh. "I'm going with you."

The laugh that left Raziel was born of pure humor as if it were the funniest thing she'd ever said. "While I'm impressed with your performance during the abduction, *absolutely not.*"

"What's to stop them from putting holes in your head the moment you roll up to the gate? No, you need something you're willing to let them hold hostage while you talk 'in good faith.'" She glared up at him, daring to meet him at his level in front of his family. "And I've proven I can handle myself, haven't I?"

"Take her with you," Mael interjected. "She's earned the right to a little vengeance."

Raziel bared his fangs, snarling at his older brother, and swore under his breath. "If she dies—"

Nadi cut him off. "Then you don't have to worry about an inconvenient honeymoon. You'd no longer have to decide whether to kill me or turn me. Your problems are solved. You don't care if I live or die. So, why *not* bring me if I want to go?"

The look Raziel gave her made her want to wither into the floor. By the lords below, she had *pissed him off.* But a moment later, his expression smoothed, and he reached a hand up to gently cup her chin, leaning in to whisper in her ear. "You want to see what happens when you join this family? You want to play at my heels, and see what kind of a monster I really am? So be it..."

He straightened up, leaving her sitting there, stunned and fighting the urge to shiver. "Very well. She comes with me. And I leave tonight before the cowards can run aground. That concludes our business. So, kindly get the *fuck* out of my home."

And just like that, everyone was dismissed. Nadi watched as everyone filed out of the room, muttering to each other.

Raziel's mood had gone from bleak to as dark as the void. She stood, getting ready to go back to bed.

He crossed the room to her before she could slip away, however, grasping her wrist. "You are playing a dangerous game."

"It seems to me that's the only kind you play in this family." She wouldn't shy away from him. And she would *not* cower. "I can handle it."

He yanked her to him without warning, sending her staggering into his chest. Wrapping an arm around her lower back, he pinned her there. Before she could react, he captured her lips in a slow but searing kiss that left her breathless.

Her stomach instantly twisted into knots.

When he parted from her, he looked entirely too pleased with himself. "We shall see. Now. Go back to bed. I have important business to attend."

With that, like the rest of his family, he walked out of the room without another word, leaving her standing there confused and unsure of what to do. Every time she felt like she knew which way was up with that man, he went and flipped the compass.

Damn him to the fucking *void*.

She was really looking forward to stabbing him.

SEVENTEEN

Sharp nails traced through her hair, waking her from her sleep.

Nadi's hand tightened around the handle of the knife under her pillow. But as she slashed at whoever was over her, fingers cinched around her wrist, stopping her before she could strike.

"Ah-ah." A voice, deep and dark, rumbled over her, followed by a chuckle. "I'm not falling for that a second time."

Raziel.

Nadi's heart was pounding in her chest as she blinked herself awake. The vampire—her *husband*—was sitting on the edge of the bed, smirking down at her. She had been about to stick a steak knife into his throat, but he had been smart enough to predict the attack.

With his other hand, he pulled the blade from her grasp and tossed it idly to the nightstand. It was clear he didn't give much of a shit about her attempt on his life. He was already standing, having let go of her wrist. "Get up. It's time."

She rubbed a hand over her eyes, sitting up, trying to wake up enough to process what was happening. And now that her eyes were adjusting to the darkness of the room, she noticed something was odd about him. Namely, the way he was dressed.

Furrowing her brow, she tilted her head to the side slightly as she studied him. Usually, he was dressed to the nines—all expensively tailored clothing, every stitch in the perfect place, his hair impeccably combed and clean. But now, his shoes were scuffed and dirty and his pants were a dark denim with gashes in the edges. He wore a dark gray wool vest over a linen shirt and a long black wool coat, none of which looked as though they had been cleaned in a very long time. A flat woolen cap was pulled low over his head, and his hair was oily, tied back at the base of his neck with a cord.

He looked like he had come from one of the steel plants at the edge of the metropolis, complete with the dark stains along his cheek and his neck. If it weren't for the fact that she'd recognize his face *anywhere*, she would have passed him on the street and thought him any other human worker—just another cog in the machine. If a particularly handsome one.

He jerked his head toward the dresser. Following his gesture, she noticed a stack of clothes there, waiting for her. Not the usual overtly sexual fare that he had for her. They looked much more functional—downright *matronly*. Without a word, she climbed out of bed and went to dress.

It was time to go to war. She still hadn't decided what to do once she got there. Would she turn on Raziel when she had the chance, and kill him? Or help him kill Luciento in the name of her larger revenge on the Nostrom clan? Bet small, or bet big? She... honestly didn't know.

The idea of slaughtering her *own uncle* in the name of her revenge was—it felt horrible. It felt *wrong*. Could she go through with it? She honestly didn't know. Could she kill her family, even estranged from them as she was, in the name of tearing down the Nostroms? At what point was it worth it?

She was so lost in her thoughts that she forgot that she slept naked. Not that it wasn't anything Raziel hadn't seen before. But his gaze was burning into her as she walked across the room.

"You heal quickly."

That was exactly what she was afraid of. He was too observant to let things like that slide. It meant she would *definitely* have to keep reopening the bullet wound.

It was a statement, not a question. And it was more of a growl than anything else. His words twisted deep inside her, feeling almost like a threat—like it was something he was interested in testing out for himself. She'd only been back from the kidnapping for less than thirty-six hours, and some of the scratches and bruises were already fading.

She shrugged, keeping her back to him, focusing on pulling on the old stockings he had brought her as part of their obvious ruse. "Always have. Grew up on a farm, lots of sunlight and fresh air. And I'm used to getting knocked around a lot, working with cows. They're big, and—"

Raziel was suddenly behind her. She gasped as he stepped close, forcing her to step into the dresser. Her hips pressed against the wood surface, trapping her between him and the furniture. She didn't know which was the harder object. She had to bite her lip to keep from either whimpering or reeling around and tearing out his eyes with her fingernails.

His nose pressed into her hair as his hands settled on her bare hips. One of his hands was directly over the bandaged wound. It itched like mad, the skin healing around the stitches faster than it should for a human.

He pressed his hips forward against her at the same time he dug his thumb into the bandage. The sting of the pain combined with the raw feeling of him behind her was too much.

The noise it pulled out of her was instinctual. It came from somewhere deep inside her. Somewhere she had no control over, somewhere animalistic and wild. Somewhere that howled in hunger. Some part of her that she didn't even know *existed* until right there and then.

It wasn't a sound of pain.

And it betrayed her.

Raziel growled.

A sound that was just as inhuman as the part of her that had inspired the moan he had pulled from her. The pressure from his hips relented only to redouble.

She dug her fingernails into the surface of the dresser so hard she swore she must have scratched the surface. It felt like the air had been pulled from her lungs.

His lips pressed to her throat, and she felt the tips of his fangs. By the lords of the deep, this was it. Maybe in a few moments, she'd be dead.

It'd solve her internal debate, that was for certain.

But the primal part of her mind had taken over, unable to listen to reason. It could only beg. Plead. Whimper.

Yes, gods—yes!

His growl turned into that unnatural purr, sounding like the rumble of a deep car engine. She tilted her head away from him, inviting him in.

When his fist slammed against the dresser, it was like a light switch had suddenly been thrown, a floodlight cast over the moment. He was gone just as quickly as he had been there, standing across the room, his hands over his face.

"Get. Dressed." Each word was bit through clenched teeth. "We have work to do."

She was trembling. It was like being woken from a drugged sleep. She was still half unconscious, still in that stupor—ready to be ravaged—and now she had been plunged into an ice bath. She shook her head, trying to wake herself. "I—"

"I'll be in the car." Raziel slammed the door on his way out.

Stunned, she finished getting dressed. Her outfit matched his—two paupers. She went to the bathroom and mussed up her hair. Taking the cork from the bottle of wine she had drunk half of the night before, she stuffed it in her pocket. Putting on the ratty shoes and her own wool cap that Raziel had included for her "costume," she sighed.

To say she was conflicted would be to put it lightly.

Heading downstairs, the guards barely gave her a second glance as she went to the driveway. Sitting there, idling, was a canvas-sided truck that had seen better days. The back was stacked with wood crates. They looked like munitions, if she had to take a guess. He'd mentioned crates of weapons from Deniel.

Raziel was sitting behind the driver's seat, his hands resting on the thin metal steering wheel. He was glowering through the dingy windshield.

She climbed into the passenger seat, holding out her hand. "I need to borrow your lighter."

That earned her the arch of an eyebrow.

And she shot him a flat look in exchange. "Oh, just hand it over."

He placed it into her palm a moment later.

Flicking it open, she lit the wick and took the cork from the wine bottle she had put into her pocket. Lighting the cork on fire, she clicked the lighter back shut. She let the cork char for a little while before blowing it out.

Using the rearview mirror, she smeared some of the black char on her face as soot, then blended it in with her fingers. "Makes for the best fake dirt. Learned it from some traveling entertainers." She lit the cork again. "Show me your hands. You did your face but not your hands, I bet."

Raziel looked down. Sure enough, the backs of his hands were spotless. Letting out a thoughtful hum, he let her smear the cork soot onto his knuckles, fingernails, and up his forearms before she did the same to herself.

She handed his lighter back to him and tucked the cork back into his pocket. "See? I'm not *just* a tempting piece of ass."

He put the truck into gear. They drove for several minutes

through the city in silence. "There's a knife and a pistol in the glove compartment for you."

Opening the metal hatch, she tucked both into her belt. The knife she figured she'd end up using more than the pistol. "Do we have a plan?"

"Luciento is at the caves overseeing an exchange of goods coming in from the Wild for trade. The guns we have in the back are a regular shipment—we're simply taking the place of Deniel's usual goons making their typical run, plus double for a peace offering." Raziel turned down a side street, taking a ramp down to a lower level of the metropolis.

The buildings got dingier and blacker with smog and dirt the lower they went. And the more tightly packed the buildings became, the windows into the abodes shrank in turn. It made the contrast with where they had just been all the more apparent.

"Wait. Deniel deals with the Iltanis?" She turned to look at Raziel. "He deals with the *fae gang*?" She knew this. But Monica wouldn't.

"Herein lies the story of how you and I arrived at this moment." Raziel sneered, disgust clear on his sharp features. "We have spent generations ensuring that Luciento was the only remaining fae in that clan of feral humans to make them as toothless as possible. But rabid dogs are still rabid and Mael mistook their complacency for loyalty. The Iltanis got greedy and decided to broker deals they had no right to, so we responded by murdering their partner to ensure they learned their lesson. In turn, they bit the hand that fed them for the last time."

Luciento was the only fae left in the Iltani clan. Nadi had suspected that, but the knowledge of it hurt. "So... we're showing up with crates... because?"

"Because my cousin Deniel thinks we don't know what he's up to. That we don't know all his little side deals with Luciento." Raziel scoffed. "We've let it continue because it's useful for us to have an extra few sets of eyes and ears with the aspiring beast-fuckers. And in the past Deniel has always made a peace offering to Luciento after there have been spats between our families—his way of saying *It's not me, it's them.* So, a few extra crates of guns will get us past the idiots at the door. Then, it will be too late for them." He shook his head. "To attack me at my wedding..."

"*Our* wedding." She shot him a look.

"They weren't targeting you for your sake," he argued back. "They were trying to murder *my* family at *my* wedding."

"Whatever." Rolling her eyes, Nadi went back to watching the city go by. She was familiar with this part of town—more than his area, to be fair. She only ever went to the expensive part of the metropolis to kill. This was where she lived. But not where she belonged. Where she belonged was down below, in the Wild.

Where Luciento was from.

With the rest of the fae.

She shut her eyes. "Why'd you *actually* agree to bring me?"

"You were right. I need a reason for Luciento to not shoot me on sight. I need long enough to speak." Raziel paused. "And someone I can trust to act intelligently."

That was interesting. She watched him for a moment. Not someone he trusted per se—but someone he trusted to act *intelligently.* "Thanks?"

"You're welcome." He smirked. "Besides. You were right on another point. If you die, it does save me a boat ride. You should know that my mother has insisted that you die during the honeymoon. You are not to be turned."

Shit. Well, that wasn't entirely unexpected. Volencia hated her, and the feeling was mutual. "And it's *her* decision to make, *not* yours?" She grunted. "Because she's the matriarch."

"Precisely."

"Huh. So I really shouldn't have told her off earlier?"

"It wouldn't have mattered. Your death is meant to send a message to your father and the humans he has working for him in the outer posts. My mother also said she doesn't need me... distracted." Raziel sneered.

Distracted. She watched Raziel for a moment before going out on a limb. "I think what she meant to say was that you're easier to control when you're alone."

He didn't respond. And his expression didn't change. He just stared out the windshield of the truck as though she hadn't spoken at all. Well, she'd tried.

"Either way, I'm glad you listened to reason and brought me along tonight. I'd rather die being useful than as a part of some... twisted blood sacrifice in a few days." Nadi turned her attention back to the street. They were getting closer to Luciento's base of operations. "They might be confused as to why you brought a woman along. And they might recognize me." She pulled the cap she wore farther down over her face.

"Eh. I'll simply say that you're part of the peace offering in case the guns aren't good enough. You can handle that."

She slapped him on the arm before she realized what she was doing. But it earned her a laugh from him that was genuine, and a smile to match it. Shaking her head, she glared out the window. Mostly to hide her own half-smile. "I'm not sleeping with any of the Iltanis."

"No, but it would get you alone with one of them long enough for you to stab them."

She hated it when he made sense. "You're assuming they're going to take turns."

He snorted. "Fair point. I'm sure you can argue that you're not *that* kind of whore."

"Ah, yes. The classy, one-at-a-time kind of whore."

"Precisely." He was clearly extremely amused by the conversation.

She paused. "What happened back there? In the bedroom? Why did you—"

His expression fell as he cut her off. "Don't."

She sighed. "I know I'm going to die soon, but—"

When he cut her off, his fangs were extended. "I have been trying to keep myself from *ripping you to shreds*."

She stopped, stunned.

"The scent of your blood is driving me *insane*." His words were tinged with a deep growl like a second voice. His hands tightened on the wheel so hard the metal creaked. He had to take a deep breath and focus on relaxing his grip.

After he paused, he continued. "I tasted you after you were shot. I have had every drug on this planet, and it's nothing like what your blood has done to me. I do not know what is—why you—but when I'm near you—the urge to—it's overpowering."

"Oh..." was all she could manage. A shiver like ice water ran down her spine.

Is it because I'm fae...?

"I'm supposed to kill you in a ritual, but I don't know if I can honestly wait that long. There is... a good chance you do not survive tonight, regardless of whether or not we're successful." He grimaced. "And whether or not that is my intent."

Shit.

He brought her here tonight because after Luciento Iltani and all his goons were dead, there was a real good chance she'd be another corpse right there alongside them. He was going to feed from her and likely kill her in the process.

Killing her by drinking her dry would shame his family... unless he could blame her death on someone else. What was one more corpse in a fight with the fae gang? Easier to cover up than in his bedroom.

Unless she managed to kill him first. Or they managed to kill each other. She tried not to laugh at the mental image of it. Whoever found their pile of corpses was going to be terribly confused. The corpse of a fish-tailed fae on land, dead beneath the body of the Serpent himself, and a sea of dead Iltani humans. What a headline that'd make for the newspapers.

Taking a deep breath, she held it, and let it out in a rush. "Well. Let's hope I don't break as easily as all your other toys."

Raziel's laugh was quiet. "You may very well come to think death is the better option. So many others have."

Her jaw twitched.

One way or another, she was about to find out. No matter what—between her uncle and her new "husband"?

Tonight was going to be a *mess*.

EIGHTEEN

Nadi did her best to keep her heart from pounding out of her chest. Vampires could hear heartbeats—and while she could excuse her fear as nerves from sneaking into enemy territory to commit murder, she didn't want to raise Raziel's suspicions any more than she probably already had.

She was deep enough in over her head without him starting to think something was up.

Doesn't matter. He just told you he's probably going to kill you tonight, anyway.

"Two things you should be aware of before this begins." Raziel broke into her thoughts, his voice barely audible over the rumble of the old, poorly maintained engine of the truck. "One leads directly into the other. Out of fairness to what you have already suffered, I want you to be as prepared as you can."

"All right?" She eyed him curiously. He'd already told her he planned to rip her to pieces out of some... blood-addiction-fueled starvation. How much worse could he think it was going to get for her?

"First. You have yet to truly experience the full power of

my... gift." The edge of his lips twisted up in a thin smile. "The one that makes me particularly useful in this kind of a scenario."

"Hypnotism. You can control people around you."

"Precisely. I have only used it on you once, and even then, it was barely a nudge. Part of why they call me the Serpent, I suppose."

"About my hair." She gestured at the messy bun at the back of her neck. "It doesn't seem to stick."

"That is exactly the point I am leading to. I can command others to do whatever I wish them to do with only the power of my voice. But once I leave their presence, separated by walls or space, it fades. It is..." He paused, clearly searching for words. "Like exposure to the sun. A little is easy to mend from. The longer you are exposed, the longer the damage lasts. If I issue you a single command, it may last for a minute—an hour—a day, at most. Depending on how weak or strong-minded the individual is." He gestured aimlessly. "It's an inexact science."

This was fascinating. She'd always been curious how his hypnotism worked. She hadn't ever really been able to pin it down, and obviously hadn't ever been able to ask the source about it. She twisted on the bench of the truck to watch him. "So, if you order someone to do something and then leave? For example—let us through this guarded door and don't tell anyone we're here..." She let out a rush of air. "Shit. Everyone has to die. That's the second thing, isn't it?"

"I will offer Luciento a chance to leave. He won't take it. And then, yes. You're correct." His ruby-red eyes glinted with amusement and perhaps more than a little bit of pride. But his expression quickly fell flat to one that was surprisingly empty. Almost, even, perhaps just a little bit *morose*. "As you aren't likely to survive this evening for one reason or another, little murderer, I want you to know I sincerely and honestly apologize for underestimating your intelligence."

That felt real. Her shoulders drooped a little. "Apology accepted, Raziel."

A faint smile returned. "When we arrive, we'll see how far we can get via deception, first. I will insist on speaking to Luciento personally." He tapped his fingers on the steering wheel. "While I have no qualms simply murdering them all, Luciento is a coward and a rat. He'll slink into the sewers if we alert him too quickly, like all fae scum."

She kept a straight face and simply listened.

"If they question why you're here, you're the second half of the peace offering." He smirked. "You've proven to be proficient with a gun. And if you insist on sleeping with a knife under your pillow, I hope you're capable of using one."

"I'll make do."

"Once we reach Luciento, I will dispatch his men. Luciento will be immune to my hypnotism. But, one on one, fae are no match for vampires. If you are not otherwise... indisposed, you should stay some fifty feet behind me."

"Why?"

"When I blanket an area, my commands are impossible to ignore by any within range. I would hate for you to mistake my command to eat the end of your gun as one I wished *you* to obey." He chuckled. "I have other plans for you this evening that don't involve watching you splatter your brains out all over the ceiling. No, stay as far back as you can until I call for you."

"Not a problem." She blanched. He was right about one thing—she'd never actually seen him use his power like that. She'd heard about it plenty of times. Whole rooms of people, slaughtered by their own hands. Or by the hands of their friends and companions. Suicide by some of the most grisly and seemingly *impossible* means. All because he had simply *told them to do it.*

The Serpent had earned his title.

Hearing about it second-hand, or seeing a few grainy photographs in a folder, was very different than witnessing it in person.

Her stomach twisted. Luckily, she was immune to his gift, same as all fae. But therein was the other half of her torment.

Luciento and the Iltanis. Her uncle and her old clan. These weren't any old gang of criminals. These weren't just some pack of low-ranking vampires or grubby human mobsters she was going to help murder. These weren't her normal targets.

These were her *people*. They had been her friends, her blood. Her family.

She was sitting in a truck next to her worst enemy—the man she'd sworn vengeance against—and planning on *murdering her own people*.

Was it worth it? Why was *her* revenge worth more than the lives of other people? No. No, that wasn't it. There was more to it than that.

She wasn't just avenging her family; she was unwinding the entire Nostrom clan.

Raziel would have to die first—his mother's insistence that "Monica" had to die during the sacrifice had solidified that. If they both survived the raid, Nadi would go to the ancestral home with him, and only one of them would walk away.

Then, she'd slink back into the shadows and bide her time to pick off the rest of the Nostroms. Because her vendetta had to be bigger than just Raziel alone.

It *had* to be.

She wasn't just picking the weed off at the ground, she was poisoning the roots. She was going to rip apart the Nostroms from the inside. Because if this "mission" was just about Raziel, she should have killed him in the truck half an hour ago. Right?

Right?

She had a knife. She had a gun. Vampires were hard to kill, but they weren't unstoppable. His guard was down. She could

have "checked the bullets" in her gun and put four in his head
before he even knew what was happening. Squeezing her eyes
tight, she leaned back in the truck and took a deep breath before
letting it out.

No, this had always been about ridding the world of *all* the
Nostroms.

But tonight had quickly become about survival. Her job was
to get through to the dawn in one piece. She could figure out the
path forward from there. She couldn't kill *any* of the Nostroms
if she herself was dead.

They drove along in silence for another twenty or so
minutes before Raziel pulled up to a large warehouse with a
sliding wooden door. The circular headlights shrank into small
bright disks on the faded, flaking paint. She could just make out
some text about *DANGER, NO ENTRY, CAVE SYSTEM,*
FAE.

Her jaw twitched. She was glad Raziel was distracted.

As Raziel brought the truck to a halt, he spoke up. "One last
thing. If you prove yourself tonight, there is a chance my mother
might change her mind. There is a chance we could delay the
honeymoon... perhaps even indefinitely."

She didn't have the time to reply. Or even register her shock
before she had to hide it underneath the brim of her cap. She
knew that was on purpose. *Damn you—*

A man in a deep green wool vest walked up to them,
rubbing the back of his hand across his nose. It looked like a tic
of his. Powder-user, was Nadi's guess. Not uncommon in his
line of work. The man tucked his hand into his belt, pulling his
brown overcoat aside, clearly showing them both that he had a
gun tucked into his belt.

"You lost, mate?" The human man sneered up at Raziel.

"Lookin' for Luciento," Raziel replied, his accent mimicking
that of a lower-metropolis steel worker flawless. She was
impressed. "Deniel sendin' gifts, I'm just the monkey drivin' the

truck." He jabbed his thumb toward the back of the vehicle and the stacks of crates.

"Who's the girl?" The man eyed her.

"Another gift if your boss decides the first ain't good enough."

She smiled from under her hat. Sweetly, but not *too* sweetly. She'd hung out with enough whores in her life to know how to smile like one on the job. It was about looking just a little bit tired and bored of it all.

Snorting, the man shook his head before walking toward the rolling door, and with a whistle, gestured his hand. From the inside, there was a thud, and the wood panels creaked and parted for them.

The smell of the Wild greeted them. Gods, Nadi *loved* that smell. She'd missed it. Crisp, and fresh, and *alive*. Utterly different from the reek of garbage and piss and dirt in the metropolis.

The cave mouths were still far from the true depths of home, but it was the closest she'd been in a very, very long time.

They were inside. A good first step. Before them, the road dipped into the ground at a stiff angle, making her wonder if the old truck could handle it. But the vampire next to her seemed unconcerned as he pressed the gas and headed farther in.

Darkness was cut into sharply by the glow of gas lamps. They meant she almost couldn't make out the faint purplish-blue glow of the threads of vines that laced along the cave walls like the thinnest of veins. The Wild. She hadn't seen it in so long. It was the only consistent source of light they had to see by, down below.

This part of the cave mouths attached to a series of tunnels that popped up in various parts underneath the metropolis— and Luciento and the Iltanis controlled almost all of them. It made him the king of smuggling items through the literal under-ground. If anybody needed anything or anyone moved quickly and discreetly—sometimes, the easiest way was down, if they had the cash.

But most of Luciento's money came from dealing in the mushrooms that were turned into the powder the humans favored so much. While it wasn't the only drug in Runne—not by any stretch of the imagination—it certainly was one of the most popular.

The road was a mix of dirt and rocks as they passed by crates until they reached a larger chamber, a few hundred feet around. Luciento's base of operations. It was a two-floor structure on both sides, with rooms cobbled together mostly of steel that had been stolen from anything and everything they could get their hands on. Corrugated metal, the sides of boats, doors that were taken from different places.

It felt like home. Colorful and bizarre, haphazard but craftily made. Nadi had to fight back a smile. And twisted through it all—not consuming it like above but mixing with it instead—were the purple-blue vines of the Wild.

Figures moved around in the darkness, the gas lamps doing little to chase away all the shadows. As they approached, their headlights caught who was clearly waiting for them, alerted by the guards up above.

There he was.

Sitting on a barrel by a wooden pylon was Luciento. The one she knew as *saestren*, as uncle and family. He was surrounded by his goons, all packing guns. Deniel's guns, provided to them by the Nostroms, she now knew.

Luckily, John—the Iltani she'd let live—wasn't among them. That would make things very complicated. But odds were still good that this was about to go south, anyway. "You *know* one of them was at the wedding," she told Raziel. "You *know* one of them is about to recognize at least one of us."

He parked the truck and turned it off. Three men were already walking toward the back to likely check the crates and make sure the vehicle wasn't rigged to explode. Raziel was already half out of the truck, and had ignored her statement.

Her heart lurched in her chest when Raziel stepped forward into the headlights and raised his hands in a show of harmlessness. "Luciento Iltani." He wasn't speaking in the accent anymore. "I'd like to talk somewhere private, if you would be so kind."

What is he doing? Screaming in her head, Nadi made sure the knife and gun were somewhere she could reach them quickly before opening the door, climbing out, and closing it behind her with a thud.

"Takes balls to walk in here, Serpent," Luciento replied. There were dozens of guns trained on them now. "With your new wife, no less." He laughed. "Do you think we're fools?"

"No. Which is precisely why I came."

Luciento snorted. "What do you want, Serpent?"

"To broker peace. Mael is willing to forgive your transgression. As am I, for the right price. Which is why I'm here with no other fighters. I have even brought my *new wife* as collateral. Take her as an assurance that I won't do anything foolish while we speak."

If Luciento had any brains at all, he would have opened fire on Raziel immediately. He *wasn't* a fool, despite what he said. So, why wasn't he attacking? Greed?

"Fine. You and me, we talk. John, Ezra, take the wife to the storeroom. Hold her there. You hear trouble? You know what to do." And that was when Luciento looked at her.

With recognition in his iridescent, whitish eyes.

He knows who I am.

Nadi glanced at the two men who walked up to her. One of whom was more familiar than she'd hoped. And he was looking at her with a strange, dire expression in his eyes.

John. She'd let John live. Of *course* he'd told his boss what he had witnessed. She'd taken the form of Raziel's bodyguard

Ivan. He'd seen what she could do. And there was only *one* shapeshifter like her in all the Wild that she knew of.

Fuck.

That was why he hadn't opened fire. Luciento knew who she was. Everything was about to fall apart at the seams.

This was going to be a *terrible* night.

* * *

Raziel ignored his little murderer's protests as two of the Iltani men rather forcefully ushered her into a storeroom. She really did know some interesting and colorful swears.

It was rather unfortunate that she was likely not to survive the night. But, thanks to his mother's orders, she was living on borrowed time, regardless.

He pushed thoughts of her from his mind for the moment. She would be fine. For now. Until he found her later and they sorted through their *unfinished business*, at any rate. Luciento's men wouldn't hurt her. They tended to be *fairly* honorable toward women when there was a business deal involved. He would give them that much.

Pulling the disgusting cap from his head, he tossed it into a garbage bin nearby. He hated the ruse, namely because the clothing itched, but it was required to get past the door.

Luciento had ten men around him, all with guns trained on him. But he was the only fae present. Raziel wondered if the bastard knew how useless the ten men truly were. In fact—less than worthless. A *liability*.

It was fascinating to him that despite all the legends, despite the stories, no one seemed to believe what he was capable of— what "the Serpent" could do—until it was too late. And it seemed Luciento was the same.

And the greedy fae scum would never pass up the chance to make a deal.

"So. Can we discuss business now?" Raziel brushed the dust from his sleeves and followed the fae ringleader into the dingy building he used as a storehouse and took quick stock of his surroundings. No windows. Wooden tables, shelves along the walls—plank floors worn by time and water and salt. But the rafters were high.

Good. This would do well enough.

"I'm surprised." Luciento kept his distance, standing by an exit door. Just because he was fae didn't mean he was an idiot. They had wonderful survival instincts. "I figured the cycle of death-for-death would go on a little longer before we had to come to an agreement. That has been the way with our families for so long."

Raziel shrugged. "The mayor has an election coming up in a few months, and Mael can't be spending time worrying about what you're doing down here. He needs you quiet. So I've been told to forgive, forget, and find a deal."

Luciento laughed sadly. "Well. We are here." He threw up his hands. "And you wished to speak."

"Yes. The deal." It was one he knew Luciento would never accept. But he had to make sure that he gave the fae beast a way out. He undid the tie at the back of his neck and combed his fingers through his hair, tidying it. "I kill a few of your men here —two, maybe three—you can choose which. You and the rest escape with the guns and supplies I have brought into the Wild. You leave for an outer city and never set foot in the metropolis again."

"*Hrippaiid, i'ika nish ba—*" Luciento laughed. Raziel didn't speak the guttural, trash language of the fae, but he knew whatever the bastard had said, it had been obscene. "What kind of deal is *that*?"

"The other option is that I slaughter you all. And none—not a single Iltani present here tonight—leave this place alive. I will finish what we should have done decades ago—and wipe your

clan from the face of Runne." He smiled cordially, holding his
hands out at his sides. "I am being quite generous."

"*Fi'ti*," Luciento snarled. "Kill him!"

Raziel laughed as the gunfire began.

This was going to be a *wonderful* night.

NINETEEN

Nadi couldn't help but swear as she was shoved into a room by two men, the door clicking behind her. The walls were cedar, and the tables that lined the walls were covered in... wow. Luciento had done well for himself while she'd been away.

The room was filled with gold and silver—jewelry and gemstones and all sorts of precious goods mixed in with high-end weaponry and stacks of cash piled on top of boxes that contained who-knew-what. The light overhead glittered off the facets of gems and shining metals.

There was a hatch in the floor that must lead deeper into the underground. That was likely her only chance of escape. She hoped it opened.

Turning, she ran a hand over her face and sighed. This wasn't going to go well at all.

John was standing some ten feet away, a gun pointed at her, a mix of expressions on his face. "Why'd you spare me that night?"

"Because you were decent." She sighed, throwing up her hands in frustration. This is what happened when she did *good* things. They bit her in the ass. She should have just killed him and been done with it. "And because I didn't think I needed to. You lot are my people."

"Then why're you working with that bloodsucking *bastard*?" the other man, Ezra, bit out. He also had a gun trained on her. That was going to make it a lot harder to kill them. A lot harder. Probably impossible. Even as a shapeshifter, she was only deadly when she had the jump on someone. Two men with guns who had her at a disadvantage? She was as good as dead.

She walked over to a bench by one of the tables covered in jewelry and gold coins and sat down. "Because I'm trying to kill him. Because I'm wearing this fake body to sneak into his family so that I can murder every last one of them. Until *you* lot keep getting involved and fucking it up!"

That made them waver, glancing at each other. "So you *are* her... Luciento told us what happened to your father... your whole family."

"I've been out to get revenge on them ever since. I saw the chance to switch places with his arranged wife, and here I am." Gesturing down at herself, she changed her shape to that of her *almost* true self. Her humanoid self, at any rate. Her own face, her own hair, her own *humanoid* body. Not her tail, for obvious reasons. But still clearly a fae.

She let out a sigh, feeling like she had finally been able to put down a jug of water she'd been carrying for weeks. She was good at holding up glamors—it was her whole life, after all—but that didn't mean it wasn't exhausting. She wondered how much energy she'd have in a day if she didn't spend half of it holding up literal appearances.

Whatever.

The two humans stared at her, dumbfounded.

"Sorry." She shook her head. "I'm a little sick of being Monica right now." She cracked her back. Monica was chestier than she was—a little fuller in the hips and the backside. It was nice to be curvy now and then, but it meant that she didn't really know how to carry all that extra front weight.

John lowered his gun. "You want him dead."

"Very badly. I'm just biding my time. I'm trying to take the whole family out. But I've lost time due to all this nonsense." She gestured at them and the warehouse. She took Monica's shape again, and let out a heavy sigh. It felt like putting on wet clothes. "Now... please. I don't want to hurt either of you. But if I have to, I w—"

She didn't get the rest of her words out.

That's when the screams began.

Nadi had heard plenty of screams in her life. Screams of pain. Screams of agony. Screams of rage. Even screams of fear.

But... there was something different about what she heard in the sound of Luciento Iltani's men. She knew they were dying. And she knew they were afraid.

It was the sheer *helpless terror* in them that twisted something in her and cut her nerves raw. It was like biting down on steel, jarring and horrible.

John and the other man looked just as affected.

She went to the door, pulling out her own gun. "Go. Both of you. *Run.* You can't fight him—you can't save the others. *Get out of here!*"

They stared at her, wild-eyed and unsure.

She grabbed John by the arm. "I can't do anything to help you this time. Take Ezra here and run. *Please.*"

John nodded weakly. "Hey. She's right. Let's go." He threw the door open. Stepping out into the hallway, he immediately took a left turn and ran in the opposite direction from the screaming.

Ezra, however, wasn't so smart. "I'm no fucking *coward.*" He ran to the right.

And Nadi knew he wouldn't come back. Fine. One less person who knew her secret. That was, if Luciento hadn't already spilled the beans to Raziel. The vampire might already know the truth—might already know what she was. Her secret might already be out, and she might already be dead if she stayed.

Letting out a ragged breath, she pressed a shaking hand over her mouth and held her gun down at her side, thinking as fast as she could.

If she ran, she'd lose her only chance at revenge. This was likely her one and only shot at Raziel and the Nostroms.

But Luciento could have told Raziel everything—betrayed her to the vampire to spare himself? That's what she would have done in his place. His men were dying in the *worst* possible ways, of course he'd offer anything in exchange for mercy.

And even if he hadn't? Her odds of survival tonight were slim.

Fuck, fuck, fuck!

Tears streaked down her cheeks.

But she had to roll the dice.

She *had* to.

Her whole life had been about this.

Stepping out into the hallway, she faced right, in the direction of the screams.

Just in time to see Raziel step from a room to confront John's friend who was running toward the chaos. Raziel looked like something from a nightmare. He had taken off the coat and vest, leaving him in only the black pants and white linen shirt. His long hair flowed like black silk down around his face. He almost always had it tied back. But tendrils of it hung down along his sharp features in contrast against his pale skin.

The man lifted the gun.

The smile that Raziel paid him in response had Nadi's blood running cold.

And all he had to do was merely speak. One word, and the man's life was over. "Kneel."

The man dropped to his knees like he was made of lead, heedless of the pain it would cause him.

Raziel's expression turned gentle. Almost *kind*. There was no malice in his expression. No cruelty. He walked up to the man and, crouching, whispered something in the man's ear.

Like a sleepwalker, he stood and headed into the room that Raziel had just exited.

Someone grabbed her by the arm, yanking her around roughly. Her gun fell from her hand, clattering to the ground, as the stranger dragged her back into the cedar room, slamming the door behind her. She heard the door bolt shut. "*Saeiga*—you fool!"

It was Luciento. She hadn't seen where he'd come from. He was already pulling her toward the hatch in the floor. "Don't—don't call me that."

"I don't know how you got mixed up in this nonsense or what you think your game is, Nadi, but we need to get out of here *now*." Luciento grabbed the ring of the hatch and gave it a yank. It was stuck. He snarled, gave it another pull, and it creaked open.

"Does he know?" She was shaking.

"What?" He looked up at her, those iridescent eyes so much like her own real eyes. He shook his head, only sorrow on his features. "We don't have time for this."

"Does he know?" she repeated, harder. She pulled the knife from her belt and shoved him up against the wall, pressing the blade to his throat. "Did you tell him who—what—I am?"

"What is *wrong* with you?" Those eyes searched hers.

"You know what he did. You *know* what he's cost me. I—I have given up my whole life to see him and his family dead in exchange—" She kept her words low, hissed through her teeth. "I'm not about to give up here."

Something slammed into the door from the other side.

Raziel, she assumed. He was a vampire—he would find his way in soon.

"I have kept your secret, my *saeiga*." Luciento held his hands up in surrender. "I haven't told him what you are, or that you are my *niece*. We do not betray our kin to those *things*."

Her hand was trembling. Her uncle's message was clear. He wouldn't hurt her. Would she hurt him? Could she kill her own kind?

Killing him would earn Raziel's trust. And his respect. It would get me closer to him. It might get Volencia to change her mind about the sacrifice. It might even get Raziel to spare my life tonight... This could solve all those problems.

"I have dedicated my entire life to this." She gripped the knife tight in her hand, forcing it to stop shaking. "I vowed I would see him and his entire family rot for what they did to mine."

Luciento's shoulders lowered. She had seen that expression a thousand times. The face of a man who knew he was about to die.

May the void take her.

"Forgive me, *saestren*."

* * *

Suddenly, Raziel wished that he had his cousin Oliren's gift of turning into mist. It would have made slipping beneath the locked wooden and metal door a breeze.

But, then, it would have made the slaughter of all the Iltani soldiers far more difficult. He slammed his shoulder into the door again, snarling, his fangs extended. The smell of human blood flooded his nostrils. The work in the other room was some of his best and most creative, he had to say. Whoever took the place of the Iltanis would be hard-pressed to forget what happened to those who crossed the Nostroms.

The scent of the blood was driving him *mad.* But it also obscured the scent of any other fresh sources of blood. He could not smell anything over the scent of the dead and dying around him. If his little killer was hurt, he had no way of knowing.

He couldn't hear her screaming or crying. But he couldn't hear Luciento either. He had seen the fae shit drag her inside as he was finishing up one of the lingering guards.

"Open the door, you *coward!*" He slammed his shoulder into the door again. It shook on its hinges. He was far stronger than a normal human. Mael would have been able to bash it down in two hits. It would take him eight. Which might be six too many to save her.

Why did he care?

I came here to add her to the pile. But only after I had my fun with her. Not before. Certainly not after Luciento cut her to pieces!

The idea of the rat hurting her sent him into a rage. He hissed, a feral growl deep in his chest forming. He reared back, certain that he would now be able to tear the door free.

The lock clicked.

The door swung open.

His little murderer stood there.

A blood-covered knife in her right hand.

Her peasant's dress was soaked at the bottom with crimson where it had dragged through a quickly forming pool. He found the source quickly.

Luciento. The fae was slumped against the wall, head tilted to the side, blood still pouring from a puncture wound underneath his jaw. It soaked his shirt. A look of sadness and perhaps... even betrayal in his eyes.

He tried to save her.

Raziel could picture it. "*Come with me—I can save you from him.*"

The opened hatch in the floor confirmed the escape route.

She had the opportunity to flee with him. Even still, she could have run on her own. She knew he planned to kill her, intentionally or otherwise. He had said as much.

But here she stood.

Fae blood on her hands.

And he had never felt such need before in all his years.

* * *

Numb.

Nadi didn't know what to think. She didn't know what to *do*. She felt numb. Empty. Tears streaked down her cheeks. Luciento was dead. She had killed him. She had not only killed her own kind... but her own *uncle*.

In the name of the greater good. To complete her mission to kill the Nostroms.

But there was no guarantee she'd ever succeed, was there?

She might die in this moment.

Raziel was standing in front of her. A vampire. Her enemy.

She deserved it if she died. She deserved the void. Luciento's soul would rejoin the Wild. He would be reborn. She would be dust—she would be like the nothingness she felt clawing at her.

"Look at me."

The words were an order. She felt Raziel's power in the room like a blanket—like a fog. He was hypnotizing what he thought was a human Monica. That confirmed Luciento hadn't been lying. She snapped her eyes up to his, obeying him. She had to keep up the ruse at all costs. And she was in no mood to try to fight him.

I deserve what happens to me next.

"Drop the knife."

She let it slip from her fingers. It clattered to the ground beside her.

His red eyes were almost black, the pupils were so dilated. His fangs were long, extended from hunger and lust. His chest was rising and falling in rapid, deep breaths. He took a step toward her, and she took one back into the room of glittering gold, silver, and jewels.

Another step forward from him, and she took another one back.

When he spoke, his voice was deep, almost ragged. "Take off the cap. Lower your hair."

She did as she was told, keeping her eyes on his the whole time. Her hands trembled. There was... something in the simplicity of doing what he said. Something *easy* about it. She didn't have to make excuses for her actions if he was ordering her to do it.

It wasn't her fault then, was it?

Suddenly, his hand shot out. He snatched her by the throat, clenching her tight enough that she gasped in pain. He dragged her toward him, his other arm around behind her waist, cinching her tight to his body. She felt his desire there, his hard length pressing against her stomach, trapped in his trousers.

He kissed her, rough and hard, devouring her lips as his hand released her throat to tangle in her hair, yanking her head back harshly to angle it better for him. She gasped at the pain in her scalp, and his tongue was instantly tangling with hers, exploring her mouth. Claiming it as his.

She moaned against him. It was instinctual. She couldn't help it. He was making it so easy just to... let it happen. Let her body answer for her—let herself simply *exist* in his arms. The strength in his grasp. The certainty in it. The sheer primal *need*.

Without warning, he threw her toward one of the wooden tables. Coins clattered to the ground as she staggered backward into it, rocking it into the wall with a *wham*. She gripped the edge of it to keep from winding up on her back against the surface, though she knew that was where she would be before long.

Raziel stalked toward her, his face a mask of lust and hunger. "You will give me your honest answers."

She nodded. She didn't feel his hypnotism there—he was simply demanding it from her. And she found she had no will or desire to lie to him.

"Did he ask you to escape with him?"

"Yes." She kept her eyes locked on his red ones. She could lie if she needed to—but he didn't know that.

"You chose instead to kill him and stay. Why?"

"I want you to trust me." That was true. "I want you to spare my life, even if your mother says no..." That was *also* true. But she knew she needed to give him something more. A confession. Something that he could believe enough to spare her. "And I—I want you." Lords of the deep, that was also not a lie. "I need *this*. Even... if it kills me."

The growl that left him went straight to her core. Shuddering at the sound and what it did to her, she shut her eyes. She couldn't help it. The room smelled coppery and metallic, like blood. Blood she had spilled. *Fae* blood.

The dim light of the room was blotted out as Raziel stepped into her, the smell of his cologne masking the smell of the blood. His lips were on hers again, taking away her ability to think or breathe as he roamed his hands over her body, squeezing and groping as he quickly tore away her clothing, shredding off the dress and ripping anything that didn't come off fast enough.

Reaching down, he picked her up by the ass and lifted her up to place her on her back on the table. She was surrounded by the trappings of wealth, coins and riches of every kind. But he didn't seem to care at all as he yanked her forward to wrap her legs around his waist.

He leaned over her, capturing her lips again in a furious kiss, as his other hand rustled with his belt and his fly. She felt his length pressing against her. Shutting her eyes, she kissed him back, as hard as he gave to her, lacing her fingers into his silky hair—wanting to taste him. Wanting to feel him.

Wanting him to take it all away.

Wanting to make it easy.

He broke off the kiss, looking down at her, studying her for a moment, those red eyes flicking between hers.

Was he asking her for *permission*? That wasn't the Raziel she knew. And not the one she wanted in this moment. Right now, she wanted the one that would make it all simple, clear-cut, and black and white.

Now wasn't the time for thinking.

Now was the time to have all those things taken from her. Lifting her head, *she* kissed *him*. Pushing her tongue into his mouth, she forced the matter. She wanted him to take her. Wanted him to consume her. Wanted him to make her not have to think about what she'd just done.

She pricked her tongue on his fang. Hard enough to make sure it bled.

The noise that left him was heaven. Her moan joined his as he sucked on her tongue, trying to coax another drop of blood from her.

When it didn't come, he pulled his head back and straightened up, standing between her legs, then let out a snarl that was part man, part animal. "You *little*—" He let out a shuddering breath. "Do you know how many people *died* this week because of you?"

That shouldn't turn her on.

It really shouldn't.

Grasping himself, he pressed himself to her entrance. She had no idea what she was in for—and he hadn't prepared her at all. And it seemed he was aware of that. "Usually, I like to work my partners in a little. But I fear you have gone and worn my patience *thin*, my dear sweet killer." He shifted his grip to hold her hips in both hands.

"Will you just *shut up* already?" She had heard enough of his talking. She needed action. *Now*.

He pulled her to him as he drove himself forward.

Her mind went white.

He was merciless. Relentless. She couldn't think. Couldn't process anything except the feeling of him inside of her—moving harder and faster than any human was capable of.

She had never felt anything like it before in her life.

It was *amazing*.

It wasn't pain that had driven her mind white when he had rammed into her, filling her to the hilt and stretching her. It had been ecstasy. It had been a sudden and instant release, a push over that cliff into pure bliss.

Even now, she lay beneath him, gasping and mewling, and when she had the air to breathe, she found herself *whimpering his name*. Twisted up with words like *more*, and *harder*, she was begging him, pleading with him to keep her where he had put her—somewhere safe from what she had done. Somewhere in this bliss, this pleasure, this cloud of ecstasy away from death and murder.

And he seemed more than happy to oblige. "Look at you..." He slowed down, if only seemingly to taunt her. He straightened up, and placed his hand around her throat, cinching his grip to cut off her air just enough to keep her from responding. "Gods, you feel *incredible*. And that *taste*. You are going to be an addiction if I'm not careful." Pulling nearly all the way out, he rammed himself forward, jerking her hard on the table, sending coins rattling to the ground.

Her eyes rolled back. He was too much for her—just *barely* more than she was made to handle. And all she wanted was more.

"My little bloody bride, my killer, my little murderer—you

like it rough, hm?" He grinned, flashing his fangs. "Do you like it when it's violent?" He rammed into her again, and she moaned as her body spasmed around him, so close to another wave of release. His hand tightened around her throat again and it only made her dizzier. "Tell me the truth."

"Y—yes," she half breathed, half moaned. "I like it..." And it wasn't a lie.

"Good." A third impact, and he nearly roared, snarling through his clenched teeth.

She wailed—she was so close. She was going to faint if he kept his grip on her throat for much longer. "Raziel—"

"Do you want to feel my bite? Do you want me to drink you? Do you want me to taste you and truly make you mine?" He leaned over her, his grasp on her throat loosening. His voice softened. "You may die. I may not be able to stop myself."

She met those red eyes of his. And by the moons, if she died like this... she didn't know if she cared. She deserved for her soul to be eaten by the void, either way. Because there was no excuse for the one word that was a whisper as he turned her chin to the side to bare her throat to him.

"Yes..."

TWENTY

Bliss. Pure, unadulterated ecstasy. Her blood burned in his veins. And he'd never felt anything like it in all his centuries of life.

Raziel carried his wife's unconscious form from the caves in his arms. He left the truck behind, there was no need for it, and should anyone want to try their hand at taking a truck full of weapons, they'd soon find it more trouble than it was worth. Besides, he felt like stretching his legs after what he had just done.

Ivan and Hank had been told to bring a car to meet them. He was happy to have all the Iltani nonsense concluded, and it had ended surprisingly well.

He had dressed his little murderer in the black wool coat he had worn on the way there. As her clothes were in shreds, or covered in Luciento's blood, it seemed only appropriate to redress her in whatever he had available.

She was alive. He had managed to stop himself from drinking her to death.

If just barely.

But the way she simmered in his body, the way every vein

and artery seemed to burn with some new kind of life? He couldn't explain it. He had heard of some vampires finding mates that had this effect—something about the blood singing to theirs. But he had thought it was only a myth. But now that he had tasted her? It was the only thing that made sense. He would have to do some research. Or ask his grandmother Lilivra about it, if he could get an audience with the old hag.

Either way, it made their situation far more complicated. Because whatever he discovered, he would still have to kill her.

There was no use attempting to delay. His mother would simply roll her eyes and see it as a sign of weakness, and demand he take the girl to the ancestral home and get on with the sacrifice. With a sigh, he looked down at the woman in his arms. She was pale, her head resting against his chest, forehead tucked against his throat. His body temperature would keep her warm, as he now had her blood in his body.

She would heal. And she healed quickly, which was convenient, seeing as he had likely bruised her badly enough she would limp for days with how hard he had rutted her. He couldn't help it. Seeing her like that, after having murdered Luciento? There was no stopping him.

There seemed to be no stopping her either. Yes, he believed she had done it to earn some semblance of trust from him, or perhaps in hopes that he would spare her life. But to confess that she had done it also out of mutual lust? *That* he found truly remarkable.

Curious, mysterious, murderous thing.

But as of now there was one thing he knew for certain.

She was *his* curious, mysterious, murderous thing.

That was what had stopped him from draining her dry. The little creature in his arms *belonged* to him. As his own ecstasy consumed him, he had filled her, claimed her, and he had made her his bride in truth. While he licked clean the bite marks on her throat and purred to her soothingly, he decided he would have as much of her as he could before time ran out.

Or, perhaps, he could find a way to stop the clock.

Because this creature felt special to him. Maybe it was how much she was still hiding from him. Maybe it was how murderous she was, and how useful that might be to him.

Because he had plans.

Big plans.

And the fun was about to begin.

* * *

Nadi woke up in Raziel's large and comfortable bed.

Her first thought was, *Well, I lived.*

And couldn't decide if she was relieved or disappointed. She was sore *everywhere*, though she shouldn't exactly be surprised. Raziel had fucked her like a train engine, and *then* drank her dry. How else was she supposed to feel? Daylight was filtering in through the lace curtains pulled over the windows, casting a dim pale glow over the expensive bedroom.

Raziel was in bed next to her for the first time since they were "married."

She still didn't really consider them married, for a lot of reasons. First and foremost, she wasn't really Monica.

He was on his side, facing her. He had showered, and judging by her slightly damp hair and the smell of soap, he had cleaned her up also. How thoughtful.

She watched him as he slept. The smoothness of his features, with their sharp edges. There was no question how handsome he was.

But this was the face belonging to someone that had haunted her nightmares for over eighty years.

Someone she'd sworn to kill.

Someone she'd made passionate love to.

There was no point in denying how badly she'd needed what they'd done. The desire had been more than mutual. There'd been no hypnotism, no ruse, no questionable situation to blame—just pure lust. Pure hunger.

Frame by frame, like the images in a zoetrope, she played the scene through in her head, searching for some reason to condemn him. Something, *anything*, he had done that she could use to pin the blame solely on him. He could have commanded her to her knees. Could have used his belief in his control over her to make her do anything he wanted. Instead? He'd asked for her honesty.

He hadn't wanted to take what would be given to him for free. With a wavering sigh, she climbed out of bed. Cringing, she arched her back and cracked her spine. Damn. He didn't mess around, that was for sure. Heading to the bathroom, she decided she needed to find some painkillers.

Did vampires even keep painkillers around? She knew drugs worked on them—but she only knew of them taking them for recreational needs. They healed even faster than fae, so why would they keep painkillers? But it was worth taking a look—her legs were sore. And Monica would be in far worse shape *elsewhere* than she was.

The first barrier presented itself when she realized his mirror was way too large to be a medicine cabinet.

"First drawer closest to the door and in the back."

Glancing to the door, Raziel hadn't moved. But it was clear he wasn't as asleep as she thought he was. "Thanks."

"I don't keep any for myself. But my... guests often need them." He rolled onto his back, folding his hands over his chest. He slept shirtless. If he had trousers or boxers on, she didn't know.

Opening the drawer in question, she rooted around until she found some basic painkillers. Nothing too strong. She didn't need to be drugging herself silly. Taking two with some water from the sink, she ran a brush through her hair and examined herself for bruises. Nothing that wasn't already fading.

There, on her throat, however—were two pinhole scabs, surrounded by darker purple-blue blotches of teethmarks. The telltale mark of a vampire bite. Touching it tenderly with her fingers, she was surprised at how little it hurt, though it was fairly tender.

"It won't scar. They never do."

"I wasn't worried." Throwing on a black silk robe that reached her mid-thighs, she headed back toward the bed. "It'd be too late to do anything about it, anyway. And it's not like I'm going to be alive much longer."

"Fair point." He reached a hand out to her, beckoning her closer.

Intrigued, she walked up to him and slipped her hand into his. He pulled aside the covers, revealing that he was wearing black silk boxers. Damn. She was rather curious to see what had been the weapon of assault from the night prior. He drew her into the bed with him, guiding her to lie down on top of him with her propped up on her elbows before pulling the sheets back over them both.

It was shockingly intimate.

She didn't quite know what to make of that.

And it was clear her confusion was plastered all over her face by the smile that appeared on his. "Hm." His fingers traced over her cheek. "I act the monster, threaten to kill you, and stage a mass murder, and it's business as usual. I show a little affection, and you act as if I've grown a second head."

"Actually? Yes. One is unexpected. The other isn't."

He chuckled. "Another fair point."

He was warm beneath her—from *her* blood, she reminded herself—and his startlingly pale skin was smooth, feeling like velvet over stone. He was *built*. Broad, but not overly so. His body wasn't *bulky*. No, he was efficiently muscular. Much like his namesake, the Serpent. Powerful. Deadly. But streamlined.

Moons, it... felt *good*. It made her want to touch him. Explore him. To roam her hands all over his body, to feel what it was like when those muscles moved and flexed. To grab hold of the thing between his legs and really give it a proper road test on *her* terms. She wondered if he'd let her get away with that.

Raziel was known for liking one thing and one thing only behind closed doors, and it certainly wasn't fairness.

He wrapped an arm around her as his other hand still gently caressed her cheek. "My family is coming over for dinner in a few hours."

"Oh, great." She dropped her head onto his chest. "More of your mother's attitude."

"You murdered Luciento in cold blood. I believe that may earn you points with her. It might even get her to change her mind about the sacrifice, who knows." He stroked her back gently. "My siblings will be quite impressed."

In cold blood. Nadi didn't need the reminder. The look in the fae patriarch's eyes would haunt her until the day she died. She lay down on Raziel's chest, resting her cheek on his bare skin. He had a heartbeat—which vampires didn't usually have. It must be because he had recently fed.

"I can't avoid it by saying I feel like shit, can I? You did nearly kill me." Now she was whining. She didn't care.

"No, but it will excuse you early. So it will make it a brief affair. And it'll keep my fangs from your neck and my hands from wandering until you tell me you've mended." Raziel kissed the top of her head.

It was another... tender gesture.

He was holding her like she *mattered* to him. Or like he *wanted* her there. It made her want to break the moment. Picking her head back up, she pushed herself to her elbows and looked down at him. "These rumors about you and your 'guests.' Can I ask questions now?"

"Mm?" He thought about it for a moment. "I suppose you've earned it. Very well. Go ahead. I will answer your questions."

"Whips, chains, straps, all that—how much of that is true?"

"Enough to have earned the reputation, but likely the more *inventive* things you've heard are fabrications." He smirked. "No one has ever been flayed alive. I save the true horrors for my enemies."

She let out a breath. "And what if I wanted to..." She paused, trailing off.

A slow smile formed on his face. "You wanted to, what?"

"What if I wanted to be the one in control?"

He sat up, forcing her to do the same. She was straddling his thighs, sitting on them as he smiled down at her. Even like this, he was still taller than her. She expected him to laugh. She expected him to scoff at the idea—to call her an idiot, a fool, to maybe be moved to anger or fury at the notion of someone like her having the gall to even suggest such a thing.

But instead, she saw only the strangest kind of *excitement*. As though what she had just said was enticing to him.

Slowly, he slipped his hand to the back of her neck and pulled her in close, lowering his lips toward hers as if to kiss her. He stopped, a hair's breadth away. His words sounded like thunder on the horizon, a whisper of a storm. "I would *love* to see you try..."

A threat and an invitation.

Open arms and a bloody knife.

What a fucked-up pair we make.

Closing the distance between them, she kissed him.

He responded in kind for a moment before pulling his head away and placing his fingers against her lips to stop her from chasing after him. "Ah, you *hungry* little thing."

Sighing, she glowered at him.

Laughing at how put out she looked, he tossed her rather unceremoniously onto her side on the bed. "I am not going to get into another round with you. Or else I will be railing you into oblivion for the next two hours. You will be a bruised and battered mess for dinner, and I will not hear the end of it from my family."

"You could tell your family to get wrecked. Say you're spending time with your new wife." The words left her before she could really consider what she was saying. What was *wrong* with her? What had he done to her? She knew humans could get wrapped up in what it felt like to be bitten by a vampire—but she hadn't even been aware of the bite. Her head was already scattered from the intensity of the sex and everything else she'd been through. The moment he'd sunk his teeth into her neck, she had passed out. She hadn't really experienced it.

Had it done something to her? Was she his thrall now?

A fresh wave of fear hit her. No, no—that wasn't possible. She was just playing the part. And he was handsome. And she hadn't been laid in a long time. And she had never in her life ever been laid like *that*.

Maybe there was also some relief in her that he hadn't realized she was fae after feeding on her. Her glamor had held up after being bitten. There was a lot to attribute it to.

Raziel was already changing, laughing at her comment as he pulled on a pair of trousers. "As much as I appreciate the sentiment, and as much as you will come to regret it later, I'm afraid I will have to insist. If you still feel the same way later, I'll take you up on your offer after a bottle of wine. How's that sound?"

"I'm just trying to avoid your mother." She flopped back down onto the pillow. "But also... we'll see." She smirked at him in the mirror.

He smirked back. "Trust me. I would much rather be introducing you to the truth of the rumors about me than listen to my family prattle on." His expression faded. "While they will be impressed with your performance, I'm certain they will find *some* reason to needle. They always do."

He pulled an undershirt over his head. She watched the muscles in his back flex as he did. Moons, she wanted to lick every single line of them. *I clearly needed to scratch more itches in my life.* She laid her head back down on the pillow. The painkillers were starting to work, and the ache in her lower back was easing up. "How long until they get here?"

"A few hours. You have time to get some more sleep before they arrive. I'll send someone to wake you an hour before to give you time to dress."

All he got in response from her was a grunt. She was already on her side and half buried in the thick comforter. When she felt him sit on the edge of the bed next to her and stroke her hair, she didn't know what to say.

When he kissed her cheek, she didn't know what to think.

"Get some rest, my little murderer. You'll need it."

When those words made her smile, she didn't know how to feel.

TWENTY-ONE

Staring at herself in the mirror, Nadi was lost in thought. Studying a face that wasn't hers. A body that wasn't hers. And a soul that... she wondered if she was quickly going to fail to recognize before long.

What was happening to her? What was she *becoming*? Was a chance at destroying the Nostroms really worth killing Luciento? It was too late now. She had made her choice. Luciento was dead. There was no going back.

Her uncle had been sacrificed on the altar of her revenge. All in the name of winning Raziel's trust and convincing Volencia that she was worthy of joining the family. Or, at the very least, convincing her to agree to Nadi's preferred outcome —that the sacrificial honeymoon simply be postponed for a while.

All Nadi needed was enough time to kill them all.

Looking down at her palms—at *Monica's* palms—there was another thought that was eating away at her, a worry in the back of her mind, a stray thought, something far more insidious and dangerous than even her wanton lust for her worst enemy.

It was a single blot of black ink on a white piece of paper in her mind. A tiny little dot, but impossible to ignore. And equally impossible to remove.

Raziel found fae *disgusting*. Beyond disgusting. Reviled them with every fiber of his being. That he made painfully clear. He found Monica attractive. That was also painfully clear.

Those two things led straight to the thought that would not go away.

Raziel would find my true self disgusting.

It was a statement of fact in her mind. There was no way around it. If he saw her real self, her oil-slick-colored scales and fins, her pale green skin, and midnight-opal eyes, he would turn away from her in revulsion.

That wasn't the issue. She knew that.

It was the fact that... it *bothered* her. It twisted something in her that was akin to pain. No—not pain, worse than that. *Shame.*

She was ashamed of what she was through his eyes.

Her jaw twitched as she clenched her hands into fists hard enough that her nails bit into her palms and squeezed her eyes tight. How dare he. How *dare* he make her think about herself in such a way! No one had that right. No one in the world, in all of Runne, had the right to make her ashamed of who and what she was. Of how she was raised, where she grew up, or what she looked like.

Anger boiled in her. She embraced it like an old friend. Let it seethe into hatred. Added it to her armor like the scales of her tail. She was letting him too close. Lust was one thing, lust was useful. She could wield that against him, and there wasn't any harm in enjoying it while it lasted. But she wouldn't—couldn't—let him any closer than that.

She wouldn't survive it.

Letting out a wavering breath, she muttered a quiet prayer to Luciento and her family in her native tongue. An apology and a plea for forgiveness she knew she didn't deserve. She wished she had an altar where she could light a candle or place an offering out for Luciento's soul. A binding of bones, or a small animal sacrifice.

But she had nothing. Nothing but her own sorrow, anger, and rage. And a promise that blood would flow in exchange for theirs—hers or Raziel's, either way, their ghosts would be paid.

Getting dressed, she decided to wear something polished, but not fully formal. Something that showed deference to the family, but that still said she had been through the wringer in the past forty-eight hours and was eager to get back to bed.

Whether to sleep or do other things remained to be seen.

She swore at herself in her head. "Idiot." Yes, fine. Sex with Raziel was *amazing*. And now that she knew what it was like? She wanted more. The problem was, Monica would be far more battered-up. As a fae, Nadi felt... not great, but not the worst she'd ever felt, honestly.

A little tired from the blood loss, sure. But once she had some food in her, she figured she'd be fine. She just had to not let on that was the case. Zipping the red and black silk dress up the side, she smoothed it down over her legs and walked up to the mirror to examine her neck. The bite marks had even faded a little over the hour she had been asleep. Damn it. The puncture wounds she could scratch at and keep fresh, but the bruises? The bruises would be hard to fake.

Blaming it on good genetics could only get her so far.

But Raziel seemed completely bought into the illusion that she was Monica. Chewing her lower lip, she sighed. There wasn't much she could do, except maybe hide it. Monica wasn't from the metropolis. She could play it off as being unsure if it was a faux pas to flash bite wounds at the table or not. Finding a thin silk scarf in a drawer, she draped it around her neck, slipped on a pair of heels, and headed down to dinner.

* * *

Patience was the word that Raziel kept repeating to himself in his head like a mantra as he poured his sister a drink. Lana was attempting to goad him into a fit of rage. She had begun by insisting on bringing her favorite pet Azazel along to dinner, which was purely to offend their mother and put her in a bad mood.

Which, in turn, was purely to put *him* in a bad mood. But delivering the jab in this way, one step removed, made sure any attempts to call her out would seem melodramatic and petty.

Siblings. Sisters were always the most devious.

Patience.

He had a prize waiting for him this evening if he managed to make it through the night without smashing a bottle of wine over the table and digging the shards into his own skull to end the banal double-speak and thinly veiled insults.

His little murderer.

What a wonderful bundle of surprises she had turned out to be.

Bloodthirsty. Not only capable of killing but able to face it with an unflappable resolve that rivaled perhaps even his own. To not only murder Luciento—to drive a knife into his skull—but then to allow him to savagely fuck her with the corpse as witness?

How wonderfully and singularly *depraved.*

Could it be, he might have found someone whose capacity for violence—if trained and tailored and polished—might match his own? But adrenaline had aided her in the kill. Luciento had likely threatened to take her by force if she didn't go willingly. He wondered how she would perform if there was no threat to her life.

"Are you going to finish making that drink anytime this century, brother?" Lana sighed dramatically.

Patience.

Walking over to where Lana sat at his dining room table, he placed the cocktail down in front of her a little harder than was polite. Mael shot him a glare as if to reprimand him for his bad attitude. Yes, because *he* was being the problem child here. Not Lana.

"Have you given any thought to the trip north, brother? And what your choice will be?" Mael was sitting at the head of the table, frowning down into his wine glass. Raziel suspected his brother had already become fond of Monica, despite only having met her a few times.

"My choice is to make no choice at all." Raziel shrugged. "I thought I might postpone the trip for a while, if not indefinitely."

"Don't blaspheme, boy." Volencia grimaced. His mother was seated at the opposite head of the table, leaning against the polished wood back of her chair, a long cigarette holder perched between painted fingernails. The smoke curled up and away from the end. "You leave on the trip as planned. And she dies."

As if on cue, his new wife walked into the room, and as she always did, her eyes darted around to take stock of her surroundings. Counting the people present, including the staff and guards, and checking for exits and windows as if always pathing an escape. As if always prepared for an attack.

It was another one of the mysteries he had yet to solve about her.

There were... many.

Volencia watched Monica enter with such scrutiny that Raziel was impressed the younger woman did not burst into flames. "Speak of the beast and there she is."

Ignoring their mother, Mael smiled, beaming in a sincere friendliness that made Raziel want to scream. Mael quickly stood from his chair to greet her. "Monica—are you well? Raziel told us about what happened."

Monica stood her ground, though it seemed like she reflexively wanted to take a step back from the mountain of a vampire who walked up to her, even if he was smiling like a teddy bear. When Mael reached out to take her hand, she gave hers in return.

Mael bowed his head to kiss the backs of her knuckles.

Raziel once more wanted to scream. *Patience. She's mine. Not his. Mine.*

"I'm all right," she replied. "Though I wish he'd warned me about exactly what he was going to do once we got there."

Ah, yes. Right. That. Raziel cleared his throat. "I was hoping you had overlooked that." He handed her a glass of red wine, namely to get her hand out of Mael's, and gave her a rather false smile of his own. "It was easier if I didn't have to explain it all to you."

She took the wine and sipped it. It was clear she wanted to ask why he hadn't trusted her with the plan—the question was burning in her green eyes. But she was also smart enough not to ask in front of his family in case it was a sensitive topic.

Moons above, he wanted to bend her over the table right there.

Gesturing dismissively, he walked to the table to pull out a seat for her. "His people would recognize me without question, and I wanted to ensure that Luciento died in the attack. He was wily and escaped us for decades. The only way to keep him there was to promise a deal."

He waited for her to sit before pushing the chair back in for her. Lana was seated next to her. Which was upsetting to him, but unavoidable at this point.

"It was still a stupid, dangerous plan." Mael headed back to his chair. It creaked under the mammoth weight of his frame. "You put her in a lot of danger."

Raziel took a long sip of his bloodwine before answering. "She is doomed to die, anyway. I thought perhaps giving her a chance to be useful might sway dear Mother's mind. Clearly, I was wrong."

That turned all eyes to his new wife.

Who simply raised her glass to them in a toast before downing half of it.

He was beginning to be quite proud of his little murderer. "Luciento tried to take her with him as he escaped. Maybe he thought it would be a perfect insult, to steal my wife. Maybe he simply wanted her for himself."

"She *is* gorgeous." Azazel winked at her from across the table. "And *feisty*."

Raziel ignored him, instead reaching over to top off his wife's glass of wine. His staff served the main course of dinner while they continued to talk. He had opted to skip a longer affair for the sake of his own sanity. "But the bastard is dead. As is most if not all of his human family. The remaining Iltanis will be like lost rats, running to ground and taking shelter wherever they can."

"Yes. We all heard what you did to the Iltanis, Raziel. Truly, did you need to end them in such a spectacular fashion?" Volencia took a slow drag from her cigarette, ignoring the steak placed in front of her. She didn't eat in public, but preferred food be served to her anyway to keep up appearances. "Did you really need to tell them to hang themselves with their own intestines? That was barbaric, even for you."

His wife's fork hovered over her food for just the briefest moment before she resumed eating.

Raziel didn't miss the hesitation—nor how short it lasted. "Another fae clan is likely to take their place at the edge of civilization. I wanted to ensure that whoever it was would remember what comes to those who attack the Nostroms."

Lana shook her head. "Each time you kill, brother, it worries me more and more. Who are you competing against in these sick games of yours?"

"I loathe to ask how Luciento died." Mael winced. "What did you do to him?"

"You would have to ask her." Raziel allowed himself to grin wickedly. This part of the story he had kept to himself for now. "She killed Luciento."

All eyes were once more on his wife.

Mael's mouth was open.

Lana laughed. "Bullshit!"

"Language." Volencia scoffed. "But the sentiment is true. You're lying."

"I'm not." Raziel sat back. "While I was dealing with his men, Luciento dragged her into a room intending to abduct her and escape. She had a choice. Go with him or use the knife I gave her to kill him. I found him dead in a corner, bleeding out. One stab up from the jaw into the throat and the skull." He put a finger against his neck where the blade would have entered Luciento's body. "The knife was on the floor nearby. Luciento's hands were clean. Right, Ivan?"

"He's right," Ivan confirmed from where he stood by the wall. "Hank and I found him right where Raziel said."

"When was the last time *I* used my own hands to kill someone?" Raziel couldn't keep the grin off his face as he sipped his wine. "I would have made one of his men do it. And the person who did it was shorter than Luciento, and I am not."

Raziel was staring at his little murderer, who was dutifully cutting up her steak. It was cooked rare, nearly raw in the middle. She didn't seem to mind in the slightest. His eldest brother shook his head. "Did you really kill him?" He paused. "I don't mean to insult you, but…"

"I know this family is dangerous," she said. "And I could hear what you were talking about when I walked in here." She put her knife down on the table. "And I knew that if I wanted to survive, I had to prove my worth to all of you." She stabbed a piece of her steak with her fork. "Killing a person isn't so different than killing a cow, in the end." Her green eyes met Mael's gold ones. "Except *he* didn't scream when I stabbed him." She ate the piece of meat.

Silence stretched over the room. Even from his mother.

Damn it all to the void—she was starting to make his life *complicated*.

Because Raziel wondered if this was what love felt like.

TWENTY-TWO

Dinner had been spent mostly in silence after Nadi's conversation-ending comment about murdering Luciento.

Which was one she was exceedingly proud of.

She wished she kept a journal, if only because she really rather wanted to write that one down to keep for later. But a chronicle of her life seemed like an exceedingly piss-poor idea, as it'd wind up being just a collection of confessions. And it would definitely wind up getting her killed.

After being excused from dinner early, which she was more than fine with, she headed back to the bedroom. *His* bedroom. She would never think of it as "theirs" or "hers." Either she wouldn't live that long, or he wouldn't. One of the two.

Her nerves were on edge, and she didn't understand why. She felt like she was going to scream. Or shatter something. Or both.

Normally, what she'd do to calm down would be to draw a hot bath, turn off all the lights, and sit in the hot water in as close to total darkness as she could and down a bottle of wine.

But she was currently *Monica*. Not Nadi.

And while *Nadi* could see in almost total darkness—Monica couldn't.

Pressing her hands over her eyes, she let out a long, ragged sigh. Maybe that was what was driving her up the wall. She was a good liar. She'd had to learn to be over the years. But she only had to be an actress in short bursts—a day or two at most, never *weeks* at a time. She never had to keep it up incessantly like this.

Even now, she couldn't just *be*. She couldn't just *relax*. She had to *literally* keep up appearances. Flipping on the light on the bedside table, she also lit a candle in the bathroom, so Raziel wouldn't be suspicious if he came in and found her sitting in total darkness.

Consoling herself with a bottle of wine that she set down on the edge of the tub along with a glass, she climbed into the hot water and tried her best to enjoy it for what it was.

Stretching out, she sighed as she leaned her head back against the edge of the porcelain. It was nice to live in an expensive home, she had to give Raziel that much credit. The tub was big enough that she didn't have to bend her knees to sink into the water and it had lovely little shelves on both sides to store things like her wine. And soap. But most importantly, the wine.

This would be perfect to almost anyone else.

And in normal circumstances, it'd be perfect to her.

Then why was she suddenly crying?

She *hated* crying.

"Fuck." Wiping angrily at her face, she stared up at the ceiling above the tub. They weren't tears of grief or sadness. She didn't *think* they were, anyway. They were tears of frustration. Or maybe stress.

Her emotions were one big angry tangled mess, however. All swarming around each other like bees in a hive that someone had kicked. So honestly, she had no idea *what* she was feeling or why.

But it didn't matter. The emotions were real, and there was

no stopping them now. At least she wasn't weeping. She couldn't stand weeping. Crying was obnoxious enough—getting congested and snotty because of it was just adding insult to injury.

Shutting her eyes, she let out a long breath and tried to let it simply run its course.

But matters went from bad to worse when the door to the bedroom opened.

Glancing over, she swore silently to herself.

Raziel. His crimson eyes glinted faintly in the dim light of the room.

Looking away quickly, she wiped her eyes again. But it was too late. He'd seen her.

"Ah." Shrugging out of his coat, he tossed it over the back of a chair and walked into the bathroom, his expensive shoes clicking on the hardwood floor. "My mother tends to have that effect on people."

That got him a single, tired, half-laugh. "It's not your mother."

"I suppose that makes it more troublesome, then." Reaching down, he picked up the glass of wine and took a sip from it before placing it back on the edge of the tub with a quiet *tick*. "Would you like me to leave you alone?"

He was such a different man to the one she'd met when she first walked in the door as Monica. It was like a curtain had been pulled away. No, something far more solid than that. Whatever it was, *she didn't like it*, and wished he'd put it back.

She shook her head.

"I honestly don't know. So I'll say... no. If you want to stay, you can stay." Wiping at her cheeks, she took a deep breath, held it for a long moment, and let it out in a rush. "But you'd better not be planning on hogging the wine."

Chuckling, he sat down on the floor next to the tub, his back against the wall closest to the foot of it, sitting opposite her. "And risk your wrath? I'll fetch another bottle if I do."

"Oh yes, terrifying me. When you can order people to hang themselves with their own *intestines*." She made a face. She was glad she was spared having to see that. "You could have just told them to shoot themselves. Why get so..."

"Creative?"

"I was going to say disgusting."

He pulled on the knot of his tie, loosening it, tugging it at an angle. "It inspires fear. The more the story about the way I made those men kill themselves spreads? The fewer idiots who will step out of line in the future."

Picking up the glass of wine, she sipped it. "I hate it when you make sense."

"Most people do." He leaned his head back against the wall, shutting his eyes. For a moment, he looked exhausted. "May I ask why you were crying?"

Pondering his question for a long moment, she shrugged again. "I'd tell you if I knew. I honestly don't. I don't know if it's any one thing. Likely just...a little bit of everything, finally snowballing into too much."

"I wouldn't blame you. This..." He gestured aimlessly at the room around him, but she knew he meant his home—his family —his world. "It breaks people."

"Does it ever get to you?"

"Which part?"

"All of it. Any of it."

He smirked. "Of course it does. But do you think I'm about to show any of that to anyone? *Please.* I'd rather be dismembered like dear old Father."

That could be arranged.

"Lana is throwing a garden party tomorrow." Raziel couldn't help but grimace as he said the words.

She stared at him blankly for a moment. "*Garden* party?"

"Lana feels that since your wedding was interrupted, you should be given another party instead." Raziel rolled his eyes. "I would rather die by teaspoon."

"No, I meant—it seems like a bad idea to have a party for vampires *outdoors*."

"Ah." He huffed a half-laugh. "You'll see." His expression fell. "And Mael seems glad for another opportunity to speak to our mother about sparing your life."

"*Is* there any chance of talking your mother into letting me join the family as a vampire?"

"Is that your goal?" He watched her keenly then, those red eyes still glinting in the dim candlelight.

"I don't want to die." No, she wanted enough time to kill all of them. Picking up her glass of wine, she sipped it and placed it back down between them. "Whether that means I convince you and your family to permanently postpone the 'honeymoon'... or convince your mother to let you turn me... I don't know if I have a preference."

"Hm." He studied her for a long moment. "I had hoped so, but... no. I fear that once my mother has made up her mind, there is little we can do. Mael's words will be in vain. Even your murder of Luciento hasn't swayed her. She says the message we must send to your father is still far more important than whatever 'perceived value' I feel you might add to the family. I believe she simply thinks I'm smitten."

"I'm sure she thinks some part of you is," Nadi muttered into the wine. It was a good cover for all the screaming and swearing she was doing in her head. She had been clinging to the hope—even some tiny little shred of it—that Raziel would convince his mother to let her stay.

But it was gone now.

And she had to figure out her options. But she'd need time to think, for that. She focused on the conversation instead. "Wait. Why does your brother care what happens to me?"

"That's what I want to know." His fangs were slightly extended, which seemed to happen when he got angry. "He's never given a *damn* what happens to any of my lovers before."

"Is it because I have your last name now?"

"I doubt it. Lana has had *three* husbands. All three are dead and dust." Raziel snorted. He went straight for the bottle this time, taking a swig from it. "No. Something else is going on."

"Maybe he's jealous." She smirked, turning in the tub to fold her arms on the side and prop her chin up on them. "Maybe he's trying to save me from his wicked, evil little brother and plans to steal me away before I die on our honeymoon."

The look that Raziel gave her sent her blood running cold. The joke she had just made had *not* landed well. He wasn't angry. No, it was worse than that. There was a frigid and terrifying *hatred* in his ruby eyes.

She shrank back, just a little. She knew that kind of hate. She'd seen it in the mirror a thousand times.

"Tomorrow, we will attend this garden party at Lana's. In three days, we board a yacht and leave for my ancestral home. There, you die." His words were flat. Empty and as dead as a tomb. Standing, he took one more swig of wine from the bottle before placing it back where he found it and heading toward the door to the bedroom.

He was gone a second later. And Nadi knew he wouldn't return that night.

Sinking into the water, her mind was reeling. What had just happened? Why was he upset with her? She'd just been joking around. *It doesn't matter. Focus. Focus!*

The fact of the matter was that her hope of convincing Volencia to spare her life was toast. She needed a new plan. Refreshing her glass of wine, she shut her eyes and leaned her head back against the lip of the tub.

Killing the whole family was no longer possible. She

couldn't get it done in three days, with human and vampire guards all around.

But *one* of them was going to continue to be alone with her. Raziel.

So... she would have to settle for the Serpent's head on a pike. At least *for now*. And he was the most important one to remove from this world. She would go on the little boat ride with him to his ancestral home and kill him there.

Then, her options were either to flee into the Wild and find a new fae clan to join or to make her way back to the metropolis to start again.

The idea of sneaking back into the family *as Raziel* popped into her head very briefly, but it was so ridiculous that she barely kept herself from laughing. She might be able to look and act like him. But when it came to being a vampire, and all the powers that came with it? She'd be hopeless.

Kill Raziel... then what? Flee? Or return?

She remembered the look on Luciento's face as he died. As the life left those iridescent green-blue-yellow eyes that were so very similar to hers. He'd died so she could kill *all* of them. Not just Raziel. If she'd been willing to settle for only the Serpent, he'd be long dead already.

Nadi's choice had already been made. She was in this until every last one of the Nostroms lay dead.

No matter how long.

No matter the cost.

Nadi was right. She saw nothing of Raziel the entire night. Which was fine by her, honestly—she nestled into the thick velvety blanket and fell asleep. While having another wild romp with her new "husband" was tempting, it was better for everyone involved if she avoided him.

Even her dreams had the kindness enough to leave her alone that night.

But the next morning, she had to brace herself for what was going to happen. A *garden party at Lana's house.* And even though she knew that convincing Volencia to change her mind about the sacrifice was pointless, Monica certainly would want to keep trying.

A knock on the door and a muttered warning told her she had one hour to prepare.

After showering and doing her hair and makeup, she picked out an outfit from the closet. Something that said she was Raziel's possession and wife, but nothing that would upstage Lana. After all, it was *Lana's* party and *Lana's* home that she was visiting, even if the party was being thrown in "Monica's" honor. A crimson dress that clung to her curves—*Monica's curves*—but didn't reveal too much skin or give away too much of the goods.

She kept her hair down, except for a few locks that she twisted into a braid at the back of her head. Then she fitted a red rose into it, one that had survived the wedding with only a small patch of charring. A nice reminder to anyone who noticed the detail.

Slipping on a pair of black stiletto shoes and a black coat, she headed out of the room. Raziel was waiting for her by the door, his expression grim. Hank stood nearby, and she didn't miss how the guard's gaze locked immediately onto Monica's *assets.*

Meanwhile, Raziel didn't even glance at her as she walked up. She knew he heard her. His vampiric hearing would have picked her up, even if she weren't wearing ridiculously loud stiletto shoes on a marble floor.

"You look like we're going to a funeral not a luncheon." She tucked her hands into her pockets. "Keep this up, and I'll start to think you don't like your siblings very much."

Raziel huffed a quiet laugh but said nothing as he walked toward the expensive black car that was idling in the driveway, waiting for them. Hank was staying behind, likely to watch the house.

The chrome of the car was recently polished and shone even in the clouded sunlight of the dreary day. Not great weather for a garden party, but great for vampires who didn't much love the sunlight, she figured. She wondered what the plan was—Raziel had alluded to something. Following after him, she climbed into the vehicle—a servant held the door for her, *he* didn't—and sat in silence in the back as they drove.

Vampires were weaker in the sunlight. Which meant gathering at a garden party—even in overcast weather—would make them vulnerable. She didn't know if she'd have time to take advantage of such a situation in the future, but she took note of it.

Hubris was a curse all vampires seemed to suffer from in spades. She would have to find a way to wield that to her benefit if she wanted to dismantle the Nostroms from within.

Raziel was staring out the window, his expression dour. Furrowing her brow, she glanced at him, and then to Ivan, who was driving the car.

Something told her that this "garden party" was going to be *miserable*.

It gave her time to mourn her bad plan of sneaking into the Nostrom family to kill them all. She had figured her performance with the Iltanis would have bought her a few weeks at least. But it seemed his mother was keen on getting rid of her quickly.

That was a detail that would be good to know. It changed her approach. "Whose idea was it to schedule the trip in two days?"

"Mine," came his simple, curt reply.

Wincing, she turned her attention out the window. "So you're ready to be rid of me, huh..."

Silence.

Why did that actually *hurt*? The sudden emotional sting made her laugh. Resting her forehead against the glass, she couldn't help it. She *laughed*.

That finally got Raziel to look at her with an arched eyebrow.

"Sorry. It's just... such a farce." She shook her head. "You never wanted to marry me. I never wanted to marry you. And yet I'm sitting here with wounded feelings." She laughed again. "It's ridiculous." Looking back out the window, she sneered at her faint reflection in the glass that wasn't even her own face. And he didn't even realize how much of the truth she was really telling him. "I actually *care*."

"There's a great deal of upheaval on the way," he said. "With the destruction of the Iltani family, the balance of power across the city is going to shift. I want this matter between us resolved before the battles begin. Even then, most of my men will be staying here. I have permission to take only two body-guards with me." Raziel's tone was unreadable. Matter-of-fact.

"Why just the two?" That would be Ivan and Hank, surely?

"Mael needs the others to secure the mayoral election. Certain parties need to be... pressured. Others, protected. So our manpower is going to be thin." Raziel sighed heavily. "I only get to keep the two with me."

Now that it was clear she was working on a shorter timeline and with a hitlist consisting of just one man—Raziel—Nadi's position had changed a great deal. She was no longer gathering reconnaissance. It was no longer about *positioning* herself within the family in order to pick them off carefully without drawing suspicion.

Now it was about making sure she could take Raziel out with a good escape route for herself. And when one could breathe underwater and had a fish tail, where better than a boat at sea?

Ivan, Hank, Raziel, and "Monica" would be the only passengers on the yacht besides the crew. That made things far more accessible, as far as dispatching Raziel went. But it'd make her a lot happier if there were only *one* guard on board.

Wheels started to turn in her head about how to rid herself of either Ivan or Hank. The decision on which one of them to kill was immediately clear. Hank, for three reasons—one, he was a third Ivan's size. Two, he'd rubbed her the wrong way from the first moment she'd set foot in the house. And three?

He hadn't stopped staring at "Monica's" body like a dog staring at raw meat. That made him a *very* easy kill.

Staring out the window, Nadi let the conversation dissolve into silence as she started to work out her plan in her head. This would work. Raziel had given her just the piece of information she needed. Maybe it was because when all you had was a hammer, everything looked like a nail...

She smiled.

But it was a *damn* good-looking nail.

TWENTY-THREE

Smile.

Patience.

They'd all be dead.

Eventually, if not *soon*.

That was what Nadi kept telling herself as she sat there at the table underneath the blackened glass panels of the enormous greenhouse that Lana owned. The decorative structure had its doors wide open to allow the fresh air to come through. Well. "Fresh." As fresh as any air in the metropolis could really be. Even as far out on the edges as Lana lived, it was still nothing compared to what it was like in the Wild.

And it was suitably bedecked in fake plants, trees, and shrubs of all sizes. Some glass, some paper, some metal—meant to represent plants from everywhere on Runne. Meant to look *exotic* and *strange* but of course, *tamed*. Anything they had that was real was ringed in iron to keep it under control.

Some of the fake plants were so delicate they were works of art in their own right. But instead of leaving her feeling in awe? Nadi really rather just wanted to be sick. Instead, she had to quietly watch Lana and the rest of the Nostrom family and friends banter and gossip with each other.

Even the mayor of the metropolis was there again, schmoozing and laughing, trying to drum up support for the election. She didn't pay much attention to politics—that was just the showy surface-level nonsense. Simply the cover for the dealings in the back, which were the true workings that she was more interested in. Just the cover business for the dealings in the back.

The focus on her was luckily over—and for that, she was *somewhat* grateful. She was now just the temporary human attachment to Raziel. Something that would be violently sorted within the week.

Just like Lana's three ex-husbands, if Raziel's story was right. There were about thirty people seated at the table—the closest friends and family from the wedding that had been rather spectacularly interrupted. Though, now it was Volencia sitting at the head, not Raziel and "Monica." Mael sat beside her at Volencia's right hand. Lana at her left. And Raziel beside Lana. And Monica beside him.

The seating was quite clearly sending a message: Raziel was third in line. He wasn't even the spare son behind the first-in-command.

She'd almost find it insulting on his behalf if she didn't find it so damn funny.

She had hoped to use the day to try to talk her way into the clan. But now that her original plan was dashed, she wasn't even sure if she wanted to bother with *trying*.

Her new plan was far more likely to succeed. And maybe more fun, to boot. Or at least, she was trying to convince herself of that.

But, she reminded herself in an annoying counterargument, Monica wouldn't have a plan to murder Hank, then Ivan, then

Raziel. Monica's only road to survival would be the approval of the family.

So there she was.

Smiling.

Laughing politely at everyone's terrible jokes.

Taking Volencia's insults aimed at her in stride.

And picturing in her head the violent and terrible ways she was going to kill them all.

"So," one of the vampires seated across from her began during a lull in the conversation. He was a cousin. One low-born enough that she didn't know his name, but to judge by the way he was wrinkling his nose at her like she was a spoiled tin of sardines, he was itching to put his name on her kill list. "I hear you were at the slaughter of the Iltanis."

"I was." She reached for her glass of wine. "They saw fit to involve me in the family business, so I saw fit to return the favor."

"Mmhm." It seemed he wasn't impressed with her answer. "The Nostrom family is the oldest and most revered vampire clan in the metropolis. We can trace our lineage back to—"

"She does not need a history lecture, Alberto," Raziel inter-jected, rolling his eyes. "Get to the point."

"Our *family business* is not for a human to be *involved in*, is my point." Alberto grimaced, baring his fangs. "And is far more dignified than killing vermin in an infested den below grounds. That a weasel thinks to even be seated at the table is—"

"Which one of us are you calling a weasel?" Nadi was the one to interrupt that time. "Him, or me?" She smiled. "Sorry to interrupt. I want to make sure I don't commit any *social blunders*, I am from the country, after all. I'd hate to open my fat mouth and take an insult the wrong way."

Azazel, a few seats down from the direct family, was hiding his laughter in his napkin. She knew he'd lied to her the first time they'd met—or at least played her sympathies—but against her better judgment she still rather liked him.

Raziel was glaring a hole in Alberto in silence.

And Alberto looked as though he was suddenly regretting his decision to speak.

Even Mael was fighting a smile.

"Enough." Volencia had the presence of mind to ruin her fun. "Leave her be, Alberto. This is not a permanent arrangement. She leaves for her honeymoon in two days, and she will not be returning."

And neither will your precious son, you rampant bitch. No one would come back from the trip. Nadi would make fucking *sure* of it.

The luncheon continued on exactly as it had started. More niceties. More obnoxious conversation. After food, everyone broke away into little pockets of conversation. She trailed alongside Raziel for the most part as that would be exactly what Monica would do. At least, until he excused himself and went to go speak to someone privately, leaving her alone in one corner of the large greenhouse by a large statue of some vampire muckety-muck whose name she didn't care to learn.

"Finally."

Turning, she found herself staring at a chest. Blinking, she looked up. Right. Mael was *tall*. "Oh. Hello." She smiled at him.

"Bastard certainly has a way of keeping me from speaking to you." The tank of a vampire shook his head. He looked like the antithesis of his brother. Every time she saw him, it struck her how remarkably different they were. Like the two moons—one light, one dark, but both belonging to the night sky. His golden eyes were hidden behind dark sunglasses. Even under the tinted glass of the greenhouse and the shady sky, it was bright for vampires. "I have been attempting to talk to you since after the wedding. He said if I didn't watch myself, he'd order me to eat my own hands."

"Can he do that?" She wrinkled her nose. "Order a vampire to do something?"

"I'm honestly not sure. He's never tried." He chuckled. "I'd hate to find out. Would you like to join me for a walk? Lana has beautiful gardens. And while the mayor is here and I have business to do, it can wait." Gesturing one of his enormous hands down a path, he started moving before even waiting for Nadi's answer.

"Sure." She *was* going to join him, anyway. But the fact that he assumed made her want to roll her eyes. Lana's fake gardens were rather pretty, she had to admit. They were beautifully designed with soaring iron arches to keep the *real* roses from consuming the building. The Wild could infect anything, if they weren't careful. But most of the plants were replicas. She supposed a fake garden was easier to keep alive—no need for a staff to take care of plants when everything was metal and glass.

But so strange that the humans and vampires felt the need to mimic the thing that they hated and feared so very much.

She kept those thoughts to herself.

"He told me you were concerned for my well-being. That's funny, considering I'm going to be dead soon. But a sweet thought, I suppose." She chuckled.

"To use a metaphor you might appreciate, just because I eat a steak doesn't mean I want the cow to suffer." Mael sighed. "And I don't think it's right, rushing you off to die like that. You showed your value. If I..."

Interesting. *Very* interesting. "If you, what?"

"Nothing." He shook his head again. "There's no point in wondering what could have been. You're his wife." He reached into his pocket and pulled out a tiny manilla envelope. "I just wanted to give you this."

Taking it, she pretended she didn't know what it was, and looked back up at him quizzically. She knew *exactly* what it was. Pills, made from the mushrooms from the Wild.

"For the pain. Of..." He made a face and looked away. "Of being with him. I know what he's like. We *all* know what he's like. And what he can do to people. If you need to dull the pain, take one. If you need it to stop... take them all."

Oh.

Oh, shit.

Well. Wasn't *that* fascinating. Reaching out, she placed her hand on his arm. "Mael? Thank you. Really. I can tell you care, and that—that honestly means the world to me."

The funny thing was, she could tell he really *did* care. Why, she didn't know. Putting the small envelope in her inside coat pocket, she let her hand drop from his arm. "I don't want to die, Mael."

"I know. And for that, I'm so truly sorry." The big vampire stepped in closer to her, making the moment suddenly intimate. Alarm bells started ringing in her head. "If there were more time, I would—"

"There you are. We're leaving."

Raziel.

Like an icy wind through an open door in the dead of winter, he shattered the suddenly too-warm moment. Mael took a step back from Nadi, and it left her standing there, stunned and confused.

"Y—yeah." Honestly, she was kind of relieved. "It was good to talk to you, Mael. I—" She was about to say *I look forward to seeing you again*, but... Monica wasn't coming back from that trip to the ancestral home. "Bye."

The walk to the car was deathly silent. And so was the majority of the ride back. It wasn't until they were halfway back to Raziel's home that he held his hand out to her, palm up. "Hand me the envelope."

"What?" She blinked.

"The envelope he gave you." The look on his face was one

that promised violence, though she didn't feel the swirl of his hypnotism in the air. "*Now.*"

Slowly, hesitatingly, Nadi reached into the coat pocket and procured it. Placing it into his palm, she felt like she was somehow in trouble. "He was just concerned about—"

Rolling down the window with the wood and ivory handle on the door, he whipped the envelope out of the gap before rolling it back up. "I am very well aware of what he was *concerned about.*"

"I... I wasn't going to take them."

"Good. They're poison." He stared out of the window.

"I mean, I know drugs aren't good for you, but—"

"No, little murderer!" he snapped without warning. Like a shattering piece of glass. Suddenly, his hand was around her throat, and she was pressed up against the door of the car. He was caging her in, his face hovering close to hers, his chill breath washing over her lips as he hovered only inches away from her.

If it bothered Ivan at all, it didn't show in his driving.

Nadi just stared at Raziel, wide-eyed, lost in those crimson eyes of his, too stunned to speak. She had no weapons. Not even her hairpins. There wasn't anything she could do except cling to the front of his coat and wait to die.

"You don't *understand, do you?*" The vampire laughed quietly. "What you're *really* up against? The games you've walked into...? The depths we'll sink to for a chance to torment each other?" His gaze flicked to her lips. "Do you know how many of my pretty little things he's killed, just to annoy me? How many of my toys he's broken just to *piss me off*? And not because he hates me, oh no... just because he's my big brother and that's what we *do.*"

"I—"

"*Quiet.*" He ground out the word, the hand around her throat tightening enough to cut off her air. "The pills he gave you are *literal* poison. Perhaps he truly thought they were an act of kindness, killing you before I had the chance to. Maybe he's even smitten with my little murderer and was being merciful, who knows. Who *cares*. You're *mine*. And no one gets to kill you but *me*. Understand?"

His hand released enough that she could gasp in air and struggle out a choked "Y—yes."

"Good." He sat back on the seat and gazed out the window again like nothing had happened.

They rode the rest of the way in silence.

And all she could think to herself was...

I'm going to make you fucking suffer.

Nadi had one day before they left for Raziel's "ancestral home." One day to make sure the boat was just a little less crowded when they left. One day to kill Hank. The question was... how?

Luckily, Raziel had a lot of business to attend to that was going to keep him locked away in his office and out of view. It would be a day trip to sail there, and likely a day trip back, and he needed to sort out his affairs.

Good.

That meant she could do a little bit of quick figuring out. The first thing she needed to discover was... where was the best place in the home to dispose of a body? Her first instinct was the trunk of a car. But with the garage under constant surveillance by multiple guards, that wasn't going to work.

Plan B. She could find somewhere in the house to hide corpses where they wouldn't be found for long enough that it wouldn't matter. The issue was, Raziel had a great many servants and guards who were always poking around and going in and out of seemingly everywhere. And if someone found Hank's corpse, the jig would probably be up. No, she needed somewhere decent to throw him.

So, she set about exploring Raziel's house, opening every

door and searching through every possible nook and cranny for places she could stuff a corpse. Luring Hank down into the basement to murder him wouldn't be hard. It was obvious Hank was attracted to Monica. But the question was, was he attracted to her *enough to risk it*? Was he more afraid of Raziel's wrath than he was horny for his boss's temporary new wife?

She could only hope that in Hank's head, it was an incursion that would sort itself out in forty-eight to seventy-two hours when she was dead. Therefore, low risk, high reward.

There were a decent number of locked doors in the basement. She had half a mind to pick the locks, but without the ability to re-lock them, she knew that suspicion would immediately fall on her once they were discovered open. She figured at least one was a wine cellar.

Another one was probably a space for Raziel's collection of... *specialty furniture and implements*.

She snickered at the idea.

Time to think of a Plan C. And fast.

To clear her head and give herself a chance to think Nadi decided to go for a walk around the yard. More fake shrubbery, trees, and grass. It was funny to her, how vampires wanted to surround themselves with the *appearance* of the Wild but loathed the idea of the reality of it. They wanted to feel in command of it.

That they were somehow superior to it.

Pacing around the edge of the property, she could at least enjoy the sunshine. That was a benefit to being out from the underground. As much as she missed her home, and how refreshingly cool the air could be down there, the sunlight up top in the city could be wonderful.

Plan C. Murdering Hank would make it that much easier to kill Raziel on the yacht. But she needed somewhere to stuff his dumb, disgusting ass. But *where*? There had to be something. Somewhere.

It was on her third lap around the property when the opportunity presented itself. Funny thing about real trees, grass, and shrubs. The roots absorbed rainwater. And when those things were removed, and dirt was replaced with concrete and stone, water had nowhere to go. And so... other drainage was required.

Nadi found herself staring down at a circular drainage hatch. It was hidden behind a row of silk and metal wire hedges and set into a depression in the false grass. More trickery to hide the workings of the house. Fake grass didn't drain into dirt, now did it?

Crouching down, she stuck her fingers through the slats in the drain and lifted, pulling the heavy metal grate from its home and sliding it a few inches to the side. The grate was some twenty inches wide, which would be difficult for Ivan. But Hank would fit just fine.

She'd known from the beginning that Hank would die first, and it was almost time.

The hole was deep. Good. Picking up a pebble, she dropped it inside. She counted the seconds before she heard it hit water. Two. Long enough for what she needed. And it wouldn't be the first time her people down below had found a few corpses floating in an underground lake or river.

She had the most important part of her plan—how she was going to get rid of Hank. And, looking up, she knew how she was going to bait the hook *and* celebrate her find at the same time.

Putting the grate back in place, she straightened up, brushed her hands off, and decided she was going to celebrate her discovery with a swim in Raziel's pool, since she'd yet to actually enjoy it.

Besides, it'd be a lot easier to kill Hank later in the evening when it was dark. She'd wait until he had a few drinks, lure him into the shrubs, pop a few holes in his lungs, and cram him into the drain.

So she had some time to kill. And if she wasn't mistaken, Hank would be on guard by the pool soon. *Perfect.*

Over the past week, she had watched the patterns of the normal servants and guards. She had their paths memorized.

Now, she just had to figure out how much time she had to do the deed. Raziel seemed distracted—but the question was, *how* distracted?

Stopping by Raziel's office, she knocked on the door.

A grunt from inside was all she got for an answer. Opening it, she popped her head in, and shot him an innocent smile. "Are you going to be coming to dinner?"

"No. I won't be coming to bed either. You're on your own tonight." He didn't even look up from his work, or whatever it was he was doing, scribbling away in a ledger, his head down. A cigarette was in an ashtray, a curl of smoke rising from it in a lazy spiral. He was walking a gold coin across his knuckles.

She had the urge to walk up to him, push his rolling chair away from his desk, climb onto his lap, and ride that perfect cock of his until the sun came up. Damn him for being so damn *handsome.* "All right..."

She pretended to be disappointed. As it was, she was smiling ear to ear as she shut the door. This worked perfectly. She'd have all night to herself with Raziel too busy squaring things away.

Heading back up to Raziel's bedroom, she rooted through drawers until she found a bathing suit for her. It was exactly what she expected it to be. Crimson and barely there. Just enough to leave something to the imagination while flaunting to the world precisely what Raziel now believed himself to be in possession of.

She changed into the crimson bikini and dug a long, black lace shawl out of another drawer, wrapping it around herself. Looking in the mirror, she smiled sadly. Monica really was a beautiful woman. She missed her own face. It was rare that she ever saw her own, *real* face in the mirror.

But Monica had curves in all the right places. It'd make it easy to tempt Hank into betraying his boss for a quickie. But she had to be careful—if Hank was too loyal or too afraid, it could blow up in her face in all the wrong ways.

Either way, she had to make sure that Hank never breathed a word of it to anyone. Whether he said yes or no, the man had to die.

Heading back to the pool, she was happy to see her target was still posted by the pool. She watched him from the corner of her eye—watching without watching—as she kicked off her sandals by the edge of the water and undid the tie from her hair, letting her brown locks fall down around her shoulders.

Hank was staring.

Good boy. *Stare.* She wanted these images burned into his brain for later in the evening. When he came on the late guard shift with a few beers in him. And let the urges win.

She took her time. Combed her fingers through her hair. Bent over, *very* slowly, to tuck her sandals underneath one of the chairs to keep them out of the sun. Making sure that Hank got a full view of her *assets*. When she stood, she let the lace shawl drop from her shoulders to drape over the arm of the same chair.

Every movement deliberate. But every movement innocent. Innocuous. Just a young woman, enjoying a private moment by a pool. Hank was just a staff member, after all—just a fixture. No more interesting to her, or threatening, than the lamp he was leaning against.

Her trek to the pool, though, had two purposes. One, seducing her target. And two... swimming. Lords below, it had been ages. She smiled, and dove into the deep end of the pool, instantly relishing the cool embrace of the liquid as it greeted her, even in her false human form.

How she wished she could shed her shape and feel the water flow through her fins. Shallow and contained as the water was, it would still feel like ecstasy against her scales.

She just had to remember to come up for air at short intervals—humans couldn't breathe underwater like she could, even with a glamor on. While she could shrug off her quick healing, her inability to drown would be harder to dismiss.

An hour in the pool turned into two, spent doing laps and just lounging about, enjoying herself. It reminded her of home, even if the chemicals did sting her eyes a bit and made her skin itch. Why humans and vampires felt the need to kill every living thing out of their captive water puddles, she didn't understand. But she supposed it was due to their need to *control* the Wild. Moons forbid anything thrive in their world.

She climbed out of the pool and headed back to her room to change the bandage on her side—the stitches on her gunshot wound were now largely for show. Eating dinner in her room, alone, she waited until it was close to midnight.

Checking the clock, it was almost time. The guards stayed up late, working in shifts. But the other servants—maids, chefs, and so on—tended to go to bed around eleven, save for a skeleton crew that stayed on call in their rooms for any special requests. But they weren't out and about, and only answered if Raziel rang for them.

The guards would be posted at certain points only. Kept out of sight. That meant she had a path she could walk where no one would see her—if she didn't want to be seen. And there was only *one* guard she wanted to notice her late-night wandering.

Pulling on some lacy underwear, she tied a black silk nightgown over it and made sure that the front was open dangerously low in the front. Into the band of her stockings, she tucked two thin fillet knives she had pocketed from the kitchen. Meant to delicately pull the flesh from fish, they would be perfect for puncturing Hank's lungs through the ribs.

As long as she didn't sit down too fast and stuff them into her own arteries, that was.

She checked that the nightgown was long enough to hide the knives but still short enough to show off what she was selling —then she went to work.

Humming a song idly to herself, she left her room and took a stroll around the gardens. Just a sleepless night. Just a poor girl from the outer cities, alone, and scared to die.

Lonely.

She was *so alone*, after all.

Sometimes, it helped to think the part to play the part.

She walked past Hank where he was stationed by the door as she headed outside, not saying a word to him as she went out into the yard. If he followed her... that was his decision. She didn't invite him. She didn't even glance at him. If he took this as an invitation? That was *his* damn fault.

If this didn't work, she didn't want him to have an ounce of anything to go to Raziel with.

Turning the corner behind the fake hedge, she went to stand in the darkness beside the drain she had discovered. It was fully obscured from the house. No one would see her there—for better or worse.

Would he bite the lure?

Leaning against the wall, she chewed her lip and waited.

She didn't have to wait long.

Hank rounded the corner into the darkness.

He was already undoing his pants.

Good boy. She opened her nightgown and beckoned him closer. She didn't want to talk to him. She didn't want to drag this out. He reeked of alcohol and cigarettes as his lips messily crashed against hers.

His hands sloppily groping her breasts only hitched slightly as she drove both knives into his lungs from the back. Once. Twice. Three times.

She tasted his blood on her lips as he coughed.

He was a heavy fuck—she had to struggle to aim him to the grate as he fell, landing with a quiet *thump* on the fake grass. She had to pull him over to the drain a few more inches until his throat was over the hole.

Yanking his head back by his hair, she slit his throat from ear to ear, holding his head back until she was certain he was fully dead. Only then, did she feed him head-first down into the hole. The deep *splash* was the loudest noise the two of them made through the whole ordeal.

The two fillet knives followed a moment later. A waste of good weapons. But she couldn't take the chance of leaving them lying about in a place where vampires could smell blood.

Replacing the grate over the drain, she examined herself for any remaining traces of Hank. Nothing. A clean kill. Save for a lingering taste in her mouth.

Nothing a little red wine couldn't cure.

Heading back to the bedroom, she poured herself a glass and drew herself a nice, hot bath, as was her tradition.

Lifting her glass in salute, she smiled.

Raziel would meet the same fate soon. And while she didn't know how long it would take, she would ensure that every one of the bastard Nostroms would die too.

Here's to you, Hank-Who-Has-Died-First.

And here's to all who'll follow in your wake.

TWENTY-FOUR

The next morning, Nadi walked downstairs for breakfast, minding her own business. Well. *Pretending* to mind her own business. She was just Monica, after all, preparing to eat her last meal in her husband's home before being shoved onto a boat and floated up to the ancestral home of the Nostroms to be murdered.

She was absolutely not, you know, a shapeshifting assassin listening to find out whether Hank's disappearance had caused any kind of stir.

Sure enough, the guards weren't in their usual positions. And the staff were going about their business a little more nervously than before. *Good.* They all knew Hank had gone missing. And they knew Raziel's second-favorite guard hadn't just walked off the job.

Walking up to Ivan, who was standing in the main hallway looking deeply concerned, she smiled. She was purposefully trying to be as obnoxiously cheerful as she could. "Hi, good morning! Have you seen Raziel?"

"Office. On the phone with his mother." Ivan frowned down at her.

Interesting. Either a good sign or a bad one. "Thanks." Putting her bag down by the door—keeping up the appearance that she was *fully* convinced that she was leaving for a cruise to her death that day—she headed back up the stairs to the second floor where Raziel's office was located.

Two guards stood by the closed door, flanking either side. That was unusual. *Good.* She smiled at them and gestured at the door. "I'd like to speak to my husband."

When one of the guards opened the door to let her in, it was clear that they'd been instructed to do so. Also interesting. Raziel was expecting her to come find him, which meant he had been expecting to be on the phone for some time.

Heading in, the guard shut the door behind her. Raziel was sitting behind his large, expensive oak desk. A whiskey glass in front of him said he had been drinking for some time, despite it being first thing in the morning—something told her he hadn't started early; he hadn't stopped from the night before.

His fingers were steepled against his temple, and the expression on his face was one of pure unadulterated suffering. The look of a man who had been forced to listen to nonsense for a very long time and was about ready to snap. A cigarette was perched between his fingers, the smoke curling lazily from its tip into the air.

It took everything in Nadi not to grin like an idiot.

"I am *aware.*" Raziel sighed and took a drag from the cigarette, flicking the ashes into an angular gold tray in front of him. He gestured at a chair across from him.

Taking her cue, she sat down and waited like an obedient little human sacrifice.

She couldn't hear what Volencia was saying on the other end of the line, but whatever it was, it was pissing Raziel *off.*

"All the more reason to leave, don't you think? Mael needs my men. And if I have a traitor within my ranks, he's better suited to 'fumigate the house' than I am." He shut his eyes, looking exhausted over the whole thing. A pause. "Ivan is plenty."

Wait, what? Now, suddenly *Volencia* wanted to postpone the trip, but *Raziel* didn't? That wasn't how she wanted this to go. Frowning, she sank back into the leather of the chair. Luckily, her dismay worked for Monica as well—if for very different reasons. From Nadi's point of view, it made no sense. It didn't change her plan—kill Raziel, disappear into the Wild. But the fact that Raziel was now keen to keep it to "business as usual" and that Volencia was the one who wanted to delay... stung.

Another pause from Raziel while his mother spoke. "Believe me, I fully understand that. My point is simply this, then—it takes fewer people to secure a yacht than it does this house. And on the chance that the attacker snuck in and was not already masquerading as part of the staff, I will be on a *boat* surrounded by the *ocean*. There will be nowhere to escape should they fail. It would be too risky for them to attempt."

Challenge accepted, asshole. I have a tail. Nadi kept herself from laughing at her poorly timed silent retort. Even if she really didn't want to.

"Oh, yes, thank you for the reminder." Raziel rolled his eyes.

She wondered what Volencia had said.

"The fact remains, however. We leave in an hour." He hung up the black metal receiver on the cradle with a *click*. His fangs were slightly extended in his anger. But, after a moment, he took a breath, held it, and let it out in a wavering sigh. Crimson eyes flicked to her. "Someone murdered Hank in the middle of the night."

"O—oh. Oh, no." Nadi blinked, feigning shock and dismay. "I—how?"

"Unsure. He went missing on shift. We haven't found the body or any blood, but... my men do *not* simply disappear. And especially not him. No one saw him leave. His things are still here." He took a long pull from his cigarette, speaking through the exhale, the smell of woodsmoke and incense filling the air with it. "Some fae piece of garbage likely getting revenge."

The fact that he was right—sans the piece of garbage bit, but she supposed that was a matter of opinion—was also *incredibly* funny to her. "Do you *really* think the boat is safer than here?"

"Nowhere is safe, my little murderer." He put out the cigarette, crushing it in the golden tray. "But on a boat, there is nowhere for them to hide from *me* either."

Slumping her shoulders, she sighed. "I won't lie, I'm not exactly excited to go off to my death. I wouldn't mind staying here a few weeks." Chuckling, she played the doe-eyed innocent card instead. Maybe that'd work. All she needed was a few weeks to murder his entire family, and—

"And yet, here we are." He stood from his desk, downed the rest of his whiskey, and placed the glass back onto the leather cover on the polished, lacquered surface. "The car is already waiting for us."

Fine. Nodding glumly, she stood from her own chair and followed Raziel from the room.

And prepared herself for a luxury cruise from which one of them would not return.

What a bizarre situation she'd found herself in.

It wasn't that Nadi didn't know the Nostroms owned a yacht.

It was just another thing to *see* it.

This was the kind of luxury that she both abhorred and yet... found herself a little jealous of, if she were being honest. Everything was shiny, polished, or painted fresh.

The ship was about a hundred feet of chrome and lacquered wood. It looked as though it could be rigged up for sails, and she thought she'd much prefer that over the rumble and chugging of an engine. There was something that seemed endlessly peaceful about *sailing*, though she'd never been. Cushioned benches lined the deck, and she saw several places to hide from the sun—a must for the vampires who owned it.

The ocean was her joy. She'd grown up in the underground lakes and cisterns of Runne, but the ocean was always calling to her. The few times her family had gone to the sea, she could feel the lure of its openness. Something in it called to the part of her that had fins and a tail.

What was out there? Who was out there? Were there other continents? Other people, other fae like her? Her family all were two-legged creatures. She was the only aquatic fae in her clan. It wasn't uncommon for that to happen, as all her people were born gifted in different ways.

After her family had died, Nadi had debated taking to those open waters. Picking a direction and just... going to the horizon. Either she would find a new home or she'd find the void. But the need for vengeance had kept her in Runne.

The need for death had kept her alive.

Raziel walked ahead of her, still not even glancing back at her as he walked aboard the large steel and wooden structure, her bag slung over his shoulder. A single, circular steam stack rose up from the center of it, a white cloud rising up from it to signify that the engine was already burning and ready to go.

The minimal crew was already hard at work. Everyone bowed their heads to Raziel as he passed. He didn't acknowledge a single one of them as he walked inside. One of the deckhands took her bag to go put it with Raziel's things, she assumed.

She wondered how loyal the crew was. How easily they could be paid off to look the other way. Or how much they even saw in the first place. Not that she had the money to pay them off at the moment—but it'd be good to note for the future.

Ivan stopped next to her. "The master suite is downstairs in the back. But I'd give him some space."

Nodding, she sighed. "Is it noon yet? Not too early for a drink?"

Ivan snorted. "You're married to Raz. You drink at any hour." He followed after his boss, likely not wanting to leave him alone with a possible assassin on board.

If they only knew.

Heading to the bar that was at the back of the boat on the deck, Nadi ordered a whiskey sour before sitting on a bench in the sun and watching the city begin to shrink as the boat pushed off from the docks.

It was at that point she realized... she'd never been on a boat before.

Well, okay, never on a *moving* boat before. There was that one hit she'd done on a canal boat. But it'd been moored up when she'd put the bullet in the woman's head. That didn't count. Nadi hadn't ever been on a boat at sea.

It felt strange. The movement was unnatural but swayed with the waves at the same time. She couldn't help but lean over the railing to watch the water as it crested in their wake. The wind whipped her hair in her face. The smell of the salt air and the warmth of the sun was just *wonderful*.

Everything was chaos. Everything was likely about to fall apart around her. Odds were good she'd be dead before long.

But this was *incredible*.

The metropolis began to shrink as they sailed away. She watched it change, watched it grow... small. Its smoke, its dirt, and its grime shrank and grew insignificant in its steel and shining glory. All sharp lines and hypermodern sensibilities. Was that how the humans saw it? Did they only see it from far away? The "big picture"? Was that why they loved their crowded structures so much?

Or was it because they made them feel safe? Powerful? In control of the Wild? There was beauty in it, she had to admit. The lines the structures made, each one seeming to compete against the others, yet somehow creating a piece of art in the inorganic, yet unplanned structure of the whole. It was an organism in its own right, wasn't it? An un-living, living thing?

A corpse filled with crawling things. Only these insects were the architects of the corpse, digging up and melting down and rearranging the body parts to suit their needs.

Moons, when did I get so moody? She didn't know how long she stayed there. But somebody came by and refilled her drink twice, and she wasn't trying to plow through them, if that was any indication.

It was probably time to face the music. She had to talk to Raziel *eventually*. Even if she still had no idea what to say to him. But the fact remained... she couldn't avoid him forever. They were on a boat.

Downing the last of her third drink, she stood and realized... ah. Yeah. She'd had three drinks. Great. Well, that'd make the conversation go a little easier. Or worse. Harder? Harder. That was the word.

Shit. She was a little drunk.

That was the problem with having staff. They were trying to be helpful by refilling her drinks without her asking. But if it was in front of her, she was going to drink it.

Get it together. She needed her faculties for this conversation.

With a breath, she headed down below decks to the master suite. The yacht was large, but it wasn't enormous enough that getting lost was a real possibility. She reached the door. Should she knock?

They *were* married.

Sort of.

All right, well, *he* thought they were married.

Ivan was standing nearby. She glanced at him. "Knock or no knock, what do you think?"

The big guy cringed as if watching someone about to put

their hand into an oven and knowing he couldn't do anything to stop them. He shrugged.

No right answer. Nodding, she decided to get it over with. Twisting the handle, she was surprised to find it unlocked. She shut the door behind her, and braced herself for the worst.

The room was dominated by a large bed directly in front of her, swathed in black silk. The room was huge for a ship, and every surface was polished wood or gleaming metal. Doors on either side went out to a large, private balcony on the back of the boat, which was likely just below where she had just been on deck. Another door to her right revealed a bathroom with no one in it.

There was no sign of Raziel.

Until a hand settled on the back of her neck. Fingers on one side, thumb on the other, holding her in place.

She went rigid.

"Started the party without me, did you?"

Stunned for a moment, she stammered. "I—what?"

His grip tightened. "You smell of whiskey."

"You left me alone and your staff is *very* helpful." She shivered at his grasp. "I didn't mean anything by it, I just... are you mad at me?" What was going on? Why was he so *pissed*?

Suddenly, a wave of panic washed over her. *Does he know? Has he figured it out?* Was she about to die?

His hand slid from the back of her neck to around the front of her throat. Grasping her underneath her chin, he pulled her back to his chest, tilting her head to look up at him. Those ruby-red eyes of his stared down at her.

There was no anger there.

Only hunger.

Only *need*.

His thumb traced along the edge of her jawline. "Are you ready?"

She felt like the floor had dropped out from underneath her. Was she?

Swallowing the lump in her throat, she let out the breath she'd been holding. "Yes."

The smile he gave her sent a chill through her. "Then let's begin."

TWENTY-FIVE

After she'd killed Luciento, when she and Raziel had made love—*fucked like animals, to be honest*—it had been in a moment of bloodlust and the shattering of the tension between them. Nadi knew that wasn't exactly what he was... known for.

This was different.

This was premeditated.

This was *controlled.*

Raziel bowed his head and kissed her temple before shifting his palm to the middle of her back and pushing her two steps forward, making her stagger. "Remove your clothes." He wasn't using his hypnotism. She couldn't feel the weight of his power in the air.

At least he wasn't trying to control Monica like that. He was a monster. But there were some lines it seemed even he wouldn't cross. What a strange relief.

Shrugging out of her thin coat, she tossed it to the corner of the room. Her shoes went next. She didn't want to rush. Namely, because her hands were shaking badly enough already. The whole time, she was afraid to even look at him. He was simply standing behind her, looming there, his gaze burning into her.

But it wasn't long before she was naked. Weirdly, she found herself fighting the reflex to cover herself. He'd seen it a dozen times or more at this point. But she hadn't ever felt this *exposed.* Even though she was wearing someone else's body and someone else's face, she felt like he could see right through her.

"Face me."

Turning, she did so.

"Look at me."

It took a split second, but she flicked her eyes up to him.

By the void, he was *beautiful.* A dark god. He stepped up to her, all in black and crimson, his expression unreadable as he studied her.

She was shivering despite the warmth of the room.

"You're nervous."

"Of course I am," she murmured.

"I'm flattered." A thin smile graced his features. "But you have no reason to be." He lifted a hand and stroked his knuckles against her cheek.

"But..." She furrowed her brow.

"This is our... complex understanding. I didn't seek you out as a plaything. You didn't come find me wishing to be broken by me. That makes this a *very* particular arrangement." He tilted his head to the side slightly. "The others were easily snapped, like toothpicks. Already small. Already fragile. You? You, I feel would be like using a machete to clean my teeth. I have to handle this with far more care."

A rare compliment. And one that she found actually *meant* something to her. Her eyes flicked between his, searching for the joke. Searching for the sarcasm. She found none. He was being sincere.

"Now." His smile turned just a little devilish. "Shall we see how far this blade is willing to bend without breaking, hm?"

Willing.

Was she willing to bend to him? *Bend without breaking.* He didn't want to shatter her. Could she trust him? Her first instinct was to laugh. The part of her that had hated him for over eighty years—the part of her who had watched him murder her family, who had despised the Nostroms and vowed revenge —swore at her and declared that he was the enemy. She couldn't trust him. Absolutely not.

But some part of her wanted to do it *regardless.* Wanted to put herself in his hands. Wanted to bend, *anyway.* Wanted to feel what he could do to her.

Screw it.

Literally.

Taking a deep breath, she held it, then let it out in a wavering rush. She nodded.

"Good." Raziel rested his thumb against the hollow of her chin. His smile made her feel hot and cold all at once. Dread and excitement warred for supremacy. His words were a growl, a promise, a threat. "Kneel for me, my beautiful little murderer."

* * *

All his life, Raziel had collected broken things.

Toothpicks, as his metaphor had gone. Things to be used, snapped, and thrown away. Sometimes, they came to him, sometimes he found them. Baubles. Vampire or human. Men or women.

Things that were already whittled down past the point of recognition. Once-great trees or vines reduced to splinters.

But this creature in front of him? This woman? This *killer?* She was no broken thing. She was closer to someone after his own heart than anyone he had ever known. Though young. Impetuous. Foolhardy.

Too naive for her good. She still had a lot to learn, though she clearly believed herself above reproach in that regard.

A lesson he would teach her soon enough.

But he had more *pressing* lessons to address first.

He had ordered her to kneel. He never used his hypnotism to coerce his partners. It was what gave him the greatest joy in the world—not having to use his gifts to get others to obey him. Watching them choose to do it instead, for whatever reason, gave him such pleasure. And their reasons were as varied as the broken souls he had collected.

Often it was physical lust. Either for him or for what he could make them feel.

Sometimes, it was from a need to make their bodies hurt the way their minds did. To feel *something*, anything at all, even if it was only pain.

Or, perhaps, it was the need to feel like the center of someone's universe—even if it was as a plaything and a toy.

More than one of his former "lovers" had come to him, knowing that they wouldn't survive the ordeal, mentally or physically. He was just a very elaborate form of suicide to them. He despised them for it, every time.

But this one?

It was precisely as he had said. Neither of them chose this. She hadn't come to him. And he had not sought her out. It would require them both to adapt. And if she was willing to bend for him? He would do the same for her.

"What if I wanted to be the one in control?" Her words to him the other night echoed in his mind. He had never once in his life surrendered control to another. Never let someone have their way with *him*. Even in a menial, superficial sense, let alone anything close to what he was about to try to do to her.

The thought should have revolted him. Or made him laugh, perhaps, at how ridiculous it sounded. Him? Blindfolded and shackled? Please! But this woman—this creature before him—

staring into his eyes, searching for something? Was surprising him at every turn.

Including, it seemed, by uncovering things about him that even he didn't know.

Because he had a hard time remembering when he had been so instantly turned on by an idea in a very long time. The idea of her, knife tip pressed against his throat, his blood staining her hands as she rode them to completion, made his already painful erection twitch inside his pants.

He had replied "*I would* love *to see you try.*" And he had meant the words. They hadn't been a threat. They had been an invitation. *Catch me off guard with a gun to my head, my little murderer, and I will kiss your feet and obey your every word.*

But that was if destiny allowed them to last that long.

Now, he was the one in command.

The one that she warred with.

Would she surrender? Would she cross the point of no return? Or would she back down?

It wasn't a matter of whether she would enjoy it. They both knew she would, deep down.

It was a matter of *trust.*

Did she trust him?

Not in politics. Not with his family. Not with her life. The answer there was a clear and understandable "no." But in some way, *this* trust was more important than that, wasn't it? This kind of intimacy?

The moment stretched on for another beat, and he was certain she would retreat. But she had one more surprise in store for him. The tension fled from her shoulders as she committed to her choice. And slowly, cautiously... his little murderer knelt at his feet.

* * *

Nadi couldn't believe what she was doing.

Had she lost her mind?

She was kneeling at the feet of Raziel Nostrom. Naked. Trembling. *Eager* for what he was going to do to her.

His hand stroked the top of her head, gently, almost soothingly. "We will take it easy on our first time truly playing together. Sorry if that's a disappointment." He walked behind her and out of her field of view.

The floor of the suite was carpeted, which made his footsteps silent. She had no idea where he was. That made her more nervous. And made it so, so much more intense. She was almost shivering in need.

"Spread your knees. Sit on your ankles." He was standing right behind her.

She did as she was told.

A pair of leather straps dangled over her shoulder from his hand. "Put these on your wrists. Cinch them tight. I will know if they're loose. But keep from cutting the circulation. That's my job."

He... wanted her to do it? Why did that feel so much worse? *He wants me to tie my own noose and put my own head in it.* This wasn't about making her do anything. This was about her doing it to herself. With a shaking hand, she took the straps. Her fingers kept slipping as she put them on.

If he was getting impatient, he said nothing. He stood behind her, waiting in silence, letting her do the task. She did exactly as he'd said. She made sure they were tight, but not so tight she'd risk cutting off the blood to her fingers. She tested them, making sure she couldn't slip her hands out.

This was dangerous. She was literally placing herself into a trap. But this was exactly what she knew was going to happen! Cussing herself out for being an idiot, she debated getting up and making a running leap for the balcony. If she jumped overboard, she could drop her glamor and escape. She could just swim for freedom.

This might be her last chance.

A larger leather strap with the same kind of attachments dangled into her view. "For your throat."

A collar. *Shit.* Oh, lords below. What had she done? What had she gotten herself into?

When she hesitated, he hummed. "Do you want to stop?"

"N—no." That was the worst part of it. She didn't. That was the last thing she really wanted. This was just extremely stupid. Taking the collar from his hand, she carefully put it around her neck and cinched it, clasping it tight.

Raziel pulled her hair gently behind her, clearing it from the edge of the collar. His touch was tender and sweet as he ensured there were no stray hairs caught in the collar's metal clasp. He rotated the collar so the D ring was at the back, and gave it an experimental tug. "Good."

Just that one tug alone sent a crash of pleasure ripping through her body that brought a gasp from her lips.

The next thing to hang into her line of sight was a stretch of black silk. "A blindfold."

She hesitated again.

"This dance of ours today is about trust, my little murderer. I want you unable to protect yourself. Unable to stop me. And unable to see what I'm about to do. I want to see how far you will let me go. But it will only be as far as you *let* me."

Her mouth was dry. She swallowed thickly. Taking the blindfold, she tied it on, arranging it so that she couldn't see. He adjusted it for her again, tightening it a little for her in a way that she couldn't do herself.

"Put your hands behind your back. Wrist to wrist. I am going to link them together." His words were deep, like rumbles of thunder. His tone was soft but painted thick with lust and need. He needed her as badly as she needed him. But he wasn't... harsh or cruel. Damn him to the pit, he sounded *tender*.

Putting her wrists behind her back, she felt him crouch behind her. He folded her arms so her hands were on the elbows of her opposite arms. Two clicks. She couldn't move her hands.

"Now... for the final step. Are you ready?" His hand grazed over her shoulder and down her back along her bare skin.

It instantly broke her out in goosebumps. She shivered, pulling in a gasp through her teeth. Nodding, she couldn't find the words to answer.

"Tilt your head back. I am going to lash your collar to your wrists. You will be completely exposed to me like this. Do you understand? I need you to say the words." His lips gently pressed to her shoulder, feeling volcanically hot against the electricity that was shooting through her. The anticipation of it all was more intense than the bindings themselves.

"I... I do." She couldn't believe what was happening. "Yes."

"Good. It's your choice."

After a pause, and more internal cussing, she did as he said. Arching her back, she tilted her head toward her hands. A click of something at the back of her neck, and he helped her the rest of the way, guiding what must be a short strap to the rings that connected her wrists.

A second click, and she was secured in place. It wasn't painful. It was just unnatural. It kept her back arched in such a way she knew she must be putting on quite the display, her legs spread like that and her breasts jutting out.

And judging by the moan that left him as he stood and walked around in front of her, she was right.

She was bound and blindfolded, helpless and at his mercy.

Raziel.

Her worst enemy.

The man she'd sworn to kill.

And she had never needed anything so badly before in her life.

"Have you ever pleasured a man with your mouth?" Raziel's belt rustled. "I'm not sure what they teach you out there in the country."

"I have..." Her head was spinning. Every nerve in her body felt like it was on fire. She couldn't see. She couldn't move. He could do anything he wanted. Anything at all. "But they weren't hung like a horse."

A deep chuckle was all she got in response at first. His thumb ran along her lower lip. "You're a quick study. Open your mouth."

Without hesitation, she did. Something primal in her was beginning to obey. Something in her was starting to answer to him that was superseding the rest of her thoughts.

He slipped his thumb into her mouth, another deep groan leaving him. The thought that she affected him like that—that he *wanted* her like this... She closed her lips around his thumb and sucked on the digit, drawing it deeper into her mouth, rolling her tongue around it. Showing off just a little bit of what she could do.

He pulled his thumb away and his groan turned into a snarl. He pressed two fingers into her mouth, pointer and middle, and slid them against her tongue. Meeting her challenge with a dare of his own. When he pushed them deeper, her throat closed as she gagged. Jerking against the restraints, she tried to pull her head back away from his hand.

"Ah-ah..." He grabbed the front of the collar, yanking her head back toward him, keeping her from escaping. Pulling his fingers almost all the way out of her mouth, he paused there. "Relax." He waited until she forced herself to do just that. "Now... deep breath."

Taking in a breath through her nose, she held it.

"Focus on staying relaxed."

The two fingers slid forward against her tongue, slowly moving deeper, and deeper, until they grazed the back of her throat. Jolting against the restraints, he tutted quietly, but kept his fingers still and right where they were, forcing her to adjust. "Focus," he urged. "Not on me. On the muscles."

It took another two attempts at her throat trying to clench around his fingers, on her mind going white, but slowly— somehow—she regained control. And he was able to slide his fingers just a little deeper without her gagging on them.

"Yes, my little murderer... see? You *are* a quick study. Oh, you and I are going to turn the metropolis *red*..." His lips were close to her ear, murmuring to her as he began to slide his fingers in and out of her throat in a slow, meticulous pattern. Each time going as far as he could, teaching her—training her— showing her what he was about to do with something far more impressive than just his fingers.

"That's it, just like that. Breathe in when I slide away. Hold when I get closer. Focus. Trust me. I won't overstay my welcome, even if you think I will. I have you. You put yourself in my palms. I won't let you fall." His deep, rumbled words were little more than a whisper. Each one was like hot lava as they washed over her.

All she could focus on was how badly she needed him. *Needed* to feel him make good on his threat. When he slid his fingers almost all the way out, ready to make another return journey, she turned her head away. "Please—Raziel—I want you..."

He chuckled. Amused... and perhaps just a little darkly sadistic. "You're just as insatiable as I am. How perfect."

Fingers twisted in her hair as he straightened up. The fabric of his pants brushed up against her sides as he stood closer to her, standing over her prone and arched body.

Without being told, she opened her mouth to him.

The moan that left him was almost enough to send her to

ecstasy on its own. He pressed himself into her, and he was hotter than sin itself. She quickly ran her tongue around him, eager to feel him fill her. His girth was exactly what she'd expected—enough that she was worried. She wished she could see him. But the *not knowing* made every other sensation twenty times more intense.

Hand resting at the back of her head, he pushed his hips forward, sliding deeper into her mouth. He pumped himself into her slowly.

"A vampire could get used to this view." His chuckle was thick with pleasure. "I don't think I'll be able to go nearly as long as I'd hoped with you today. For shame."

He pressed his hips forward, and a growl started to form in his chest as he deepened his strokes, little by little, retreating almost all the way just to push forward a bit more each time.

Helpless. Exposed. Bound. Blindfolded. At his mercy.

The words kept repeating over and over in her mind.

He was taking her. Making her his. And she was surrendering to him. Obeying him. Calming her throat and allowing him to push his girth down inside her in a way no man had ever done before in her life.

"That's it, yes—" His praise came between sounds of pleasure. "Moons, yes—" He started to use both hands then, guiding himself a little faster as he pushed a little deeper each time. "You can take it all, little murderer... you can. Come, little killer —I know you can."

If she could have crested the peak of ecstasy from words alone, she would have. Her body felt alight with it. Crackling with pleasure. Why did this turn her on so much? He was driving himself relentlessly forward. She had no idea how much longer it took before suddenly her nose was pressing against his body.

Clutching her head to him, he let out a muffled roar as if trying to push himself somehow deeper, though there was no more left to give. Slowly, agonizingly, he removed himself from her.

"Again."

She took a deep breath.

"*Again*."

The pattern repeated.

"*Again!*"

Each time, the word became more feral, more animalistic, and less human. She thought she was going to lose her mind. If this was insanity? Let it happen.

Suddenly, she was on her feet. Raziel had grabbed her by the front of the collar and hefted her up.

He half pushed, half threw her onto the bed. She landed on her side, unable to stop herself with her hands lashed behind her back. Strong hands grabbed her and rolled her onto her stomach.

As if she weighed nothing, his hands grasped her hips and hefted her up onto her knees. Hands still tied, back still arched, face on the sheets, and now her ass in the air, she was once more on full display.

A palm came down on her rear with a deafening *crack*. "Knees apart."

Letting out a small cry at the impact, she shuddered and did as she was told.

His fingers wound into the collar at the back of her neck, and he lifted her up until she was kneeling. "Let's play a game, shall we?"

She was shivering. What was he going on about? Couldn't he just *fuck* her already?

Something pressed against her lips. Something small. She couldn't tell what it was. "Open your mouth, my little killer."

When she did, he placed a coin on her tongue. One of his many coins from his collection, she realized.

"Shut your mouth."

Obeying, she couldn't possibly guess what was happening.

He buried his head into her hair. "If you can keep your mouth shut while I *fuck you senseless*—without ever saying my name or pleading for more? You'll get your wish. I'll let you take a turn with me in the straps."

Without any more warning, he doubled her back over. Grabbing her by the elbows, keeping her suspended in the air with his strength, he rammed himself inside of her to the hilt in one hard, unforgiving stroke.

Ecstasy, somehow more impossible than what he'd brought her before, threw her over that cliff and never let up. She had no idea how long he went at her like that. At some point, he put her head down, pinning her to the sheets, and used his height to his advantage.

It felt like the sheer pleasure would never stop.

The feeling of him. The sensation of him with her. In her. Surrounding her. Taking her. She couldn't see. She couldn't move. There was only *him*. Only *Raziel*. Only the vampire over her, claiming her, taking her, making her *his*.

Yes. She was his. She belonged to him like this.

One of them would kill the other before long.

His life belonged to her.

But like this?

Like this, she was *his*.

When his thrusts became uneven and desperate, he grabbed her by the hips and yanked her back against him, snarling. With all his strength, he seemed intent on burying himself as deep into her body as he could possibly go. She felt him twitch and spasm inside of her, felt the flood of warmth as he met his own release.

He roared into her hair, and the feeling of him inside her sent her to her own crescendo. The next few minutes were a blur as she tried to catch her breath. But when he took the blindfolds and the straps off, she was lying on her side, her chest heaving. Raziel was fetching her a glass of water.

And sitting there on the nightstand was a single gold coin.

She sighed. "How fast did I lose?"

Raziel handed her the water with a grin. "Less than ten seconds."

"Shit." She sipped the water, glad for the cold liquid.

He laughed. His own chest was rising and falling with the exertion. "You still earned a reward. We will arrive at the estate tonight."

Shit. So soon? She thought the family estate would be farther away, not a single day of sailing!

"I have a special dinner planned for us tonight. Very private and romantic. Just Raziel and Monica." He watched her thoughtfully, gauging her reaction.

"Where you plan on murdering me, right?" She arched an eyebrow at him.

"The ceremony is tomorrow, this is something for us, before the inevitable." Raziel kept his expression unreadable.

Shaking her head, she sighed. "Don't lie to me, Raziel. I know what's about to happen to me."

"Hm. We shall see. Dinner, first." If he was lying, he was just as good at it as she was. Which was quite possible.

Smiling half-heartedly, she took another sip of the water he'd handed her. "If you're going to kill me tonight, Raziel, just give me a quick death." She paused. "And maybe a shower, first."

He laughed—and it sounded genuine. Her bit of morbid humor had surprised him. "Mmh." Leaning in, he kissed her. Slow, but deep. It was sensual, and when he pulled away, she had to blink her eyes back open. She hadn't realized she'd closed them. He smiled. "I would say you more than earned both of those. For now, I'll leave you to your shower, my little murderer."

His little murderer.

And soon, she really would be, wouldn't she?

It was time. Nadi stared at the estate on the edge of the cliff. The castle looked skeletal from the yacht—a bleached skull on a cliff with empty eye sockets for windows, staring, unseeing, at the world around it. The roof had caved in over one wing, it seemed—the tower collapsing into the main structure of the building. But for a structure that was well over a thousand years old, it seemed... in shockingly good condition.

Especially now that it was sitting so far outside the reach of civilization and was left to the Wild.

Ivan had gone ashore with some of the yacht's staff with hatchets and cans of gasoline to hack and burn away the vines and anything dangerous from the Wild that might interfere with the "ritual sacrifice" of Raziel's bride. She could see the curling white smoke of the fires that they had built.

Dressing in a short, thinly strapped black dress and thigh-high stockings with garters, she brushed out her hair.

And slipped the two sharp paring knives she had stolen from the bar into the lining of her bustier, one under each armpit. They were flat enough that they wouldn't leave a bulge or be noticed. As long as she didn't curl into a ball or have to do any random crunches, they wouldn't puncture through.

Raziel was insisting on them being the only two in the estate for the sacrifice. Just him. And her. Not even Ivan would be there. He likely thought he was giving her privacy in her last gasps of breath.

Little did he know, he couldn't have given her a better wedding present if he'd tried.

TWENTY-SIX

The castle was a foreboding structure, the closer Nadi got to it. Even standing on the pier, it was a haunting sight. The more details of its ruined carcass of a structure Nadi could see, the less she had any desire to enter it. Something about it made her skin crawl. She didn't know if she believed in ghosts—but if she did, *that place* was haunted.

The wooden pier was old, and the steep and rickety stairs to the building some fifty feet up were built out of the same material. The planks were gray from sun and salt, the softer wood peeled away and leaving only the grooves of tougher woodgrain behind.

Taking off her high heels, she grumbled something about trying to make it upstairs in stilettos and splinters. But the wood was smooth beneath her toes, worn by sand and salt wind. The worst she'd have to worry about would be a stray nail or two.

Reaching out, Raziel tucked a strand of her hair behind her ear, smiling at her griping. He had been in a strange mood since they had reached their destination—the Nostrom ancestral estate. He didn't seem to want to be there any more than she did.

After the chefs had returned to the shore from preparing their meal, Raziel had then gone ahead alone. He said he had "setup to do" ashore by himself before sending for her and Ivan.

He'd meant it when he said he wanted them to be alone. Not even waiters would be there with them. Even Ivan would apparently be staying down by the pier with the skiff, alone.

It meant that she had her chance to kill Raziel. Just the two of them. But could she actually take him, one on one? She'd only get one chance. She'd have to wait for the right moment to catch him unaware and take her knives and stab them into his throat. It would take a little while to saw his head off with a paring knife, but... where there was a will, there was a way.

The mental image of having to kill him suddenly twisted something odd in her. It wasn't pain. Not exactly. But it was *almost* regret? It was something to do with the way he was smiling at her, with some *real warmth* in those ruby eyes... something felt like it had changed between them.

Hadn't it?

What is wrong with me?

"Come. Before dinner gets cold."

What was she going to do if Raziel decided to go against his mother's wishes and "turn" Monica? Of course, the vampire would choose to simply sacrifice his inconvenient human wife and obey his matriarch, not keep her around. He'd drain her dry on some altar and throw her corpse into some pit with the remains of sacrifices past.

Nadi hadn't really expected him to consider turning her, so she hadn't ever really planned on what to do if he *tried.* The mental image of trying to pretend to turn into a vampire in front of him almost made her laugh in a way that would be entirely inexplicable.

Raziel let her climb the stairs first, gesturing for her to lead the way.

She started up the stairs, smiling to herself. "What a gentleman. Or are you just enjoying the view?" The steepness of the climb put him at a perfect line of sight to enjoy her ass.

"It can be both." When she glanced back at him, he was smirking at her.

When they reached the top, she stared up at the grand castle and felt dread roll over her in a wave. It was made out of enormous stacked and carved stone blocks that had been overgrown with Wild vines until Ivan and the crew had charred and chopped enough back to allow them entry.

Vines were slowly attempting to disassemble the stone and iron walls that had been erected to keep nature at bay. Some things were slow going—but inevitable. The Wild would win, in time. It always did. It was just a matter of how many years it took.

"Did you grow up here?" Nadi couldn't help but stare at the enormous structure.

"Hardly." Raziel huffed a laugh. "The Wild made that impossible."

The structure soared high overhead, the looming black windows once holding glass now largely shattered and empty. The building was far, far older than anything in the metropolis —and in fact, any of the human buildings she'd ever seen. She wondered suddenly about the history of Runne. About how much of it was fiction and how much of it was fact. Once they reached the top of the stairs, she put her heels back on.

"Look." He stopped her before they went too far away from the cliff's edge, and pointed toward the ocean. "Not often you get to appreciate a sunset quite like that."

Turning, she let out a breath. He was right. It was something else. She'd never had the chance to see a sunset over the ocean. The light was glimmering on the blue waves in stunning reflections of white and gold.

Not a bad last sight, if she was about to die. "That's beautiful..."

"Indeed." His mood deflated quickly. "My grandfather was the first vampire who helped overthrow the fae and drive them underground where they belong." Raziel was walking beside her as they headed into the cavernous, almost castle-like estate with its weatherworn gray blocks.

"And it was from here that he made those first pacts with the humans." The front door was stuck ajar, the large metal slab long since trapped at an angle, vines and rust ensuring it would never move again. Raziel went in first, stepping over a vine, before offering her a hand over it.

But all the privacy was bothering her. It felt... wrong. She knew she was harmless little Monica—just a pathetic little human who could be mind-controlled into doing anything—but it still felt *odd*. "If you aren't planning on doing the sacrifice tonight, why not just eat on the yacht?"

Raziel was bringing her toward the back of the house, the golden rays of the setting sun casting sharp shadows across the once-grand wooden floor. Now, it was covered in detritus—dried leaves, bits of flaking paint and plaster.

His expression was unreadable. "Now and again, isn't it nice to be... who we truly are without pretenses?"

Fear pricked at the back of her neck.

Turning to her, he smiled faintly. "I am not a good man, my little murderer. I enjoy the terrible things I do to people. I won't make excuses or blame what I've become on my family or on the world at large. But sometimes, just *sometimes*, I wonder..." He turned his gaze back to the direction they were walking. "What I would have become if they didn't make me into a monster."

There was an emptiness in his face. A hollowness that suddenly made her heart ache. Was he playing her like a fiddle? Or was this real? Frowning, she stepped closer to him, and wove her fingers into his. She didn't know what else to do.

His hand tightened slightly around hers. "Lilivra Nostrom. My dear old *grandmother*. The oldest vampire still 'alive' in all of Runne, who pulls the strings of all humanity and vampire kind alike." He rolled his eyes. "From the very beginning, she whispered to my mother that I would be a great 'asset' to the family, but an asset to be kept on a short and spiked leash. Volencia told me this *verbatim* when I was a child. That I was blood-mad, that I was a murderer, that I was destined to be what I am now. So... was it destiny? Or was it the work of two women who crafted a child into a weapon because they wished to stay in power?"

After a long pause, Nadi let out a sigh. Raziel was forcing her to admit something out loud that she very much didn't want to. Because it made everything messy—complicated—and that was something she didn't need. "Everyone has reasons to be the way they are. Everyone is a product of their context."

It would be easy to believe Raziel was pure evil. Once she had believed just that. For a very, very long time, in fact. And maybe he still was. But she was beginning to see what he was in a new light.

He was a monster. He didn't feel remorse for killing. He would keep on doing it. His whole bloody family would leave a trail of bodies in their wake unless someone stopped them.

Nadi was going to kill him. She wanted her revenge more than ever. That hadn't changed. It wasn't a lie. But when she picked up his hand and placed a kiss to his fingers, and knew it came from a place of affection... that wasn't a lie either.

"Enough melodrama." He huffed, shaking his head. "I'm too sober for this bullshit."

"Seconded." She chuckled.

Turning to face her, he tilted her chin up to look at him. "I realized something, earlier today—you have not truly felt what it's like to be bitten by a vampire. You fainted the last time."

"I didn't f—" She went to argue.

"Yes, you did."

"Yeah, I did." She sighed.

"Come." Still holding her hand, he took her toward the house.

"I—I guess this means—this is how I die." She winced. "You drinking me dry." Was this the opportunity she needed? Closing in on her neck, he'd be too distracted by his bloodlust to notice her pulling the knives from where they were tucked into her bustier and slicing open his throat. Then, it'd be the simple matter of removing his heart, then his head...

"It is also how vampires are turned. I would drain you to the edge of death, and you would drink my blood in exchange." He studied her expression thoughtfully as if reading every flicker of emotion like a clue. "But no. I am not going to kill you in this moment, or turn you. No matter how addictive your blood threatens to become."

How oddly flattering. "Thanks?" She paused, furrowing her brow. "What do you mean, addictive?"

"I admit... after tasting you, I could not imagine letting you go. My own personal stash of a drug more potent than any powder?" Raziel led her into what looked like a grand parlor. The furniture was still there, though it had seen better days. It was clear the staff had come through and tried to clean it, or at least make it usable—drop cloths had been thrown over sofas and chaise longues. "I had brief thoughts about turning you into my own thralled fountain of blood, but my family wouldn't have it."

That shouldn't twist a knot of excitement in her stomach. But it did. "So... you keep saying you aren't planning on killing me, but... seriously... I just want to know how panicked I should be right now."

"Not until after dinner." He chuckled. Raziel brought her over to a sofa in the center of the parlor, closest to the windows where they could see the ocean. He sat down before pulling her in front of him.

"What if you don't stop? What if this *is* the sacrifice and you're just tricking me?" She felt the same eager anticipation twist in her stomach. There was something so inherently sexual about his bite, it felt just the same as when he was threatening to tie her up and have her.

"Then, I suppose I will eat dinner all on my own." His lopsided smile didn't make her feel any better. It bloomed into a laugh as she glared at him. "I'll stop. I give you my word."

"Right..." If he was going to kill her, though, maybe this was the best possible way. She had no idea what it felt like to be bitten. But she'd heard stories of it from humans who had been turned into thralls, addicted to the bites of their masters.

What would it feel like to be bitten? Would it hurt? Maybe it was agony to her kind. That would make more sense than not.

His hands slid up her thighs, riding her black silk dress up her stockings. Pulling her forward, he urged her to straddle his legs. She did, kneeling on the sofa before sitting on his lap. He was still taller than her like this.

"You're nervous again." His fingers trailed through her hair, combing the strands, the points of them scraping against her scalp.

Gods, that felt good. It lured her eyes half shut. "Hard not to be, when you're likely planning to kill me at any point."

Let him get in closer... let him just get a little closer...

"I gave you my word. In this moment, you are safe with me..." Leaning in, he kissed her throat. It was the same spot where he had bitten her before. The mark had almost entirely healed. Too fast. He hadn't brought it up. "I have more plans for us this evening to simply let it end here, I promise you."

That twisted a knot in her stomach that was part fear and part anticipation. *He just needs to be a little more relaxed...*

Resting her hands on his chest, she took a deep breath and tried to relax. He slowly stroked a hand up and down her back, shushing her quietly as he kissed her throat. With his hand in her hair, he gently tilted her head away from him, giving him more room.

That's it. Kill him now! Kill him n—

He began to purr.

She'd heard it from him before. But she'd been concussed the last time. And it hadn't felt *real*, blending into the scenery like everything else. Fuzzy and dreamlike.

But now, there was no question about it.

The sound rumbled in him. Deep and primal, resonating through her. It robbed her of breath. But like some kind of magic, all tension fled from her limbs at the sound of it. His hypnotism didn't work on her—but *that* did. It was like a lure, calling her closer. Shining in the deep, whispering *It's safe. It's okay. Come here. Come to me.* And she did, powerless to resist. Unwilling to even try.

Resting against him, she surrendered to his strength, no longer fighting against his grasp. All thoughts of resistance left her. All thoughts of hurting him fled. All she wanted was *him*.

He rolled his tongue over her throat, sensuous and slow, taking his time. How long he lingered like that, both of them basking in the moment, she had no idea. Her thoughts were muddled.

Then it happened.

A brief sting.

And for the length of a single heartbeat, nothing but the purr.

Then he *pulled*.

And a moan escaped her lips.

He drank from her and she *felt* it. Gods below, she could feel it happening. She could feel her heartbeat begin to thud in time with his rumbling.

It had no right to feel like such total and utter bliss.

Another pull, and she thought she might lose her mind. No wonder she fainted the first time. If he was going to kill her—let it be like this. Please, let her die like this. Instinctually, she ground her hips against his, needing to feel more of him.

But his purr was beginning to change into a growl. His bite was beginning to deepen—become harsh. His arm at her back cinched tighter. But there was nothing she could do to stop him; she was caught in his web.

This was how she died. Right here. In his arms. Drained dry.

But the *pull*. With each draw from her, a wave of ecstasy rolled through her, sending her deeper and deeper into the warmth of it all.

Just when she thought it was over, he ripped his head away from her. She heard his jaws snap shut, heard him mutter a curse to himself under his breath. He shuddered beneath her, his hands still clutching her tight.

Gasping, she placed a hand to her head. "Shit—"

"You are fine. It feels like I took more than I did." Raziel leaned his head back on the sofa, his hands sliding to her hips. He pressed his own up into her. It was clear that she wasn't the only one who found the bite sexual. "Oh, my little killer... you are a dangerous addiction. Oh, I wish we had time to go another round."

"We don't?"

"Mmh. Dinner will be spoiled if we wait much longer, I fear." He laughed in a strange way. Did her blood make him high? He sounded a little loopy. Giddy, almost. The idea that she was accidentally drugging him was funny enough that she had to keep from laughing.

She rubbed her throat again. It was sore but didn't sting. And her lightheadedness had cleared fairly quickly. "That was... wow."

"How do you think Lana has so many pet humans?" Sitting up, he nudged her hand from her throat and kissed the wound before rolling his tongue along the bite marks. She shivered at how sensitive it was.

He patted her ass. "Can you stand?" He was clearly still a little loopy. So was she.

Standing was a wobbly affair, and she had to lean on the sofa for a moment to do it, but she managed. He was right—at first, it felt like he'd taken a lot more than he had. But now that she could take a second to breathe, her head was starting to clear.

"Dinner is on the back patio."

Raziel led her through a large set of doors that must once have been beautiful to an enormous stone patio overlooking the ocean.

Nadi froze.

A table was set for two in front of her. White linen was laid out, with plates under silver cloches.

But there were three chairs.

Only two of them were empty.

In the third position was a woman. Wrists tied to the wooden arms of her chair. Ankles tied to the legs. More bindings around her waist. A gag muffling her whimpering cries.

Nadi was staring into the terrified eyes of Monica Valan.

The real Monica Valan.

A click from behind her. The sound of a pistol's safety.

Nadi felt the weapon being pressed to the back of her head.

Raziel's voice was as cold as ice. "Do sit down. I think it's time that we become properly acquainted. Don't you?"

TWENTY-SEVEN

Nadi began to tremble almost instantly. She had failed. Whatever was going to happen next, it was clear—by staring at the poor girl in front of her—that Nadi had *failed miserably*.

"I'm so sorry," she murmured to Monica.

"Take the knives from your bustier and place them on the table. Then, sit." Raziel pressed the gun harder into the back of her head. "I hate using guns. But for you, unfortunately, I have to make an exception. I'm sure you understand."

Swallowing the sudden rock in her throat, she took a step forward. She slid the knives from her bustier under each of her armpits, placing them on the table. Pulling out the chair that was in front of her and to the left of Monica, she sat down. She expected Raziel to restrain her. Or to just kill her, right then and there.

But he... didn't.

Instead, the vampire walked around to the other side and took his seat. He placed the gun on the table in front of him, business side facing her, and picked up a bottle of red wine.

Pouring them both a glass, he set the bottle back down. "Let's start at the beginning, fae. What's your real name?"

Nadi stared at him in silence. What was *happening*? He was questioning her? Why hadn't he just clubbed her over the back of the head and started torturing her? Why pour her a glass of wine and just... ask?

It seemed like her confusion was written all over her face.

"If you prefer we do this the more violent way, I can oblige." He sneered. "Though we both know how much you enjoy it when I make it hurt."

Her face went a little warm, and she looked away.

"Oh, now that is fascinating." Raziel sat back, wine glass perched between his fingers. "Have I ever seen you *blush*?" He laughed. "I don't believe I have."

That made her want to punch him in his smug goddamn face.

"Name, please. Or else I will be happy enough to start breaking Miss Valan's fingers one by one."

She was ready to continue ignoring him until she replayed what he just said to her in her mind. "Wait. Her? Why?"

"Ah, there's your voice." He sipped his wine. "Yes. *Her.*" He gestured at the real Monica with his glass. "It's clear you're ready to die for whatever... crusade you believe you're on. But I'm curious to see how far your fae morals go."

"My first name won't do you any good. You won't know it." Nadi met his gaze. She still hadn't dropped her glamor and wore Monica's form. She didn't know why. It felt like a shield.

Because I don't want him to see the real me and be disgusted.
Because I hear how he says the word fae.

"Would you rather I keep calling you 'fae' or 'my little murderer'?" He huffed. "Surely you noticed I stopped referring to you by name a few days ago."

She hadn't. Fuck. Nadi swore and looked off toward the ocean again. She wouldn't cry. She refused. But she was frustrated and angry—no, she was *furious*—with herself for being such a gods-damned fool. "How long?"

"The clues were there, but you played the part beautifully. Each mystery was small enough to ignore on its own, but together?" He reached out and picked up a bread roll, tearing off a piece and dipping it into a bowl of oil. "I truly began looking for answers after the Iltanis kidnapped you. You told my mother you killed three men. But to me, said you shot two. Something didn't add up. *Someone* was missing."

Wincing, she sighed. "Fuck. *John.*"

"Precisely. And when you let him live a second time? When I saw him run from the docks? Oh, then it was so beautifully obvious. It was easy enough to pay him for the answers after that." Raziel laughed, joy flickering in his ruby eyes. "Everyone is for sale. Especially when they have no home left to return to." He put the piece of bread into his mouth.

"Fuck you."

He swallowed and sat forward, grinning like the cat who ate the canary. And she was the canary. "Tell me—killing Luciento. Did you plan to do it? Did he know what you were? Did he look in your eyes and see a fellow fae betray him? Or did he go to his grave thinking you were just a poor, misguided human?"

When she shut her eyes, her face twisting in reflexive pain, he had his answer.

His laughter was like a knife in her side. "How wonderful! He *knew.* I wonder if you even were familiar with each other. Wouldn't that have been such a wonderful twist of fate."

"Fuck. *You.*"

"You misunderstand, my little murderer! I'm impressed! You must despise me more than any other thing in Runne, living or dead, to go *this far* for revenge." He gestured at the table before them. "Look at the steps you've taken. The dangers you've exposed yourself to. I assume you've done all this in order to murder me."

She stared at him flatly, part of her hoping that maybe he'd drop dead by that method alone if she looked at him just right.

"That would be a yes." He began to spoon what looked like a raw beef and vegetable salad onto another piece of bread. "So. Who did I kill? Who did I wrong that you would go so far as to sneak into my life as my *wife*, sleep with me, carry on such an enormous ruse, and betray your own kind in order to put a knife in my back?"

Silence.

"My dear, sweet, wonderful little murderer." Raziel sighed and placed the toasted bread down. "You really have to understand—your game is over. You've lost. How this ends is entirely up to you, however."

"What do you mean? You're going to kill me."

"I could. That is definitely one of the outcomes I have in mind, yes." He glanced at the real Monica. "But this is a curious situation. You must be asking yourself... if I knew, if I have known for some time now, then why haven't I killed you yet? And, therefore, I ask in return—why haven't you killed *me*? Or at least attempted to. There have been plenty of moments when I underestimated you, and you had your chance."

She stared at him flatly. She wouldn't give him that information. Though, she was curious as to why he hadn't killed her once he knew what she was.

He sighed. "Of course, for me, killing you now would be exceptionally clean. I could kill you both, throw you into the ocean, throw her corpse into the pit in the castle's chapel. The sacrifice is complete. My new wife is dead. Nobody need ever know there were two Monica Valans."

The real Monica wailed into her gag, weeping.

"Let her go. She doesn't deserve any of this."

"It was an entertaining challenge trying to find her. Luckily, money doesn't buy you intelligence. She stayed in the metropolis and started spending that nest egg you gave her. It drew attention. And that made her easy to find." Raziel picked up the beef and toast and ate it. He chewed and swallowed before speaking again. "You really should eat, darling."

"I'll answer your questions if you let her live."

"The fact that you think you're in any position to cut deals with me is positively *adorable*." He began to make himself another snack. "No, you will answer my questions if you want to have any hope of her surviving this at all."

She stared at him flatly.

"Very well." Putting down the toast, he stood from his chair and moved to Monica. He reached for the restraints on one hand. "I wonder how she'll like it when I command her to eat her own fingers on toast."

"Stop! Stop." Nadi wanted to scream. Squeezing her eyes shut, she put her hands over them. He was right. She'd lost.

She heard him sit back down in his chair. "You played the game extremely well, if it's any consolation, darling. I almost overlooked all of the strangeness—I *wanted* to. But didn't you think I'd notice how you tasted?"

"I hoped my glamor would keep it hidden."

"Ah, so you *are* a shapeshifter. I had hoped this wasn't a one-time illusion of yours. To your credit, you fooled me incredibly well." He hummed thoughtfully. "But now, I'm extremely curious as to what *exactly* I am married to. Let's start with that, then, if you'll tell me nothing else. Show me your twisted, disfigured face."

Nadi stared down into her lap. She'd lost. It was over. What did she care if he saw her face? What did she care if he found her a hideous, disgusting fae? He was her enemy. She'd done terrible things in an attempt to kill him, and she'd failed. She knew it was the most likely outcome when she had set out on the whole endeavor. But she'd tried. And she could die honorably knowing that.

"Come now, I'm sure I've seen far more grotesque things in

my years. Stand up and show me what you really are." Raziel smirked at her over the edge of his wine glass.

"I… can't stand, in my real form." Having an eight-foot fish tail made standing rather impossible.

"Fascinating! Now I'm even more curious." He laughed. "Then get up, sit over there, and show me." He picked up the gun on the table and pointed it at her. "Now I am picturing you as some terrible viscous blob."

With shaking hands, Nadi stood and walked to a bench on the deck some five feet away and sat down. She refused to cry. She would meet his disgust with hatred of her own.

This was the monster she had come to kill. And now, he would send her to the void. Soon, she'd be at peace, one way or the other. And she could meet his revulsion with defiance.

Raziel stood in front of her. "Go on."

Taking a deep breath, she held it, and slowly let it out. And dropped her glamor in front of a vampire for the first, and likely the last, time in her life.

* * *

Raziel had not known what to expect from his fae murderer. His little assassin, his spy, his infiltrator. The one who had snuck into his bed, who had been let so close to him. The one he delighted in taking to his bed, even as he knew what she really was.

He'd known since the bullet had been pulled out of her that something was amiss with "Monica Valan." But the pieces had been there all along, now that he knew the answer to the puzzle. But how many times had she had the opportunity to kill him, yet she hadn't?

How many times had she looked at him with a desire too raw to be a lie?

How many times had he met her desire with his own?

A creature full of surprises.

Raziel watched as his fae assassin walked to the bench and sat down before the shape of Monica shimmered and fell away.

And Raziel could only stare.

Long, jet-black hair reached down to a narrow waist. It curled in waves that reflected the setting sun in shades of green and blue. Her skin was pale, with a hint of sea-green if he looked closely.

Where Monica was curvy, his fae was lithe. Muscular. Meant for movement. For agility. To move through the water with strength and speed like a shark. But still with curves in the places he wished to dig his fingers into.

Her lips were black, and he knew they weren't painted that way.

But her most notable feature was… her tail. From the waist down, the transition hidden by the black silk of the dress she still wore, she had the long, tapered tail of a fish. Her scales were oil-slicked black, shining in every color of the rainbow.

Her fins resembled torn black lace. He wondered what they looked like floating in water.

Suddenly, he wanted to see her nude, like this. Wanted to see her in all her glory. Wanted to study her. To touch her. She was eerie, but graceful. She was like a spectral thing, haunting, and ghostly. In the waves, she must look like a spirit come to lure wayward sailors to their deaths.

She was the single most beautiful thing he had ever laid his eyes on.

When she cast her gaze up to him, expression full of hatred and spite, black eyes that glittered like opals in every color under the moons, he wanted to kiss her and taste that fury. Wanted to feel those tiny fangs of hers prick his lip. Wanted to feel her unbridled *loathing* for him as he claimed her throat again as his own.

He had come here fully intending on killing his little assassin.

Now? He supposed they both had a choice to make.

* * *

When Raziel did nothing but stare at her in silence, expression blank, Nadi sighed and looked away. She shifted her form, wearing a glamor of herself in her human form. "The tail is inconvenient on land," she muttered.

She stood, and suddenly she very much wanted a drink before he killed her. Ignoring him and the gun he still had pointed at her, she walked back to the table and sat down in her chair.

Picking up her glass of red wine, she chugged it and poured herself another. "Let Monica go."

He shook his head. "Unfortunately, she has to die. I can't have loose ends. John is already dead, I'm afraid."

Cringing, she looked away. He was right. Nadi hated it, but she couldn't argue against his logic. It was her loose ends that got her caught. If she'd killed Monica and John, she wouldn't be in this mess. And to a vampire with no morals, there was no point in leaving them lying around. "At least make it quick, please. She doesn't deserve any of this."

Monica screamed, muffled into the gag.

"Only because you said *please*."

He moved faster than she expected. Damn vampires. A blur of motion, and a *crunch*, and Monica's head was twisted at a horrifying angle. Her eyes were wide, caught in a moment of fear—but no pain.

"Fuck." She sighed. "I'm sorry," she murmured to the dead girl.

"Mm." He patted Monica on the head. "I liked your version of her better. This one wept too much. She was *precisely* what I had been expecting. You were not. That should have been my first and loudest alarm." Sitting back down with a sigh, he went back to eating like there wasn't a corpse sharing the table with them. To be fair, they'd already done worse with a corpse in the room. "Name."

"Nadi."

"Nadi." He repeated it as if testing it on his tongue. "Lovely. I much prefer it to Monica." He glanced at the real woman. "No offense." He looked back to Nadi. "Clan name?"

The look she gave him would have lit the void on fire and frozen it over again. After a long, painful pause, she finally let it hit like the brick that it was. "Iltani."

Raziel cackled in laughter. "Oh, that's too good! What was Luciento to you, then?"

"My uncle. You killed my family eighty years or so ago. Maybe a little more."

"Oh, yes. I remember now! Some parts of it. A warehouse under one of the road junctions, I believe? I can't even tell you how many I killed that night." He ate the food he had prepared and abandoned minutes prior. "You'll forgive me if everything runs together after all this time. I don't remember. But you murdered your uncle in the name of revenge for me. How *wonderfully* complete your hatred must be."

She stayed silent and only stared at him in venomous silence.

"Which only deepens the mystery." Raziel studied her. "You had plenty of chances to kill me. Instead, as far as I can tell, the only one of my people you've managed to murder so far has been Hank. And I wouldn't be surprised if he made a move on you and forced your hand."

"I baited him. But you're not far wrong." She was already halfway through her second glass of red wine. She didn't care. "I figured it would be easier to kill you with only one of your guards on this trip."

Raziel chuckled. "Fair." Grasping the bottle of wine, he topped off her glass. "Which still leaves me with the question, why haven't you killed me yet? You're a practiced assassin, clearly. So, it isn't nerves."

"I'm an assassin because you murdered my clan. I wanted to know what I was doing before taking you on."

"Smart. Now, answer me. Why not kill me when you had the chance and be done with it? Why drag it out? You put yourself in danger, and now you've failed."

"You murdered my entire family in front of me. I decided I wanted to do the same for you. And... besides. You're just a symptom, not the cause of what happened to me. The Nostrom family line is a plague." Nadi glanced at the poor dead human girl. What a waste.

"A symptom not the cause. I like that. Well, then, my darling Nadi. My wife. I would like to propose a deal."

"A... deal?" She furrowed her brow. "Let's hear it." If it was a way to survive—even just for another hour—it might be worth taking. There might still be a way out if Raziel was foolish enough to let her live.

But *why* would he let her live? What could he possibly have planned for her?

"I have need of someone with your particular talents." Raziel's eyes shone almost amber in the setting sun. "So here is my proposal, Nadi. I will let you live..."

The next words out of his mouth changed the path of her life in a way she would never quite be able to comprehend.

"If you help me murder my entire family."

To be continued...

A LETTER FROM KATHRYN

Dear Reader,

I can't thank you enough for reading *The Serpent's Bride*. Honestly, when I set out to write "vampire versus fae, mafia, dark fantasy romance," I had no idea what to expect. And flowed onto the page is one of my favorite stories I've ever penned.

If you enjoyed reading it as much as I enjoyed writing it and want to keep up to date with all my latest releases, just sign up at the following link! Your email address will never be shared, and you can unsubscribe at any time.

www.secondskybooks.com/kathryn-ann-kingsley

Some authors can write books and leave them in a drawer, never caring how people engage with them. I am not one of those authors. I love to hear from you, and how the book made you feel. Did it make you laugh? Cry? Did I surprise you? Did you fall in love with Raziel and Nadi as much as I did? Stop by and let me know or leave a review.

If you like my style of writing and want to see more of what I have to offer, check out my links down below. Thanks again.

Wishing you the sweetest nightmares,

Kathryn

KEEP IN TOUCH WITH KATHRYN

www.kathrynkingsley.com

facebook.com/KathrynAnnKingsley

instagram.com/kathrynannkingsley

bsky.app/profile/KathrynKingsley

ACKNOWLEDGMENTS

To Jack, for tirelessly calling me out on my nonsense and helping me edit this book into the best version of itself.

To my husband, Evan, for all the patience and encouragement while I type away on my laptop for hours upon hours.

And especially to Reb, whose love of the gothic, strange, macabre, and sexy helped turn my dream of being a "real" professional writer into reality.

This one is for you.

PUBLISHING TEAM

Turning a manuscript into a book requires the efforts of many people. The publishing team at Bookouture would like to acknowledge everyone who contributed to this publication.

Audio
Alba Proko
Melissa Tran
Sinead O'Connor

Commercial
Lauren Morrissette
Hannah Richmond
Imogen Allport

Cover design
Damonza.com

Data and analysis
Mark Alder
Mohamed Bussuri

Editorial
Jack Renninson
Melissa Tran

9 781836 187363